Echo Valley

A power hungry politician, his burning secret, and the unyielding young mother caught in the middle.

Jennifer Vaughn

Published by Waldorf Publishing
2140 Hall Johnson Road
#102-345
Grapevine, Texas 76051
www.WaldorfPublishing.com

Echo Valley

ISBN: 978-1-945171-86-4
Library of Congress Control Number: 2016957015

Copyright © 2017

All rights reserved. No part of this book may be reproduced or transmitted in any form or by any means whatsoever without express written permission from the author, except in the case of brief quotations embodied in critical articles and reviews. Please refer all pertinent questions to the publisher. All rights reserved. No part of this book may be reproduced or transmitted in any form or by any means, electronic or mechanical, including photocopying, recording, or by an information storage and retrieval system except by a reviewer who may quote brief passages in a review to be printed in a magazine or newspaper without permission in writing from the publisher.

Cover Art Courtesy of Greg Kretschmar Photography

This book is dedicated to a dear friend who has shared laughs, secrets, and stories with me for over fifteen years. Joellen Cowette, I adore you for so many reasons. Most of all, your enormous heart and your will to overcome. It is by no means an accident that my brave Bo is loaded with so many of the wonderful qualities I see in you. Thank you for your friendship, and all the colors you bring to my hair, and my life. I love you.

CHAPTER ONE

She was cute in a needy, three-legged kitten kind of way. Never one to be rude, especially to someone I'd be sharing such close space with for the next year, I gave in to her. I told my hyperactive, hair-tossing college roommate I would join her one night down at the campus hangout. She pulled her wide lips into a giddy grin and threw her arms around my neck.

"Oh, Bo, thank you!" Stella Chapman trilled against my shoulder. I knew we'd never be friends in the true meaning of the word, but this buoyant girl could still be amusing. "We'll have so much fun," she chirped, darting toward the mirror over our shared bureau to check her pretty face. "Like, let's get totally wasted and dance till our boobs fall off!"

I warned Stella that I was facing my first organic chemistry quiz the next day, had no plans to lose my boobs on the dance floor, and I'd be heading out long before midnight. She didn't care, Stella was perfectly fine with whatever—and whomever—the night brought her way.

We were a bad match, Stella and me, because her lust for adventure carried her far away when I needed her the most. My only ally in a dark bar that smelled of stale peanuts and Axe body spray took off when a swarthy lacrosse player climbed onto the barstool just to my left, ordered himself a shot of tequila, and offered me one. I declined. If beer would fog my brain for class the next day, tequila would have blowtorched the poor thing right out the back of my head.

When I excused myself to go to the bathroom, I had hoped to come back and find the frat boy long gone. Instead, he had settled right in, was working on his second tequila shot and handed me a glass with dark liquid and a lime. I declined again, but he insisted. Maybe it was exhaustion eviscerating the outer layer of my senses, because I became dangerously aware that his cute half-smile had touched off a small dimple next to his full lower lip. Even though I had a boyfriend at home whom I adored, this stranger had a sultry kind of appeal I had never experienced before. I was the smart girl, resolved and focused, a million times better than some ditzy flirt, so why was my spine starting to settle back into the wooden slats of the barstool and my resolve to go to bed early steadily slipping away?

"Come on," he replied. "Have a drink with me. I'm just trying to be nice here because it looks like we'll be in the wedding together." He jerked his head backward. I followed the motion, finding Stella and some blond-haired dude dry humping on the dance floor.

"Ugh, I knew she'd do that," I groaned, trying to sound disgusted.

"Well, that guy is my ride which means we're stuck here for a while. Cheers!" He offered up his shot glass, and I good-naturedly lifted my own.

Clink.

Echo Valley — Jennifer Vaughn

The first sip tasted like rubbing alcohol dipped in lime. I never drank anything more than an innocent glass of white wine, and this was pretty potent stuff. As I watched Stella grooving with her new boy toy, I made small talk with this unnervingly attractive new acquaintance. His name was Riley O'Roarke, he was a junior and lived off-campus. A few gulps later and I shocked myself by beginning to imagine how his huge hands would feel on my body. I reminded both of us that I had a boyfriend back home, trying to put some self-serving emphasis on the fact that I was *not* doing what we both knew I really was doing. He went along with me in theory, giving me what I needed, even though I could feel him starting to press his thigh against mine under the wooden bar. It felt like steel. I took another long drink of the vile liquid, disliking it a little less, and chewing on some small, square ice cubes. My stomach spun as I noticed him slide a tongue over his lips as he watched the grinding movement of my mouth. If my boyfriend was safe and familiar, Riley was edgy and disturbingly sexy. The dark allure of young lust worked its elicit magic, and I fell under its spell. My knee fell open beneath the bar, swallowing up any leftover space between us and inviting Riley's thigh to stay exactly where it was. My shoulder dipped toward his, seeking to touch and feel. Liquid courage made my boyfriend seem too far away. I was cool, beautiful, and drunk, my ego pixilated into something I could no longer control.

In between giggles that sounded foreign even though they were coming from me, I told him I was a pre-med major and learned that he was business management. We chatted lightly about professors, the sawdust spaghetti they served in the cafeteria, and whether I was getting used to dorm life. The words were second-hand because I didn't really give a shit what Riley was studying. All I could see was skin the color of summer, tawny and golden, and eyes that shimmered like glazed chocolate. When he told me that I was beautiful, I knew that I should cringe with the typicality of it, but instead, I preened.

What was I doing?

Suddenly, my voice sounded disconnected from my body. Riley's laugh was a thousand miles away down a dark hole. His face was blurring. I tried to explain that I didn't feel right, but my neck was getting weak, floppy, overexerted by holding up my head. I tried to put my chin on my hand, and my elbow slipped right off the bar. I could see colorful shirts collecting around me, and high-fives exchanged between Riley and his friends. Stella looked like a kaleidoscope of exploding movement as she whispered something in my ear that sounded like, "Have fun, see you in the morning."

No! Didn't they understand that I had never been drunk before in my life? I tried to argue, to squirm away, but my body was jelly, and this boy was determined.

I woke to filtered sunlight through the cracked window of a rented house. I was in some lumpy bed, my clothes splayed across a tattered rug with orange and green zigzags. Riley was snoring from the bed across the room, one arm was thrown over the edge, one leg sticking out. My insides felt raw, achy and abused while white hot pain pulsed through my skull.

Fumbling to get dressed, and feeling like my kidneys were burning because I had to pee so badly, I wound my way through an unfamiliar living room that stank of man-sweat, and stepped out the rickety front door. It was still early; no one was around. When I slipped back into my dorm and stumbled up two flights of stairs to the room Stella and I shared, I wasn't entirely surprised to find her lower bunk empty. I didn't let myself feel contempt for her because I had just done the exact same thing.

I punished myself with a blisteringly hot shower, trying to rid myself of the lingering residue of dirty sex and self-loathing. My chest heaved with shame as I was assaulted by images of my sweet boyfriend, Jackson, the man I loved with all of my heart.

Any hope I had of burying this stupendous mistake died several weeks later when everything I had envisioned my life to be changed.

I was pregnant.

Riley's once endearing dimples weren't so attractive when the mouth they encircled sneered at me and tossed insults like, "whore," and "slut." He had dreams, too, you know. Dreams of endless parties, a steady stream of nameless nighttime partners and the full college experience his deft physical skills on the lacrosse field had earned him. He had absolutely no intention of getting benched by a girl he barely knew and a kid he didn't want.

To Riley and probably most other college students who stumble into an inopportune fertilization, the common conundrum had an easy out. Scientifically, it should have made perfect sense to me, too. This tiny being was only a jumble of cells, conceived by accident and unwanted by both parties. I told myself there would be no guilt, and that I would be sparing it from a life of desperation and disappointment. But as week after week went by, time was running out. Maybe I did it on purpose, because in my heart, I had already allowed love to take seed.

The last time I saw Riley O'Roarke, he was in the middle of a drunken crowd barking out, "whazzup dawg," while rubbing up on a girl I recognized from my physics class. I was on my own, and I knew it.

When it became apparent that I was in the family way, I dropped out of school, handed back my full academic scholarship, and came home. People around Echo Valley would look sadly at me and shake their heads. "That's too bad," they'd say as I pretended not to hear them. "She seemed so much better than her parents."

Good ol' Mom and Dad lived up to their reputations as parental delinquents. The thought of taking back their now expectant adult daughter didn't quite jibe with their plans to becloud their golden years with steady intoxication. They moved out of their dingy apartment, bought some shitty, broken-down motor home, and hit the road in search of sunshine and some sweet southern ganja.

I went ahead and stomped on my boyfriend's heart. Jackson Nichols had been the best thing I'd ever know. He had loved me in spite of the neglectful cretins I'd been born to, celebrating my dream to become a doctor and restore some honor to my family name. We had shared precious days at my favorite place in the world, my grandfather's musty, old, northern New Hampshire farm. I had known true love for a man, and letting it go brought such pain, the only defense I had was to go numb.

I didn't beg for forgiveness or even explain what had really happened. I'd already had a vision of my new life, and I knew Jackson deserved better. There would be no way I would take him down with me. I needed to make sure that once the hurt of my betrayal subsided, he would go on to have a wonderful future, with children of his own from a woman who would never have allowed herself to be compromised. I owed him as much for everything he had meant to me.

The following year, my son, Bailey Carmichael, was born with dark hair and even darker eyes, just like the father he's never met. I am not a doctor; I am a hairdresser. I haven't seen Jackson or Riley in over four years. I don't have a boyfriend, my parents are never around, and my apartment here in Echo Valley is small and overpriced. My beloved grandfather is long since gone. I am regularly overwhelmed and underprepared for life as a single mother. I am a living, breathing after-school special, the film parents show their teenage daughters before they go ahead and smash up all their potential with a wrecking ball.

What crumbled away for me the night I met Riley in a dark bar is being slowly rebuilt. Even though I am not the person I thought I would be, and the new foundation of my life may have some cracks in places, I'm doing okay. We're doing okay.

I am happy, madly in love with my little boy, and God helps anyone who tries to hurt him.

CHAPTER TWO

I hear my house phone chiming from the other room. 6:45.

Who could be calling me at this hour? Climbing up from my sleep haze, I struggle to recall the last time I saw my parents. Are they all right? I dismiss that thought, I already know better. My parents are like Teflon. Nothing sticks to them, especially not Bailey and me. Besides, since when does a hangover burn off before noon?

I grab the phone and glance quickly at the number on caller ID. I squint to make out the words—Gerry's Salon. I squeak out a hello.

"Bo, it's Gerry. Big meeting today, I need you in here pronto."

Pronto? I can't do pronto. Gerry knows that.

"What time are you thinking? I have to cover Bailey, and Annie doesn't come till nine." Gerry hates excuses, and I think underneath it all, hates kids, too. He puffs out some air on the other end, so early in the morning and he's already full of bluster.

"Get here as soon as you can, it's important." With that, he hangs up on me.

Jesus Christ, is nothing ever easy? I do a mental inventory of all the people I could ask to cover my four-year-old for a couple of hours until his babysitter gets here. Asking her to come in early is as simple as swallowing the steak knives in my kitchen. Most of my neighbors are still sleeping off whatever they poisoned their bodies with last night. My friends are limited in both number and availability. I have no one. Bailey and I are entirely on our own.

No, we're not. We have Peter. His phone number is among a very short list of contacts I have saved into my cell phone, and the one I probably shouldn't have at all.

I pluck the cell from the pocket of yesterday's work pants. There are no messages waiting for me. There never are. No one wants to hang around with an overtired single parent who can't even afford dollar draft night down at the bar. I stifle the guilt I feel by having the Echo Valley police chief on standby. Who does that?

6:54.

I know he'll be up, but do I really want to wake Emily? I am not Mrs. Brenner's favorite person. I imagine this has caused a rift of sorts between husband and wife, but whenever I broach the subject, I get the palm in my face. Peter's way of shutting me up and avoiding a discussion he does not wish to have. I don't feel good about the idea that Emily Brenner probably thinks I'm trying to force my son upon her still grieving husband. People around town have told me she has never been the same since losing her only son, Tucker, but I think when it comes to me there is more to it.

I punch up Peter's number, saying a little prayer that he picks up instead of Emily. *Please, please, please.*

"Chief Brenner here." Thank you, God.

"Hi, Peter. It's Bo. I'm so sorry to bother you this early."

"Not a problem. Is Bailey okay?" I am not surprised my son is his first concern.

"Oh, yes, he's fine. But I'm not. I'm stuck. Gerry wants us in early for some big meeting, and I can't ask Annie. I don't think she'd even know her own name this early in the morning."

"Say no more. I'll be over in ten minutes." Before I can even reply, he clicks off.

I get myself ready quickly, jumping into the shower but not washing my hair. I tuck the dark blonde strands up into a high bun and pull some wisps out on either side. I head into Bailey's room and find his head buried under the covers.

"Good Morning, Mr. B.," I say softly. "I have a surprise for you." He rises up like I just stuck a firecracker under him.

"What, Momma? What surprise?"

"Well, I have to go to work extra early today, so guess who's coming before Annie gets here?" I try to build the momentum a little, but the list of potential visitors is short. Bailey gets it in one guess.

"Peter?" he giggles. "Peter is coming here now?"

"Yes! What a lucky boy you are today." He bounds out of bed and heads for his dresser to pull out some clothes. As he races to get ready in time to greet his friend at the door, he throws this over his shoulder at me.

"This is good, Momma. Now I won't have to call Peter on the phone. He'll already be here."

"No, Bailey." I come back around to hold him by his shoulders. Even though that statement fits perfectly with his kid logic, I realize I am right back at square one. I suspect Bailey intended to do exactly what I have been telling him not to.

"I thought we were done with 9-1-1? I thought you understood that Chief Brenner is a very busy man, and we will get in big huge trouble if you don't stop calling him." He is far too excited to focus on what I'm saying, so he merely nods at me as he rushes into the kitchen to wait by the door.

"How 'bout some waffles?" Bailey isn't listening, he's running like a dog from the door to the window, window to the door. Just as we hear a knock on the door, the waffle pops up sufficiently browned along the edges. I cut it up into Bailey-sized pieces and put it on the table. I squeeze out some syrup on the side and turn to greet Peter. He has already scooped up Bailey and is giving him a hug so tight his voice is muffled against the crook of his neck. When my son pulls his face back, it is full of joy. I imagine that would be the greeting he'd give a grandfather who showed up with a giant lollipop wrapped in a bright red bow. If he had a grandfather, that is.

"You better get out of here, Bo. Don't want to keep Gerry waiting. Take as long as you need, or I can just wait here until Annie shows up. Either way is fine." Peter's tone is light and happy.

"This is above and beyond. I hope you know if I had any other choice, I would never bother you ... or Emily ... this early in the morning. I'm so sorry." The palm goes up.

"Good gracious! This makes the fifth "*I'm sorry*" in twenty-four hours. Enough already. Get out of here." He takes the same hand he just shut me up with and motions toward the door. He and Bailey hustle over to the couch to watch the high school kids wait for the bus at the stop sign just outside our driveway. As I reach for the doorknob to leave, I hear him tell Bailey, "That'll be you one day, a big kid almost all grown up heading off to high school." I lower my head, wondering if he's thinking of another little boy who used to stand at the bus stop with him a lifetime ago. The same little boy who would tell him, "I love you, Daddy," just before he walked up the steps and disappeared into the seat that was taller than he was.

I close the door behind me, feeling the rush of chilly air. The early morning temperatures are already flirting with fall. Bailey loves fall. Even as a toddler, he dances around our yard, picking up fallen leaves and holding them up for me to see the specks of red and orange along the edges, trying to wrap his juvenile mind around a concept that is as old as time.

His little face grows serious when he asks me how the green knows when it's time to leave.

I usually make up something that will satisfy his rapid-fire attention span, but I do wonder myself how trees really do know when it's time to let go. If they spend so much time nurturing every leaf that sprouts from their branches, how can it be so easy to let it go as if it were never there in the first place?

Of course, this natural progression from life to death covers people, too.

Peter Brenner came to us at a time when his most precious leaf had just drifted away on a fateful wind.

CHAPTER THREE

The sweet relationship between my son and the Echo Valley police chief began with a phone call. It was as simple and as complicated as that. Now, after serving the people of this small New Hampshire town for the better part of three decades, Chief Brenner is hanging up his holster soon. He jokes that the timing coincides perfectly with the torrent of AARP pamphlets that now target his mailbox on a regular basis.

"I get it," he told me once. "I get that when your hair either falls out or becomes the color of bone, it's time to hand over the reins." Peter may be aging, but one would never call him "old." More like wise and well lived.

In any case, we must adjust quickly. The straight-laced do-gooder who is replacing him is about two decades fresher and wound one hundred times tighter. This guy will consider repeated 9-1-1 calls from a four-year-old about as acceptable as bringing a dart gun to a water balloon fight.

"Here's the thing," Peter said recently, after yet another incident involving Bailey, our home phone, and his oblivious elderly babysitter, Annie, who sleeps more than she babysits. "You have a month left to get a handle on this. The new guy has already told dispatch he wants daily logs kept of all incoming and outgoing calls. All calls, Bo. *Especially* 9-1-1 calls."

Oh, shit! Daily logs? His secretary doesn't even take notes. She simply taps her finger against her head a couple of times, saying everything she needs to know is right there. She and the rest of the Echo Valley Police Department are in for a shake-up and my son's antics certainly will not make the cut.

I struggle with how to do it. How do you take away your child's best and only male role model? How do I tell the man who has stepped into our lives as guardian and protector that he needs to go away?

It started over a year ago, just before Bailey turned four and the fascination with the phone began. Three-thirty in the morning and I heard my name being hollered through the thin wood of my front door. I rushed into Bailey's room, throwing back his thick comforter but finding only blankets and a pajama bottom tucked into the space between the mattress and the footboard.

No Bailey.

I stumbled over to the kitchen, unlatching and unbolting the cheapest locks Home Depot had to offer one by one. Before I threw back the final deadbolt, I put my ear closer to the flimsy molding and asked again, who was there.

"Miss Carmichael, it's the police. What's your emergency?" I heard heavy boots scuffle back and forth. *Emergency?* Was I having an emergency? Other than not being able to cover my rent that month, I couldn't think of anything else.

"Bo, open the door. It's Chief Brenner. We have to respond to every 9-1-1 call the department receives. Please, let us in."

Peter Brenner walked slowly into my Lilliputian living room until I heard his deep voice purposely perched between silly and stern saying, "Is this the rascal?" I darted back and peered around the edge of the worn sofa cushion.

"Come out, with your hands up."

I saw his dark head poke around the side of the couch, his tiny fingers wrapped around the off-white tangled cord of the phone.

"Hi, Chief," he lisped in his little boy, middle-of-the-night voice.

"I was just trying to talk to you and the other officers." His eyes were huge as he looked at all of us looking down at him. In that moment when a hard reprimand could have been handed down to the kid, and a nasty reminder issued to the airhead mother that children need to be watched, we got neither. Instead, Chief Brenner reached for Bailey and plucked him up against his barrel chest.

"Oh, don't you worry about us, young man. We weren't sleeping anyway. Did you know that Mrs. Brenner just whipped up a batch of her world famous chocolate chip cookies? I'm going to run out to my cruiser and grab you one. Then you have to promise me you will go back to bed and let your mom get some sleep. No fuss, right?"

"Yes, Chief, no fuss, but can I have two cookies? Please?" His face broke into a mischievous grin as he pushed off on Peter's forearms and hopped down from his grip.

Maybe if I had insisted on one cookie that night, I wouldn't be in this mess now. Maybe if Chief Brenner wasn't covering for a colleague who was home with his sick wife, he never would have formed that immediate bond with my child. For whatever reason, Peter Brenner was brought to us that night, and now I have to figure out how to teach my son that he can't just dial up his beloved friend through the Echo Valley emergency dispatch.

As in, *9-1-1-what's your emergency,* over and over for months on end.

I've apologized more times than I can count, I've threatened to pull the phone out of the wall, and I've coerced solemn vows from my son's tear-streaked face until I almost believed he knew what he was saying.

Now, they are best buds, even though Bailey can never replace what's been lost. As one family was falling apart, another was coming together.

The story of Tucker Brenner is like small town folklore, a patchwork quilt of a tale that may twist slightly from one ear to the next but always ends the same.

The only son of Peter and Emily Brenner had been a leftie pitcher with a golden arm. A perfect blend of humble hero, Tucker volunteered at the soup kitchen, drove his dad's cruiser in the Old Home Day parade, and stole hearts before his female admirers even knew they were gone. He was nailing ninety-one-mile-an-hour fastballs and putting up the kind of stats that made folks wonder if his talent was on loan from God.

Before his potential could be fully realized, he was called in to repay it.

News of the good or horrific variety travels fast in towns where everyone knows everyone else. Once the coffee shop opened up before dawn, and friends gathered to greet each other on a brand new day, they heard of the spectacular crash on the other side of the river. The car that had melded like Play-Doh against an old oak tree unleashing pure horror on first responders who had watched the boy mangled behind the wheel grow from tow-headed toddler to rocket-armed athlete. They returned to their jobs but were never the same.

Echo Valley lost some of its innocence the night Tucker Brenner died. An unspeakable loss that, to this day, still serves as a relentless reminder of how deeply a good man and his loving wife have suffered.

CHAPTER FOUR

"Thank you all for adjusting your schedules and coming down early. I assure you, it is for a very good reason." Gerry takes a deep breath and tries to settle himself before continuing. It's a little weird seeing him like this. At least when he's at his snarky best, I know what to expect. This newfound vigor is throwing me off. We are perched on the black leather chairs typically reserved for our clients, still rubbing the sleep from our eyes.

"As I'm sure you all know, our state is about to be front and center in the national spotlight." I notice some of the more moronic nail technicians passing glances, clueless as to why New Hampshire would suddenly become a hotbed of activity.

"The primary is coming up," I whisper, getting blank stares. "You know, the *presidential* primary."

They seem to make a slight connection. I turn my attention back to Gerry, who seems to be going from pink to beet red right before my eyes.

"I am proud and honored to tell you Gerry's Salon has been selected to prepare the family of United States Senator Declan Anderson ... *for their annual Christmas card!*"

Faces scrunch up in a kind of disappointed surprise, including my own. I realize this is quite an honor for Gerry, but in this room full of various tattoos, piercings, and multi-colored shocks of hair, there aren't a whole lot of party loyalists. Gerry notices there is dead air, so he rushes back in trying to whip up the excitement.

"Let me explain," he starts, looking slightly pissed that he even has to. "I understand that some …" slight pause as he looks around at his employees, "… er … *most* of you don't follow politics." *You think?* "Senator Anderson is a southern senator who is the leading candidate for president. He, his wife and kids will be here for several events over the course of a weekend next month. One of those events will be a photo shoot at an apple orchard that the family will use for their annual holiday greeting card." Deep breath again as I see him trying to find a way to get through to this dimwitted gathering of non-voting deadbeats who probably think CNN is a new designer drug.

"We have been hired to spend the entire day with the family. This means hair, makeup, the whole nine yards."

I immediately start thinking about how I can get out of it. There is absolutely no way I can ask Annie to cover a weekend. Unless the senator-who-wants-to-be-president can bounce Bailey on his knee for eight hours on a Saturday, I'm not sure how I can pull it off.

Maybe Gerry will consider me unfit for duty. Surely, far more experienced stylists here deserve this more than I do. Gerry reaches for a clipboard and starts doling out assignments.

"Jessie and Ari will cover Mrs. Anderson. Start Googling her, find some magazines with her picture on them, do some research. Be ready to duplicate exactly what you see her look like most of the time." He pushes a page over the top of the metal hinge, counting off a few more stylists, filling them in on their assignments. I'm almost off the hook for the weekend-warrior, presidential-primping bullshit. My fingers are crossed so tightly they start to twitch.

"Bo," he says. *Shit, shit, shit!*

He pauses, walking toward me and sporting a subtle grin. Is he trying to make a point here? Drop a bomb on me? I consider the possibility that the Andersons have a dog.

Am I about to be told that I'll have to coif a canine?

"You have the most important assignment of all. *You...*" pausing again for emphasis. I beg him with my eyes to reconsider whatever he's about to drop in my lap. Remember, it's *me* here, single mother slacker who gives you fits! Remember who you're talking to!

"... are assigned to the man himself. Senator Anderson is all yours."

I feel my shoulders slump forward in defeat. I feel my face go hot, then ice cold.

"Uh," I come up with throaty warbles, trying to strike a balance between horrified and humbled. "I'm deeply grateful, but honestly, not entirely sure why this would be okay with you?" I motion wide with my arms, trying to draw his attention to the bevy of loyal, more experienced employees he is bypassing.

The bottom half of his face finds something close to a full smile, setting off a flash of tiny white pearls just behind his curled up lips. "Bo," he says, lowering his voice into what I imagine is his version of being earnest. "We've been through some ups and downs, you and me. While I admit you threaten the safety of my aging heart on an almost daily basis, I see great talent in you. If you can stop fidgeting around in your own skin long enough to focus on this guy, you just might have a future in this business."

A future? In this business?

I don't think I should admit to him that at one point in my life, I thought hairstylists were about as bright as the flickering light bulb in the oily garage my parents used to smoke pot in. Now, I am one, getting what could be my only shot at the big time. I should feel elated, on top of the world, ready to attack. Instead, I feel like shit.

Saturdays with Bailey are as precious to me as the elusive four-leaf clover on my grandfather's farm. I would spend hours gently plying back each blade of grass, looking for the one extra petal hidden in the endless stretch of green. Once all the chores were complete, he would join me in the field, kneeling down beside me while his deteriorating joints popped and groaned the whole way.

"Don't worry about me," he would protest. "You're going to be a big city doctor someday, those hands will do far more important work in this world than what I'm doing here. Better yet, they won't smell like cow dung every darn day of your life." We would laugh together as his callused fingers reached out and tousled my hair. They were happy days spent on the vast expanse of rolling hills alive with sweet air that tickled my nose but made me feel like I was home.

Grandpa died several years ago. The sun set on his well-tended fields and his tractor went silent. Even though I miss him like I would miss my right arm, I am grateful he wasn't here to see our carefully laid plans swallowed up by my own stupidity.

Gerry has not budged from the space just in front of me. The other stylists have dispersed, and I realize I have been sitting here lost in my own head for too long.

"Gerry, I'm flattered, of course. I'm just a little …"

Shocked, dismayed, completely convinced you've lost your mind.

"… um … a little … nervous." I go with that because it would be logical. Here I am, about to get hold of a potential future president's entire head of hair and he just happens to be a total George Clooney knockoff. The Andersons were on the cover of *People* magazine not too long ago, the senator's arm casually slung across the shoulder of his stunning wife as she held one small child on her hip and another by the hand. Although I can't afford cable, even my fuzzy television set can't tone down the golden loveliness of this all-American family.

As luck would have it, he'll probably win.

No pressure. It's just the family Christmas card. Don't even think about the fact that along with every friend and relative this couple has accumulated along a fantastic voyage through their uber-spectacular life, it will probably be mailed out to heads of state, former presidents, celebrities, federal judges, and maybe even God himself.

Sure, I think wryly. No pressure at all.

Gerry is doing his best to reassure me that I have the goods to handle this. Maybe self-deprecation is a talent I inherited from my grandfather, because right now, not even the whiskey he used to brew behind the barn could force his aplomb down my throat.

"Listen to me. You can do this. I chose you for a reason. It's your time. It's now or never. Think about it. I've been around this block longer than I care to admit, and you don't fit in on this street." I nod at him while I look down. "Go get some more coffee. You have several weeks to work this out, get ready for the shoot. You got questions, you ask. Hear me?"

I nod again. My stomach is rolling like a churning white cap cresting a wave. I hoist myself up and take slow steps toward the coffee maker in the back hallway. Everyone else is hustling around, mixing colors, cleaning scissors, folding towels. They smile at me as I walk by, most of them genuinely. I smile back, although what I really want to do is apologize. Especially to the few of them who've been here longer than I've been alive. Why can't they take Mr. Fantastic? They deserve him.

I'll need to come up with a plan. The shoot is still a month away, and it just might take me that long to figure out who can watch my son while I attend to the man who could soon become the leader of the free world.

CHAPTER FIVE

"Bailey," I call from the kitchen. "It's time to go, honey. Let's hit the road." I try to hustle us out the door. One of Annie's great-granddaughters is home from college for the weekend and will watch Bailey until I can escape the apple orchard photo shoot. It's going to cost me three-quarters of what I'll make today, but she's honest, doesn't do drugs, and promised me she'd only text if Bailey took a nap.

"Comin' Momma!" I hear him get a running start down the hallway, then see him fly around the corner holding one shoe and wearing the other. "Can't tie this right, need your help." I bend at the waist to inspect the knot he has inserted into the matted lace of his shoestring. I know from experience that undoing the intricate tangles along his shoelaces requires the patience of Mother Theresa and a physics degree.

"Come here, pal," I say to my son, as he plops his rear end down on the floor and holds up one foot. I snip off the impossible jumble of coils. "I know this is early, but you're going to have a really good time with Bethany. She's looking forward to playing with you today, and before you know it, Momma will be home again." I scoop him up under his arms and hoist him close to me for a hug. I kiss the back of his neck, breathing in his smell until he squirms in my arms and giggles.

"Let me down, Momma. That tickles!" He moves his head back, reaches his tiny hand out and grabs my nose.

"Got it!" he exclaims, as he pretends to put it into his back pocket, just like Peter does to him. "I'll save this for later. When you get home again, I will give you your nose back."

"Okay, Bailey, you take good care of it for me." I grab his bag that holds a change of clothes and his favorite Red Sox sippy cup filled with milk rapidly approaching its expiration date.

"Momma," he begins as we take quick steps down to the back lot where my car is parked.

"Yes, buddy?" I say.

"Does Peter know you are working today?" he asks on quick puffs of air as he tries to keep pace with me.

"Um, I'm not sure, sweetheart. I haven't talked to Peter in a couple of days. Why?"

"Because if Peter knew you were working, he would want to take me, wouldn't he?"

Here we go again.

I have him by the crook of his elbow, with my bag on one shoulder, his on the other. My hair is hanging across my eyes, a few strands sticking to the gummy wetness of my lip-gloss. I am physically uncomfortable under the weight of everything in my arms, and mentally drained from the stress of preparing for this assignment today. I am not ready to deal with the question that is as loaded as the potato skins we sometimes splurge on at Applebees.

"Honey, remember, this is a Saturday. Peter is probably spending the day with his wife, mowing his lawn, or raking the leaves in his yard. He is too busy to take care of you all day long. He is not your father, he's not my father. We can't expect him to always be here for us, honey."

Bailey deadweights on me, plants his heels and holds his ground.

"Momma, stop!" The arm that was holding his elbow falls, followed by the overstuffed bag that spills out on the blacktop.

"Bailey! What is wrong with you?" It comes out way too harsh, triggering an immediate swell of tears in his eyes. His chin dips so low it almost meets his chest, as his body slumps into itself. My normally strapping boy suddenly looks so small.

This is all my fault. He's barely had a chance to experience life, and I'm already ruining it for him. Instead of being shuttled off to yet another unfamiliar face today, he should be playing in the green grass of his own backyard with a sandbox and maybe a brother or two to throw a ball with. Bailey deserves so much more than being rushed out of his undersized apartment by his overscheduled mother on what should be a lazy weekend morning spent in pajama bottoms and bare feet.

"Honey, we have got to go. You know that I have an important job to do today." I have five minutes to drop Bailey off at Annie's and make it to Gerry's Salon where Jessie will be drumming her acrylic nails in near panic that I will make everyone else late. We all know that if we show up at this stupid orchard even a second past the time all the important people have plugged into their phones, Gerry's head will explode and we'll all feel the shrapnel.

I pull Bailey into his car seat. Tears are streaming down his face, his cheeks are red, and his forehead is loaded with sweat. I brush back his bangs and wipe his face with the back of my sleeve.

"I can't do this today, buddy. I need you to be a big boy. I promise I'll be home as soon as I can. This is important to me. Do you understand?" I pull his chin up with my finger, so he is looking me in the eye. He nods back to me, but sadness makes his brown eyes darken.

"I'm sorry, I don't want to make you late." He drags his fist across his cheek, looking beyond me and out the window. His voice is forlorn, and I wonder if he's even aware that he's speaking out loud. "I miss Peter." A soft sigh escapes on a rush of breath. "It's okay, I be a good boy. I promise."

"Let's just get through today. If you can be good for Bethany, no trouble, then I will call Peter and ask him if we can go for an ice cream. Okay?"

It is a total bribe, but it works flawlessly. In a flash, the tears stop, his eyes beam with delight, and he grins so wide I can see entire rows of baby teeth gleaming in the morning sun.

"Pinky square, with sugar on top?"

"Pinky swear."

I hold out the pinky on my right hand, his much smaller one reaches out from his left. We meet in the middle. Just like always.

CHAPTER SIX

The backseat is abuzz with small talk, sloshing coffee cups, and an abundance of nervous energy. I stay mostly quiet as we turn onto the highway, lost in thoughts that center mostly around my little boy.

Muffled words find me from the backseat.

"… not like Bo. Bo? You asleep up there?"

"Sorry, guys. I was spacing. What do you mean, not like me?" Two girls stare back at me from the space just behind Jessie's head, and William from the seat behind mine, his expression absurdly incredulous.

"Seriously, Bo?" he barks at me. "Have you *seen* the senator? Or should I say the *sex*-ator? I would like to see how far he'd be willing to go to get my vote." He puckers lips fully primed with high gloss color. "And I can't believe you get to touch him *all ... day ... long*."

"I'm just glad I didn't get stuck with his bitchy little wife," Carly Swenson pipes in. Carly has the supreme honor of French braiding the Anderson daughter, who is about seven years old with hair so blonde it looks like angels dribbled sunshine over her head. "I was reading in the *Enquirer* last week that she has four nannies and three personal shoppers."

"And two new boobs," Jessie trills from the front. "Clearly, after popping out two brats, her boobies can't be that perky on their own." She looks over at me, the only parent in the car. "Sorry, Bo," she says. "No offense, your boobs still look great, of course."

Of course. I try not to laugh at her severely backhanded compliment.

Ari murmurs something about the next exit, which I double check from the directions Gerry left for us that it's the one we want. I tell Jessie to take a left off the ramp. Just a few miles north the fall colors are bursting. The sky is a pristine blue with a couple of puffy white clouds that appear almost painted on. The red of the old-fashioned barns that dot the landscape are as picturesque as a postcard.

Days like this remind me why I'm still here. The dead of winter reminds me that I'm still too poor to move anywhere else.

I reach for my bag on the floor and check my cell phone tucked into the front pocket. I switch it to vibrate for the remainder of the day. Gerry sternly reminded each of us to do so, telling us Senator Anderson was not to be subjected to our various ringtones of choice.

Although I have the most important Anderson to attend to, he is thus far the least complicated. I have had only one phone call from his adviser, which was just to pass along contact information directly to me in case something unexpected came up. I was anticipating a deep, authoritative voice when Gerry pulled me into his office the other day to take the call, but the caller was female, and she sounded quite young. She told me her name was Mackenzie Mason, she'd be escorting the senator, and I'd need to have him ready in thirty minutes or less.

It all seemed too easy, which had me wondering what I was missing. Dare I hope that as long as I don't step on him, spit on him, or give him a cowlick this day might go off without a hitch?

We cross from blacktop onto a dirt road with a big sign that announces we have just arrived at *Bloomfield Orchards, Home of New Hampshire's Oldest Family Farm*. As we drive around a corner and up a small hill, I notice a line of catering trucks with workers clad in white aprons unloading large square pans covered in aluminum foil. Just the sight of all that food makes my stomach growl.

Jessie tries to avoid a line of muck developing on the grass as heavy trucks rip up the moist but not yet frozen morning grass. We park, climbing carefully out of each door, holding onto the sides of the SUV to avoid face-planting in the sludgy water. William is horrified that the bottoms of his hundred-dollar pants are about to be compromised.

"Jesus frickin' Christ," he mutters as he slogs his way around the back of the car where his supplies are stacked on top of mine. "Are you freaking kidding me here? As if Mrs. Sex-ator herself is going to put one Manolo Blahnik covered toe in this slop? I think not!" He passes back my smaller bag. "Here, save yourself."

The other car carrying the rest of Gerry's crew pulls in next to ours. I wave to them as I hoist my bag onto my shoulder and lean part of my weight onto William's extended arm to move to more solid ground. The barn looks all spiffed up with fresh plantings along the foundation and bluestone pebbles covering the matted down walkway. As we enter, I see the first floor divided into stations. Gerry told me to set up next to the window that faces the orchard. There are decorative barrels of mums carefully placed next to fat, orange pumpkins without a hint of rot on their stems. Fresh apple cider sits on another long table set up between wooden support beams, and there is a fancy looking crock-pot throwing out a deliciously subtle mix of cinnamon and nutmeg. Quintessential New Hampshire appeal is everywhere you look.

I find my spot and hoist the bag off my shoulder. I begin to set up brushes, gels, and sprays on the small counter next to the window that offers an unobstructed view of apple trees in full bloom. My colleagues are also setting up at their own stations, but the most action is taking place at the area where Mrs. Anderson will be. She likes things a certain way, and the hired help had better get it right. I silently thank Gerry for sparing me the endless delights of the lovely Mrs. Anderson.

With everything in place we take a seat and wait, and then we wait some more. The Anderson family is now over a half hour late. The caterer's eggs are getting too crispy, and the bacon looks like strips of wet leather spread out on a bed of grease. I complain to William what a waste all this is. I tell him I could eat for a month off this spread.

"Why must you always feed, Bo? It's so primitive of you." William is among the non-eaters at Gerry's salon. He prefers to fit into clothes meant for prepubescent boys.

I risk a quick run to the bathroom. The coffee I gulped down this morning is worse than water when my nerves are firing. After what feels like forever, I finish up, quickly wash my hands and run back over to my station. I find my place just in time to see a line of black SUVs approaching through the windows facing the parking lot. I lean in next to William, who is pressing his face onto the pane of glass.

"Where, oh, where are you, Mr. Man? Get out here and give William somethin' fine to look at."

"Remember, it's all smoke and mirrors," Ari reminds him. "They never look as good in person as they do on TV." Typically, true, though I suspect in the case of the Andersons, she has it all wrong. They really are that fabulous.

We hear heavy footsteps approaching on the rocks just outside the barn door. We scurry around to make sure we are standing directly next to the empty seats that will be filled by Anderson rear ends. Three tall men in dark suits scan the room, each taking off in a different direction to check the corners, look under the tables, and finally, grill us. They stop at each location where the stylists are patiently standing by, confirming our names and double-checking that we all know which Anderson we'll be working on. The guy that comes up to me is dark, with an olive complexion and brown eyes that are just one step below pitch black.

"Bo Carmichael?" he asks.

"Yes, that's me," I reply, trying to keep my voice on par with his.

"Do you know who you are assigned to today?"

"Uh, of course. I'll be working on Mr. Anderson." I don't know why I go with the less formal title. It makes the tan man narrow his eyes.

"We would prefer you acknowledge him by his title, which is *Senator* Anderson."

"Yes, of course." I defer the point, but I don't break eye contact.

"The family will be here momentarily. Is everything in order?"

"Yes, I believe we're ready to go. We've *been* ready to go." For some time now, asshole. It's your guy that's messing with the tightly orchestrated agenda.

A muscle along his jaw clenches. I guess he's not used to sarcasm. His eyes bore into mine. By the time I really need to blink, he decides there is nothing left to say to me. He turns on his highly polished heel and heads back to the door.

Whew, that was weird.

I try to shrug off the uncomfortable encounter as I look just beyond him, to the parking lot, trying to get a glimpse of the family as they exit their caravan. I see two towheads, running away from whoever is trying to keep them out of the mud. Kid giggles waft through the air, which makes me smile and think of Bailey. He'd head straight for the mud, too. I see several well-dressed aides, butchering their loafers and stilettos as they chase the children toward the barn door. Senator and Mrs. Anderson are not the owners of the elbows grasped by tiny hands to lead them over the rest of the matted grass and dirt. The kids are settled into side-by-side seats at the table set up just for them.

I see a pair of long, toned legs approaching the barn door. The skirt hits just above the knee, and the shoes are designer, for sure. Black, sleek, with a heel that is completely free of the mucky dirt the rest of us will be scraping off later. The sweater is fitted, the waist is miniscule, and I do believe Jessie was right about the two new additions to the middle of her chest. Her blonde hair is pulled back into a simple ponytail, but it is shiny, healthy, and untouched by chemicals. Her face is hidden behind huge dark sunglasses, and she does not greet a single person as she marches behind the handlers who are directing her path as carefully as the guys with the orange lights on the tarmac of a runway. She walks right by both of her children without even breaking stride. They don't seem to notice her, either. There is no exchange between them at all, which makes my initial disdain for her swell even more.

What kind of mother walks by her children as if they aren't even there?

Mrs. Anderson gives everyone the silent treatment as she slinks into the chair, takes off her glasses and holds them off to the side for someone to swoop in and take them from her.

Jessie and Ari quickly go to work, wrapping her long locks in hot rollers, not speaking to her or each other. It is an uncomfortable silence, which makes me especially thankful for the regular bursts of laughter coming from the Anderson kids.

I hear more heels hitting the wood floor. The team captain appears, casually carrying a leather jacket over one arm. He is slightly windblown, with a ruddy complexion and an easy smile. Unlike his wife, he immediately stops and begins shaking hands with everyone.

"Hiya, nice to see you … y'all have a beautiful place here."

Warm handshake, clasp on the elbow, moves on to the next.

"Good to meet you, y'all live nearby?"

"Y'all save me some of those apples out there, they sure are purdy."

His teeth are gleaming white; his cheeks pivot in places that would dimple if he carried any more body weight. His jaw is square and strong, his limbs long and lean, his back stick straight. I imagine his handshake feels like a vice grip; this guy wants you to acknowledge him, feel him, *love him*.

I immediately get a bad case of the creeps. He moves past the station where his kids are busy playing games and eating pizza, tousling their hair and saying loud enough for everyone to hear, "Y'all stop spoilin' them now."

Chuckle, laugh, wink. I watch him work the room. This man is a total fake, completely manufactured. He moves in behind his wife, admires her in the mirror directly in front of them and says, "You look beautiful, darlin'. 'Course, it's hard to mess up perfection."

Someone is moving around them taking pictures that I assume will soon hit his website to declare to the world that this genteel southern family can slum in New Hampshire just fine.

Mrs. Anderson barely looks up as her husband saunters off. I sense trouble in paradise. I'd bet these two don't even like each other anymore. As for love, that probably walked out a lifetime ago. But how do you divorce the future president? And why would you dump the nation's next Jackie Kennedy? They're stuck with each other until he either loses or she can slip away after his first term in office. Once he's a lame duck, divorce rumors will become remarkably palatable for a nation with a short attention span and a lustful urge for the next big thing.

Senator Anderson is now walking toward me. I watch his gaze start at my legs and slowly make its way up to my face before he flashes the gleaming smile that never quite reaches his eyes. *He's checking me out!* It's all I can do to keep my mouth from turning down in disgust. Before he reaches me, and with the nimbleness of a jungle cat, Mackenzie Mason materializes. One look at her, and I know exactly why the Anderson marriage has gone cold.

"Hello, you must be Bo." It's more of a statement than a question, she is telling me she's already one step ahead. "May I present Senator Declan Anderson. Senator, meet Bo Carmichael. She comes highly recommended from the premier salon nearby."

Fake smile on full display, hand outstretched waiting for me to close the deal. His fingers wrapping around mine feel like a death grip. I pretend I have vaseline on my teeth and open wide. "Hello, Senator Anderson, it's a pleasure. Won't you have a seat?"

"Don't mind if I do. You already met Mac?" He motions with his head backward to Mackenzie. She answers for both of us.

"Yes, sir. I have spoken to Bo already. She is aware of our time constraints and promises she will have you ready to go very quickly."

"Now, Mac, don't you go puttin' any pressure on my new friend, here. I need a little more work than I used to. Can't go rushin' what nature is slowin' down. Right, Bo?"

I make some noise that isn't a word, throw the cape on him and get to work. Self-deprecation falls flat while his lazy southern accent does nothing to soften the hard sell of pure bullshit.

While Mr. Big Shot settles into the chair, I glance over at Mackenzie Mason. She is exquisite. Her black hair is cut bluntly to her shoulders. It hangs perfectly, far enough from her face and with enough sway to allow a loose strand or two to sex it up a little. Her body is slim, with muscled calves and ropey forearms. Her skin is clear and her lips full and even. I notice just about everything when it comes to a person's face. It's how I decide what to do with their hair. I've refined my ability to scan someone's features so innocuously they don't even know I'm doing it. I can't get a firm feel for her eyes because they're buried in her phone. A slight furrow appears across her brow. Not yet a wrinkle, but it's the only giveaway that she may be older than she looks. I put her in her early thirties, but very well-preserved.

"Mac, be a life saver and go grab me some coffee. Nice and hot, you know how I like it."

Mackenzie jumps, tucks the phone into the pocket of her fitted navy blue blazer and scans the room for the coffee table. I tell her it's near the front door, and she is off like a rocket. Mustn't keep the big man waiting. His eyes slide up to the mirror in front of us to watch her walk away. There is an icy expression on his face. He doesn't know I'm watching him.

What has she done to him?

No words pass between us while Mackenzie is at the coffee table. Does he sense that he makes my skin crawl? Is he royally pissed that his typically bulletproof southern charm seems more like a smarmy act, or does his sullen silence have nothing to do with me at all?

I start to fill in some blanks.

He and his wife are done. Anyone with the slightest sense of intuition could see that.

His right-hand man is a smokin' hot chick.

And I think she's done something that he doesn't like. Not one little bit.

CHAPTER SEVEN

The Andersons' annual Christmas card will be perfect. The family was carted out to the perfect location, under the perfect Granite State apple tree, with just the perfect amount of sunlight filtering through the thick branches. The kids looked adorable, the wife drop-dead gorgeous, and the senator handsome and presidential. During the shoot, the rest of us back in the barn packed away our supplies and helped the caterers polish off the untouched spread.

Just as I'd suspected, I had the easiest job of all. The senator's hair fell into impeccable waves that required nothing more than a couple dollops of gel, and one quick spurt of hairspray. I was almost done with him by the time Mackenzie had returned with his coffee—nice and hot just the way he liked it. He thanked me curtly, spared me another crushing handshake, and walked off. Shortly after, his wife joined him, followed by the kids, and off they went in two golf carts for the jaunt into the orchard.

Now, the golf carts are sitting idle next to the barn, and the Andersons are tucked back into their SUVs. His people are still milling about, taking photos of the landscape, and punching away on the tiny keypads of their cell phones. Even though none of the black cars have snaked their way back down the bumpy farm road yet, we figure it's safe for us to head out.

The owner of the orchard made a final sweep through the barn, a nice old man who thanked us for being careful with the place. "Come back anytime," he'd instructed. I just might, Bailey would get a kick out of picking apples, especially if I let him climb the ladder to the top branches where the apples grew the fattest. I get a warm feeling just thinking about him. I look forward to a lazy night at home with my son by my side and an old movie playing on my old TV.

That reminds me to check my cell and give Bethany a quick call to say I'm on my way back. As we pile into Jessie's car, I reach for my bag and slide my hand into the front pocket where I left the phone. It's empty. My phone isn't there. I quickly pull the bag open in the middle, rifling through combs, brushes, bottles of hair spray, and elastic bands.

No phone.

"What's the matter?" Jessie asks, her hand stopping the key in mid-turn in the ignition.

"I can't find my phone. I'm positive I put it right here."

"Do you think you left it somewhere in the barn? Did it fall out?"

"I don't think so." I try to remember if I had my bag when I went to the bathroom that last time. "Maybe."

"I'll go check for you." William reaches for the door handle, willing to risk another helping of mud on the cuffs of his pricey pants.

"No, it's okay. I'll just retrace my steps. It can't be too far. Sorry guys, I'll make it quick. Be right back."

I hop back through the trenches, being far less careful this time to avoid the trouble spots. The barn door is still open, but all the tables have been removed, and it's getting dark inside. I step over the wooden threshold and inhale that familiar farm smell taking back over.

The windows to the left are losing light fast, but I can still see the Anderson SUVs. I wonder why they're still here, didn't Mackenzie say something about an incredibly busy schedule to keep? I look around each corner, and head toward the bathroom.

My flat heels are silent, so I guess they never heard me coming.

Not quite voices at first, just mumbles off to my right. I walk over to where I hear the noises coming from. As I get closer, the voices get louder. Do I hear crying?

Suddenly, they shoot around the corner. He reaches roughly for her arm to pull her back.

"Don't you dare walk away from me! Who the fuck do you think you're messing with here?"

"Declan, let go. Please. I just want to go."

"You will take care of this, and you will do it right now! For Christ's sake, Mac, this will ruin everything. Don't you get it, you stupid bitch?"

She is looking backward, pulling her body away from his grip with such momentum I can't move out of her path fast enough. We slam into each other. She whips her head around as her perfectly set hair becomes a black sheet over her face.

"Bo!" she shrieks at me. One hand tries to pull her hair back and wipe her face dry at the same time. Her eyes are swollen, red-rimmed and teary.

"Oh my God, what are you doing here?" She wants to know this from me. Guess what, Mac, I was about to ask you the same thing. More importantly, what are you doing here ... with him?

My brain screams at me to get out of here. Fast!

"Uh, I was just looking for my phone." My eyes go from Mackenzie, who looks like a baby bird dumped from her nest, over to Senator Anderson, the hungry fox waiting for the poor thing to crash to the ground.

"Nothing to see here, Ms. Carmichael." His voice is gritty and mean. His eyes are blazing as short bursts of air push through clenched teeth. "Mac and I were just having a little meeting of the minds, weren't we, Mac?" He flashes between anger and total indignation at having to deal with me at a moment like this. He will demand to know which member of his team fumbled the ball by letting the hairdresser back in. Or maybe I fumbled the ball, during a play I should never have been out on the field for.

Shit!

"Uh, sure you were," I say, trying to back up a little, so Mackenzie and I are no longer touching. She uses the back of her other hand to wipe her eyes, which are still wet with fresh tears.

Jesus Christ, she's a mess! What has he done to her?

I get such a rush of fury I can't move. In spite of knowing better, I reach for her arm and ask her if she needs some help.

"She's fine!" he explodes at me, snatching her back from my outstretched hand. Mackenzie is silent as she lets him take her arm and pull her away. Her other arm can't move as fast, it hitches on my torso and makes her wrist slump downward. In the span of milliseconds, her expensive leather purse, no longer supported on a sturdy appendage, empties out onto the old wooden planks. Lipstick, pens, a small wallet, and loose change skitter across the floor. But something square falls directly onto my mud-covered shoe. We reach for it at the exact same time. I get there first. I pull the cardboard box up, and before I can hand it back over to her, I see exactly what it is. She watches my mouth drop wide open. I see her trying to make a deal with God.

Please don't let this simple woman from this hick state have a clue as to what she's looking at right now.

Amen.

I wish I didn't know, either. But I do. Four years ago, I stuffed the same cardboard box into my purse. I had told the doctor I wanted it, *needed it*, because I was completely unprepared to be a parent. With nothing more than a scrawl across his prescription pad he ordered it up for me, told me to follow the directions carefully, and make sure I was within a hundred miles of a hospital with an emergency room.

Just in case.

Just in case there were any complications from the pills I would take to abort my fetus.

CHAPTER EIGHT

I need to see the exit that will lead us home, to feel that relief when we're back on familiar territory. I do not tell my colleagues in the car what happened inside the barn. I use every ounce of restraint I can muster to pretend that I had not just witnessed the fiery self-destruction of America's next great hope.

He had reached for me so violently I had gasped. His fingers wrapped around the upper part of my arm, pulling me in so we were chest-to-chest. His body felt like freshly laid pavement on a sweltering day: hard, sticky, and completely disgusting.

"You listen to me," he began, his voice threatening once it became clear that I knew what kind of pill he wanted his baby mama to pop, his accent only fueling the absurdity of the situation. "This has nothing to do with you. No one will believe whatever story you try to make up. I can guarantee you, Ms. Carmichael, that if you feel compelled to tell lies about what you *think* you saw here today, you'll find yourself wishing you never laid eyes on me. Do you get what I'm trying to tell you?"

In other words, are you too thick to feel the full force of the threat I'm making right now?

I did feel it. And I had every reason in the world to dumbly nod my head, chalk it all up to the ultimate case of bad timing and then walk right the hell out of there. Go back to my deplorable apartment, and my pitiful bank account that hovers in the negative more often than I'd like, and my future that holds no real promise.

For some inexplicable and not entirely wise reason, I stood my ground. From some place deep inside where my reasoning works overtime to remind me that Bailey has been worth everything I had to sacrifice, and that I made the right choice—the only choice that I could live with— came a whisper. A soft prod at first, a nudge that was trying to get my attention as the fight versus flight signals did battle in my head.

Well, Mr. Wannabe President. Who the fuck do you think *you're* messing with?

I yanked my arm back. Forever the politician, Senator Bonehead shifted tactics and tried telling me to calm down, that maybe we could work out some kind of deal. I half heard him choke out something that sounded like, "What would it take for you to keep your mouth shut?" I felt every ounce of my pride rise up alongside the hairs on the back of my neck. Was I being bribed? For real? Dear God, could this get any worse?

"Do not touch me, Mr. Anderson!" I purposely demoted him that time. I went on, with borrowed bravado I'll surely have to pay interest on. "I am not stupid, and I will not be threatened, or *bribed!* Let me tell you this. I am registered to vote here in New Hampshire, and even though I don't have much spare time these days, I will happily do everything I can to support the candidacy of whoever has the pleasure of taking your ass down."

After that defiant declaration, I hauled myself right out of there. I did not look back. I didn't even allow my hands to start shaking until I burst back through the barn door and breathed in the air that was free of corruption, pomposity, and nefarious activity.

Jessie had moved her car to less muddy ground, and was sitting with the engine running waiting for me to return. I threw myself into the seat, slammed the door shut, and told her to go.

"You all right? You look green. Uh-huh, I told you not to eat that last scallop. Don't call me when you're heaving until midnight," William joked, and I tried to laugh. It came out like a donkey bray.

"No, I'm fine. I'm just ... uh ... really upset ... my phone is gone. It's not there. I couldn't find it anywhere. Step on it, Jess, let's get out of here already."

We are rounding the corner to the dirt road. Everyone is mourning the loss of my phone, offering their own if I need to call on Bailey, asking if I had insurance, or need a few bucks on loan to replace it. They don't pay a lick of attention to the SUVs, or to Senator Anderson who is walking out of the barn just as we are passing by it. I look across Jessie, even though I know I shouldn't, as he approaches the open door of one SUV and says something to the tan man waiting to close it behind him. Both men look up as Jessie's car rattles by. Instead of dismissing the carload of undesirables, they both stare. The conversation around me drones out, my ears dull it down until I hear nothing except the rapid-fire tempo of my own heart.

Holy shit, what have I just done? I have made an enemy out of a man who could annihilate me. I feel that last scallop and everything else I woofed down start to come back up. I get a headache and my mouth waters from my back molars down. We are barely onto the main road when I tell Jessie to pull over. The backseat groans with horror as my overloaded stomach heaves and the caterer's fine creations wind up wasted along the side of the street.

CHAPTER NINE

By the time we pull into the parking lot at Gerry's salon, I feel achy and miserable. My stomach is sour, and my tongue feels like its lined with Texas tumbleweed. Streetlights are starting to come on and Jessie tells me that in the shadows I look positively ghost-like.

"You look like you could sleep for a week," she says, watching me climb out of her car.

"Thanks for driving, Jess. I'll see you guys next week." I am so looking forward to a full day off tomorrow. Some quiet time for me to go over all the ways I just set myself up for some serious hurt.

"Better keep that stomach bug to yourself," Ari yells behind her as she walks off toward her car.

"I'll take it," William shouts back. "Gotta shake some flab off to squeeze into those new Diesel skinny jeans I got my eye on."

"Fashion slave," I mutter to him.

"You know it, girlfriend," he says, winking. "But seriously, I hope you feel better. And I'm sorry about your phone."

We are all barely getting by. We feel each other's pain because too often it is our own.

"Thanks. I appreciate it."

He hangs back, looking out over the lot to make sure the other two have pulled out. One of his skinny hips juts out as he leans against the hood of someone else's car.

Forget the overpriced Diesel jeans, he could probably pull off Bailey's Gap Kids.

"Now that the gossip hounds are gone, tell me what's up. 'Cause if I know anything in this life it's trouble, and you got that written all over your face."

"Nah, I'm good," I begin, although the thought of unloading the events of the day onto another set of shoulders could feel as good as the hot shower I'm going to take the minute I walk through my door.

"*Good* as in, I'm-just-tired-William-leave-me-alone, or *good* as in, something-terrible-has-happened-and-I-don't-trust-you-enough-to-tell-you. Which one is it?" He rolls his wrists up, as his waxed eyebrows arch with impatience.

William already knows so much about me already. He has listened to me at my very weakest, when I am frustrated with Bailey and convinced I'm an even worse mother than the one who smacked her kid around over wire hangers. He knows about Bailey's obsession with 9-1-1, and Peter's effort to rein it in before he gets hauled off to juvi.

If anyone could understand the ghastliness of the barn encounter, it would be William. I know he wouldn't repeat a word of it, swearing himself to secrecy and telling me only Ashton Kutcher would be able to tickle it out of him. I hold back. I don't want him knowing what I know about United States Senator Declan Anderson. I'm getting a sickening feeling that this is the kind of information important people will do just about anything to keep under wraps. Perhaps even eliminate the risk of it ever getting out.

Maybe I do have that written all over my face.

"Honestly, William. I'm good. I'm tired, just like you are. I guess I felt sort of, umm, sort of inadequate today."

"Huh? *Inadequate?* Really? What, like, just because they have money, and crazy good looks, and people standing by to wipe their asses? Are you forgetting that you are Mother Superior with a mind as sharp as my fashion sense? Come on, Bo, have you checked your own look lately? You match up just fine, and besides, a chick like you wouldn't be caught dead letting some skinny, blonde, bee-atch make you feel bad about yourself."

He watches me for a moment as his eyes squint in concentration. "Go home. Go give your boy a squeeze and call it a day. She's got nothing on you, hear me? Nothin'!"

"Thanks, you always make me feel better." I lean in to give him a quick hug and walk in the other direction. I hear a couple of quick beeps, and turn to see William climbing into a car driven by a young guy with jet black hair. William dates like he's dying, one right after the other, no time to waste in between. He lusts for all of them, commits to none of them. A far cry from my own social life, which is pretty much on par with the nuns who spend their lives in patient servitude at the convent on the other side of town.

I pick up the pace. Night is falling fast, and the streetlights haven't hummed to full strength yet. Long shadows fall across the pavement, and I feel an unease as the wind blows the collar of my jacket against my cheek. I am almost to my car when I see a dark sedan pull to the curb across the street. I cross the final few feet, unlock the door, throw my bag in the back and climb in. I throw the heat on high and then look in my rearview mirror before putting it into reverse.

The sedan is idling, white smoke coming from its exhaust pipe. The windows are tinted. I can't see inside. I watch for a few more seconds, tell myself I'm being paranoid, and pull out of my parking space. I cut to the right to get to the main street, but have to brake for the stop sign. I am now directly in front of the dark sedan with just a dozen feet or so between us.

The heavy door swings open, as a tall man wearing a brown trench coat exits and goes to stand directly under the streetlight. He leans casually against the metal post, his face hidden in shadows but faintly familiar. The dusky light cuts almost black swaths across his deep cheekbones; his hair made darker by nightfall. His shoulders are wide under the coat. As it blows open in the wind, I see a straight pleat running from thigh to ankle.

No, it can't be. Can it?

I narrow my eyes, pulling down my visor so I can stare at him more intently without him noticing.

He notices all right. He's staring right back. His right hand comes slowly from the pocket of his coat. Five fingers go up; three go down until only two of his fingers are left. They move in slow motion, turning in toward his shadowy eyes and then pointing straight back at me.

It is an unmistakable warning, meant for no one else but me.

We're watching you, Bo.

The tan man gets back in the car, pulls away from the curb and heads up the quiet street disappearing from my view.

Message received, loud and clear.

CHAPTER TEN

"I'll have a double scoop of Mocha on the bottom, Moose Tracks on the top," Peter says with the kind of authority that tells me he's ordered this a few times before.

"Really, Peter?" I ask, with a half-smile. "That sounds kinda gross."

"Don't knock it till you try it. Live with gusto is what I've always said and that certainly extends to ice cream."

"I'll have what the chief is having," Bailey says, as he slips his hand inside of Peter's. I notice the girl at the counter giving them a broad smile.

"If he likes it, then I will, too." He grins up at him.

"Right on, Mr. B," Peter confirms.

Two lopsided cones appear. Peter reaches for the first one and hands it over to Bailey who dives in and comes up with a nose-full of creamy white and brown. Peter takes a gigantic bite off the top, almost completely wiping away all evidence of Moose Tracks ever being there.

"Ah," he sighs aloud. "Good stuff, huh, my man?"

"Ahhhhh-huhhh!" Bailey's mouth is too full to speak.

"What'll it be, Bo?" he asks as he digs with one hand into his back pocket to pull out his wallet.

"Oh, nothing for me, thanks."

"What? Who in the world can resist ice cream? Your mom is cuckoo, Bailey." He rolls his finger in small circles next to his head, crossing his eyes, and making Bailey hiccup out a laugh covered with chocolate morsels. I try to step over him to get to the girl first, thrusting a twenty-dollar bill over the counter. Peter won't have it.

"Don't do it, Megan," he warns the high school girl whose parents he sits with at the occasional Bingo night at the American Legion Hall. "I'm covering this today."

He shoots me a look and opens his wallet to extract some money. Several bills come back in change, but Peter drops it all into the small glass jar with the paper label that says "Tips" on the far side of the counter.

"Come on, let's go sit outside. It's a beautiful day." He walks ahead of us to open the door, which makes the bell on top sing out. I flinch, and Peter notices.

"What's going on with you today?" he asks, in between giant licks of his mountainous cone. "You've been jumpy and quiet. Is everything all right?" He has already asked for every little detail from the shoot at the orchard. I gave him enough to satisfy his curiosity about Senator Anderson, without going into the impregnating-his-staffer-and-threatening-my-well-being part.

"Of course, everything's all right. I guess I'm still tired from all the commotion. You know, a long day like that sets you back."

"You are too young, my dear, to get *set back*. Unless it's by a handsome man who buys you a steak and keeps you out till the sun comes up." Peter guffaws through steady gulps of his cone. I roll my eyes at his familiar jab at my self-imposed solitary confinement. He is forever warning me that I can't let the only men in my life be a child, an aging ex-cop, and a gay coworker.

I pull out the back of a chair set up on an outside terrace, help Bailey settle into it, and then move to the chair opposite of him so Peter can sit directly next to him. The clank of the iron legs on the bricks below shoots through my head. I try to hold in the shudder that follows. Peter is way too perceptive for a man, there's very little that gets by him and he notices my subtle flinch. Maybe it's all those years of searching haystacks for the needles he would need to solve crimes.

"I would hope you know that you can confide in me if something is bothering you. In my line of work, there's virtually nothing I haven't heard already."

"I'll bet," I chuckle.

Peter is watching me like a hawk. Even though he's keeping up his side of a deep conversation with Bailey about turtles and frogs and other swamp creatures, he is multitasking, trying to figure out what I'm hiding from him.

He asks Bailey to run back to the counter and grab him a few napkins. His eyes never leave Bailey's back, but he directs his next question at me.

"No bullshit from you, now. Something's wrong, and I want to know what it is. Has something happened to your parents? Something you need help with?"

"No. They're fine. At least I think they're fine. They haven't called in a really long time. I don't even know where they are right now." Even though he is watching Bailey stretch up on his tiptoes to reach the napkin canister, he continues speaking as intently as he would if we were eye-to-eye.

"What is the matter with them?" Now that Bailey is making his way back to our table Peter allows himself to look away. He leans in on his elbows, moving his head back and forth. "It's a damn shame. Look at what they have here," he motions to Bailey, but I know he means me, too. "How do you just walk out on all this?"

There is no good answer, not even an adequate one when human nature runs amok. Parents are supposed to be wired to stay, to raise their families into capable beings and then joyfully wait for the next generation to take seed. Peter and Emily Brenner had done everything right, and yet for them, there will be no next generation. Their wiring was spot on, they just never planned for the hand of fate to reach in and pull the plug.

"Sorry. It's none of my business anyway. You just let me know if there's anything you need. Promise?"

"Of course, but don't you worry about us. We're good, right buddy?"

"Good, Chief. Momma and me are good. Except sometimes when Momma thinks I'm sleeping, I can hear her cry. She was doing that last night."

To a four-year-old, this is just banter, something he knows that he wants someone else to hear. He's far too young to understand the dangers of full disclosure.

As I feel my fake smile fall, I reach over to take Bailey's chin in my hand and say gently, "Bailey, Peter will worry about us if you tell him things like that."

"But it's true, Momma, you did cry. You cry a lot."

Peter is watching us go back and forth, his mouth pulled into a tight line. Needles just about popping their way out of my haystack now, I see his mind working, trying to put the pieces together.

Bailey is blissfully unaware of the big, fat, juicy clue he just handed the seasoned interrogator who does not take kindly to someone trying to pass off a version of the truth that would hold as much water as a teaspoon on a crooked finger.

"Come on, Peter, he's *four* for God's sake, he probably heard me laugh at something stupid on TV last night and thinks I was crying. You know how kids get, they hear all sorts of things that aren't there …" I trail off, immediately regretting the clumsy reference. I can almost hear Peter say inside his own head … "Yeah, sure I know kids. I used to have one, you know. Until he went and died on me."

"Uh, I'm … I'm sorry, Peter. I didn't mean to …"

Make you think of Tucker. Make you remember your dead son.

The hand goes up.

"Now, stop it right there. You didn't say anything wrong and, yes, I do know that kids make up stories all the time. But this young man is different. He may be four, but I would say that he knows the sound of his mom crying when he hears it. This is not about Bailey. This is about you. Something's up, Bo, and I can promise you this. If you don't spill it, I will force it out of you one way or the other."

He means it; I know he does. He will be relentless until I agree to tell him what's going on. Instead, I sidestep.

"Peter, how's Emily doing? Now that you're both home together all the time, well … how is she?"

Chief Brenner had wanted to slip quietly into retirement. The small town he had served the better part of his adulthood, however, had different ideas. On a sparkling day not too long ago, the townspeople marched along Main Street toward the Echo Valley Police Department. The mayor did the honor of proclaiming it Chief Peter Brenner Day, reading a prepared statement that listed so many accomplishments it stretched on for fifteen minutes.

Laughs, cheers, commendations, the mood was celebratory and happy. The final speaker stepped up to the top of the stairway. Looking out at her neighbors and friends, Emily Brenner took a deep breath. I was standing far back in the crowd, holding Bailey low so she wouldn't notice us there. It's not that I felt unwelcomed, I just sensed her displeasure. I think in some way, Peter's growing affection for us embodied her emptiness. I held Bailey tighter as I heard her soft voice begin.

"Peter and I first met on a day just like this one. I fell in love with a great man, and together we created a perfect little boy. He loved his daddy very much, and always worried that his job would take him away from us. I used to worry about that, too." The wind had rustled enough to sway the leaves above us and make Emily Brenner pause to give it some time to pass. When it faded back to a gentle whistle, she continued.

"Peter always came home to us. I felt blessed every time I heard that front door open. I still feel blessed, even though the door doesn't open now as often as it should."

You could have heard a pin drop. Tucker's name unspoken but hanging in the air around us.

"Our boy was almost a man. What makes me most proud today is that he laid his head down on his pillow every night of his life, knowing that his dad had come home. His dad always came home … for him."

I did not stay for the high school band's performance on the front lawn or the enormous cake with buttercream frosting, or the fireworks that followed even though they would have made Bailey giddy with excitement.

Peter had asked me why I left.

I had lied then, too. Just like I am lying to him right now.

As he mutters something about Emily doing fine, volunteering down at the library, and taking yoga three days a week, I make a promise to myself. I can never let Peter know the truth about what happened to me inside that barn. I can never tell him about the menacing shadow that stood beneath the street lamp waiting to make sure I noticed him. Because if I did, I know he would do everything in his power to keep me safe and I'm not entirely sure that's possible.

He is a man who always came home. Decades of police work that could have killed him, and yet he came home to his wife and son every day of his life. He came home even after his son couldn't hear the front door close anymore.

I'll be damned if I become the one thing that keeps Peter Brenner from ever coming home again.

CHAPTER ELEVEN

Gerry pounces like a seagull on a half-eaten hot dog roll the moment I step through the door.

"Tell me everything," he starts before I can even take the sunglasses off my head. Apparently, Mackenzie Mason had pulled herself together enough to call Gerry with commendations. She informed him the Anderson family was quite pleased with the efforts of his team, and he was to thank each of us for our time. Gerry was hungry for more, though. He wanted the real scoop, the dirt.

I wish I could tell you, Gerry. I wish I could unload the fact that Senator Declan Anderson is a full-blown asshole, married to and cheating on a frigid witch who treats people like they're disposable diapers. I also wish that I could tell you that he's hiding a dirty little secret that in a few months' time will take him from presidential hopeful to family court defendant.

Could I tell him? Sure, I could tell Gerry exactly what happened, and I could tell Peter that I fear for my safety, and I could call the brand new Echo Valley Police Chief and tell him the presumed next occupant of the White House has me in his crosshairs.

I am spared the truth or anything else I could have come up with by the sound of the front door swinging open, and the light banter of colleagues greeting each other. Jessie and Ari arrive together, followed quickly by William who immediately notices the box of treats Gerry brought for us sitting on the counter.

"Paws off, William," Gerry orders. "Those can wait a minute." He looks around the room, counting heads until he gets the proper number of employees present and accounted for.

"I won't keep you. I know many of you have clients arriving any minute." He looks like the proud papa—granted of an unconventional family—but this is a good moment for Gerry.

"I got a call from Senator Anderson's aide. She assured me of the family's satisfaction and asked me to thank you for a job well done. I never had a doubt … well, only a little doubt … that it would go any other way. To celebrate your hard work, help yourselves to a box full of greasy delicacies. On me."

High-fives all around, even a kiss or two on the cheek as Gerry makes the rounds to each employee. He finds me off near the corner.

"Jeesh, Bo. What are you waiting for? I figured you'd be first in," he says, motioning to the table holding all the food. He's right. Under normal circumstances, I'd be all over that box. This morning, I have no appetite. Gerry shakes his head at me. "Remember what I told you. I hope you use this to make contacts and start putting yourself out there. In the meantime, you're still mine. Can you take a two forty-five today? My sister's friend is passing through and needs a blowout."

I try to remember if 2:45 is open. I hustle off to check my calendar, but I find a note I scribbled to myself that Bailey has his check-up today at 2:30. It's his yearly, which is hard to schedule in the first place and impossible to cancel on such short notice. Not only can I not take the sister's friend today at 2:45, now I have to ask if I can leave early.

Fabulous. I could either risk the receptionist threatening to charge me for the appointment because I didn't give a 24-hour notice, or I can face the wrath of Gerry, which may be tempered slightly because he is feeling generous toward me right now. I go with Gerry, only because Bailey has to come first. It's just the way it has to be.

I find him near William, who is turning his head around to inspect his tighter than a nine-year-old girl's rear end. "See," I hear him say. "I tell you all it takes is one stinking bite and my ass blossoms like a giant blooming onion. Ugh!" He takes the remainder of his raspberry turnover and covers it with a paper napkin.

"Do me a solid, Gerry?" he asks in between chews. I can see Gerry doing a mental evaluation of what in the world William might mean by that.

"Excuse me?"

"A solid. You know, a favor?" William throws a little sarcastic trill on the word, making sure Gerry feels sufficiently old and entirely square.

"Sorry, William. I guess I'm not hip to the lingo these days. What kind of solid would you like me to do?"

"I was going to ask you to send all this crap straight home with Bo. She'll eat every last crumb and not give a shit what her ass looks like." He doesn't consider it an insult. Neither do I.

"Speaking of asses," he continues. "Did I mention how juicy the sex-ator's looked all packed in nice and round in his khakis?" He is angling for a response from Gerry, who knows better than to engage. He just shakes his head and walks off.

"Incorrigible," I hear him sputter.

"Incorrig-a-what?" William snarls back.

"Nothing, it just means you're ... kinda bad," I say with a smile.

"Well, at least you're smiling again. You were downright miserable, girl."

"Not miserable, just ... tired." The old line does seem overused by now. Sure enough, William isn't playing along.

"Bo," he starts, putting a skinny wrist on either side of his scraggy waist. "I get that you are a momma and all, and your sweet little baby boy probably needs to get up and go wee-wee at all hours of the night, but you are too young to be so tired. Snap out of it, for God's sake." He sucks in his breath, like he's had an epiphany of some sort.

"Oh no ... *you ... did ... not!* Tell me you are not still hung up on Mrs. Hot-to-Trot." His head retreats a few inches back.

"Hardly," I say firmly.

"Hmmm," he drawls, still unconvinced. "I'm onto you. If you don't trade in this attitude *toot sweet* ... I'll call Peter. I mean it, don't test me."

It's a funny, yet sad thing for him to say. Funny, because really, what's Peter going to do, send me to my room? Sad, because William knows the real deal. I don't have anyone else who gives a crap.

Gerry hollers over, tells me that I have a phone call, some guy who asked specifically for me.

Strange. The only "guy" who would ask for me is Bailey. Then I feel myself tense as I realize my small circle of male acquaintances has grown lately, even if they are undesirable additions. Would the tan man dial me up right here? Would he dare? Gerry is holding the phone out for me, the black cord stretching to its full length.

My footsteps over to the desk feel heavy and awkward. My back feels like it's on fire, as a single bead of sweat starts a journey between my shoulder blades and winds up somewhere near the elastic band of my underwear. I feel lightheaded as my first few sips of coffee do laps in my stomach.

I thank Gerry before I put the phone to my ear, hoping he'll take the cue to give me some privacy. I clear my throat, testing my voice.

"Hello, this is Bo." I hope I sound like someone who doesn't want to be messed with. I probably sound more like a timid twelve-year-old.

"Hey. It's me."

The voice is familiar and almost makes me cry with relief.

"Your cell phone must be dead, I'm sorry to bother you at work but you weren't picking up, and it wouldn't let me leave a message."

I reach into my back pocket for the cell, temporarily forgetting it's either lost in a floor board of the old barn, or being dissected by some techie on Senator Anderson's payroll who will soon find out my life is about as exciting as watching paint dry. The lies begin to flow, because Peter can't know the truth about where my phone really is.

"Ah, Peter. I'm sorry. I must've forgotten to charge it last night. What's up?"

"I wanted to take you and Bailey out for pizza tonight. You around?"

When am I not around? Given that we just saw Peter not yet twenty-four hours ago, I figure he's still worried about me.

"Well, yeah, we're around, but you have ulterior motives, Chief Brenner. You think I was born yesterday?" God love this man for caring about me.

"Nah, I assure you I am pure of heart. Emily's gone to visit her sister in Vermont, and I'm playing bachelor tonight. Thought it would be nice to see you guys, that's all."

My throat feels thick again, although this time for an entirely different reason.

"Sure," I whisper. "We'd love to. I have to leave work early to run Bailey to his appointment with the pediatrician so how about Luca's, say five o'clock?"

"Super, I'll see you there. And Bo?"

"Yeah?"

"I am well aware that pizza is your all-time favorite food. You'd better eat tonight, or else I will begin to work those ulterior motives you're so concerned about."

"Got it, see you soon. And Peter …"

"Ah-huh?"

"Thank you." It comes out a bit too husky, too emotional.

"Don't mention it. Bye now."

CHAPTER TWELVE

"Healthy, head to toe. Although speaking of that toe, what the heck size are you in now, Bailey?" The doctor asks me with a smirk.

"Well, he's busting out of the twelves I got him at the beginning of the summer. So I'd say maybe a one or two."

Doctor Fontaine nods, types a note into Bailey's online chart.

"Well, I'd say given your height and um, his ... father's approximate height ..." he doesn't make eye contact with me, and I don't blame him. All the medical information I've been able to provide about Riley has been "approximate." On the line that asks for paternal height at full maturation, I simply wrote in "extra-large."

"... I'd say this young man is going to be somewhere in the vicinity of ten feet tall." He shakes Bailey's knee good-naturedly, getting a strong giggle in response.

Doctor Fontaine reminds me to pick up a medical history form for Bailey's pre-school registration packet. He tells us he'll see us next year, and jokes with Bailey, "If you can still fit through my door by then."

We leave the doctor's office with a clean bill of health. "Ok, Mr. B. I would like to go home, get you changed into some nice clothes and then we'll head over to meet Peter, sound good?"

"Sounds good, Momma." He skips alongside, gripping my hand and gushing about the Tonka truck sticker the nurse handed to him on our way out.

"It's got these big wheels, Momma, like it can roll right over our house and then over Peter's house and then over …" Bailey stops talking so abruptly I check my hand to see if he's still hanging onto me.

"What's the matter, honey?"

He has stopped walking, and he uses his other hand to point towards the parking lot.

"Momma, what's the police doing here. That's not Peter."

I follow his finger, scanning the parking lot and expecting to see an officer helping open a car door someone accidentally locked with the keys still inside.

"Why are they standing at our car?"

They are. About four uniformed officers are flanked around each door of my car. One is cupping his hand on the window and peering inside.

"What the *hell*," I mutter as that shaky, nervous feeling returns. What do they want with me? I doubt this is to present me with an outstanding citizen award or recognize my stellar parking skills.

One officer sees us standing there, spreads the word to the others. They move in shoulder-to-shoulder, beefy arms crossed over broad chests. Guns holstered, but present on each hip. I grip Bailey's hand tighter as I walk toward my car. I'm not sure if I should speak to them, or wait for them to speak to me. I don't have to wonder long, they decide for us.

"Bo Carmichael?" one of them asks.

"Yes," I say back, coming to stand next to the driver's side door, my fingers digging into Bailey's. He doesn't make a peep.

"We're going to need you to come with us."

"Huh?" I sputter. "Why would I need to go anywhere with you?"

My first thought is that something has happened to my parents. Finally, after all these years, their luck has run out. I wonder if they're dead. I never thought they would have the presence of mind to list me as next of kin.

"Is this about my parents?" I try to speak delicately, without giving Bailey a reason to react. I motion down to him, hoping they get the message to keep it cool.

"No, but I would decline to say much more right now." The officer who responds does get it, because he points his chin downward to indicate that he sees Bailey, and would prefer not to upset him.

"Okay, I guess. I'm getting the feeling that I don't have a choice in the matter. Do I?"

A firm shake of the head. "No, ma'am. You don't."

"What do I do … with …" I can't finish the sentence, trying to speak again in kid-code, so Bailey doesn't freak on me here.

"Is there anyone you can call?"

"No, there isn't." I'm pathetic, I know.

"Well then, I guess he'll have to come. There will be someone at the station who can keep an eye on him." Keep an eye on him, while you *do what* to me?

"What is this about? You're making it sound like I'm um … I'm …" I try to inconspicuously put my wrists together and mouth the words … "*under arrest.*"

"Technically, yes you are, although I will spare you that right now."

The words feel like buckshot. *I am under arrest!* Oh my God, I am being arrested right here in the parking lot of our doctor's office with Winnie the Pooh posters staring out at me from the windows, and my child's fingers wrapped in a death lock around my own. What have I done? There must be some mistake.

"Um, I am admittedly a little unprepared for this. You must have the wrong person. Do you realize I'm a hairdresser? I'm, like, a nobody. You get that, right?" I tuck Bailey into the slope of my hip to muffle out what he can hear.

He lets out a disgusted sigh. Not worrying so much anymore about my little boy, he spits out allegations so disgusting and off-base I wonder if I'm being Punk'd. I toss my head from side to side, waiting for the hidden camera crew to rush out to save me. I lean forward to make sure I'm really hearing his remarkably ridiculous statement.

"Say again?" I mutter through frozen lips.

"*…we have probable cause to show you sold illegal substances to so and so on this date…*"

Wind blows through my brain making noises become vacant and dull. Three of the officers are staring at me from crooked poses, probably wondering if I'm about to drop.

What? How? Who? I chew through the outrage. When I'm not with Bailey I'm working. When I'm not working, I'm sleeping. This is crap!

The youngest-looking among them drones on about my "special circumstances," meaning Bailey, and the fact that I'm pretty lucky he's willing to be compassionate and not cuff me in front of him. He also tells me they will allow me to drive myself over to the department with one cruiser in front of me and another in back to ensure I arrive exactly where they expect me to.

"Now, don't you take advantage of my good will, it will only make things much, much worse," he warns, as my horrified reflection beams back at me from the rounded frames of his aviator sunglasses.

"Uh, no. No, I'm not doing this …" One arm releases my son as both palms go up in defensive mode. They hit a brick wall.

"Either you do this," he interrupts. "Or we do it for you." His tone zings like sandpaper on a blister. I shuffle through my options. I have none. Why is there no handbook on how to handle an all-out assault when you're alone with your kid in a pediatrician's parking lot?

Maybe I should just go with them. When I can calmly explain, I'm merely a college dropout with no husband and an overused debit card they'll decide the moron who dropped a dime on me obviously flubbed the facts.

Right?

"Okay, please, just don't upset my son. I'll go. Should I just, uh, drive up to the front door?" Do I knock three times and utter a secret password?

"No, we will escort you in. Follow the cruiser ahead of you, and be sure to park next to it." He steps back. His officer friends watch me open the back door, haul Bailey inside and buckle him up. I feel like a zombie, just going through the motions but mentally suspended in a pile of mush.

The dull thud of car doors closing triggers a wail from the backseat. Bailey hiccups and sputters, almost fully out of control. I reach behind me to put my hands on each cheek. He is a million degrees, so fiery red he's almost purple.

"Honey, it's okay. I'm sure this is no big deal, and we'll be just fine."

Will we?

"Momma, they not nice like Peter, they scary and mean. Why are we in trouble?"

I bite my lip hard because if I don't get a hold of something solid, I'll break down right along with him. Yet again, I face a moment when a lie would be best. I could make something up, something funny or silly that a four-year-old would understand. I could tell him that the police are always our friends, and we'll still make our pizza date with the other police officer who is never scary or mean. For some reason, I can't bring myself to do it. I can't lie to my son. I tell him the only thing I can right now that is the undeniable truth.

"I don't know why we're in trouble, Bailey. I have no idea at all."

CHAPTER THIRTEEN

We are two hours deep into our "conversation" in the bowels of this police station, the cement walls sweating with humidity. I have tried the hostile witness angle, demanding to check on Bailey, even threatening to get up and leave, but all I get are stern suggestions not to dare try. Peter will consider us dangerously late by now, and it's killing me to imagine him sitting in a booth at Luca's, his eyes following a path from his watch to the glass panel of the front door, wondering what's keeping us and worrying more as each minute passes. Even though that one phone call is still available, and his digits are scrolling through my head like a breaking news bulletin, I can't bring myself to do it. I get a flash of his stony face breaking into that twinkly grin he gets whenever Bailey is around and what that face would look like if he knew what was really going on. No, Peter can't be hurt any more than he already has been and especially, not by me.

I look around at the various expressions of boredom. They've had enough of me playing this remedial game of shakedown hardball. I've been fingerprinted, and have defiantly dismissed my right to an attorney because I was entirely convinced someone was a millisecond away from slamming through the door and breathlessly admitting that some rookie just fucked up. Besides, why would I enlist an attorney to do nothing more than charge me a ton of dough and then bid me farewell?

Tension ripples through my fingers, clenched in a steeple under my chin. We've already covered the predictable questions about my life. I've described the extensive shortcomings of my parents while insisting we don't speak much. They've inquired about my job, my neighbors, and my friends. When they pushed me on the low-level scumbag who allegedly rolled info on me, I told them the person whose name I can't even pronounce is a stranger I've never met, let alone sold illegal substances to. Occasionally, one of them would nod, scribble onto a notepad or offer me coffee that smells like road tar. One time I even caught one of them staring at my boobs.

Time ticks on. I wait for something, anything to move this forward. My old TV may not get all four hundred cable stations available, but it does let me watch repeats of "Law & Order" which means I have basic knowledge of how interrogators roll. I almost expect one of them to start barking at me, slamming his fist on the table to rattle me into stunned compliance, callously manipulating my threadbare psyche until I'm exhausted enough to agree to just about anything to get the hell out of this room and back to my child.

"Yes, yes, yes, I killed the butler in the pantry with the candlestick. Just let me out ... of ... here!"

"Getting tired, Bo?" one of them asks suddenly. He holds out a paper cup brimming with warm pond froth pretending to be coffee. "Sure you don't want some?"

"No," I snap back. "I don't want your coffee, or your water, or anything else. What I want is to go home. I want my son, and this ridiculous standoff needs to end. I've answered your questions and am very close to insisting on that legal representation." My head falls listlessly between my shoulders. I wonder if that means I'm playing right into their hands, giving them a sign that the end is near.

"Can you tell me if Bailey is okay? Please."

The other officer gets up so suddenly the scrape of his chair on the concrete floor makes me jump to my feet. "Sit down."

"Sorry, the noise startled me. It's not like I was trying to escape, you know." I exhale noisily and sit back down, but not before getting a tingling feeling in both butt cheeks. My ass is falling asleep.

"Officer Lacey will check on Bailey for you. Have you thought about posting bail?"

I have no words. I think this may be the slippery edge of rock bottom. Instead of answering him, I can do no more than shake my head. He sighs gently and then leaves the room without speaking. I am alone. I walk the length of this narrow, shadowy room. I close my eyes and try to channel Bailey. I hug him in the dark of my mind, apologizing for this monumental mess while mentally working back to the mysterious tangle of how this could be happening.

Un-fucking-believable!

I focus, laying out my boring life like a template and then plugging in the details. This is math, my strong suit. If you apply the logic, the numbers should fall right into place. I start with Gerry's Salon. I know that a few of my coworkers buy pot on a regular basis, but would any of them finger me? No. There's no fit there. If my parents happened to be in New Hampshire right now, I'd almost believe they were the ones setting me up. But that makes no sense, either, and they're a time zone away. I think. My neighbors barely acknowledge me, so that's a no, too. The equation is off. I have nothing but remainders and zero balances.

I rake my tongue roughly over cracked lips, trying to latch onto a possibility.

Goddamn it!

Everything brings me right back to the beginning.

Ten minutes or so go by before they return and sit down. I reluctantly return to my side of the table and slide my butt back on the rigid chair, but this time I'm ready to shut my trap and insist on legal representation. Bring on the public defender who is probably younger and poorer than I am. I don't care. I have to get out of here.

"Bailey is fine." A rush of relief swirls through my abdomen. "He's sleeping upstairs. We have a female officer watching over him."

I nod at the nameless policeman. I can't think about what Bailey has been through just yet. I still have to focus on making sure I see him again. A loud knock on the metal door prompts the officer on my left to rise from his chair and open it only slightly. He says, "Thanks," to some person I never see, and then pushes the door closed. It locks automatically behind him with a grating noise.

A square Ziploc bag is tossed onto the table. It lands closest to me, making me pull myself back until the plastic seat back cuts into my shoulders. The baggie is disgusting, smeared with some stringy substance along the edges. They are all staring at me, waiting for me to react, one of them salivating like he's about to get a lick of my blood. I look at the baggie, at them, back at the baggie again.

"And... so?" I begin, my voice high and suddenly very alarmed that no twenty-five-year-old with a legal degree is sitting next to me.

"Why don't you start with where you got it. Then we'll work up to who you were about to unload it to."

What? They think that's mine! I don't even know what it is. Where the hell did they find it?

"Where did that come from?" I croak, realizing I probably shouldn't say anything at all but unable to stop myself. This is getting preposterous.

"Where do you think?"

"The cesspool out back?" I squint at it.

"Not exactly. This was found inside your purse. Clearly, it compounds your problems. There will be an additional charge for possessing an illegal substance inside a police facility."

My jaw goes soft as my mouth falls open. My jugular pulses as sweat beads push through the front of my hairline. Jesus, this is major shit! I shudder, remembering how I handed over my purse as we entered the department. "This is a lockdown facility, Ms. Carmichael, and you are under arrest. We need to search your belongings."

"Go ahead," I told them, thrusting the imitation Gucci bag I bought last year at a flea market toward the officer while reminding myself that I had nothing to hide. "There's some gum on the bottom, help yourself." Now, I have no caustic remark, no resources left to match wits. My fingers wipe the bottom of my eyes and settle on each cheek. I stare at them until my vision blurs.

Breathe, I tell myself, think, stay clearheaded, use my brain. If I fall apart now, they'll pick through me like vultures on a highway carcass.

Okay. I hover over the bag. I look closely at the junk inside. What is it? I start with what it's *not*. It's not the heroin that has gripped our state with relentless suffering. It is also not cocaine. That, as I recall from seeing on TV, is a sugary kind of white powder. It is clearly not pot because it bears no resemblance to all those homemade cigarettes my parents made. I lean forward some more, staring down at thin shards of something that looks like ice. Furious indignation bubbles up. Catching me off guard with my kid is one thing. Throwing the book at me is quite another. Even my parents never went through an inquisition like this, and they *were* doing drugs.

"Again, and this is the last time I'll say it so listen up, people. I have no idea what that is. But it *did not* come from me. As in, that fucking shit is not mine! Get it? Hear me? This is bullshit, and we're done!"

They barely blink. They're stone cold quiet, waiting me out, accusatory in their silence. It drives me wild.

"Look!" I bellow, rising up again on my frozen quad muscles. "This is unholy what you're doing to me right now. It's horseshit! I trusted you. I gave you my stupid bag because there was nothing in there. No money, no drugs, no nothing! You think I'd do that if I was hiding that shit in there? I have never seen that crap before in my whole life. I can't even tell you what it is. You have humiliated me in the parking lot of my kid's doctor's office, made me miss a dinner date with someone who will be very worried about us, and you're scaring the bejeesus out of my son. I know I waived—or whatever the hell you call it—about a lawyer, but I promise you that I will find a good one, and sue all your asses for harassment! How *dare* you do this to a tax-paying, upstanding citizen, for Christ's sake!"

I inhale sharply and immediately get dizzy. I plop back into the chair before I keel over. My heart punches the bony length of my ribs.

A see a barely veiled smirk across the table and realize I'm an idiot. They know I've done everything backward. Losing control now is tantamount to defeat in this crowd. I slump back down, shriveling under the weight of an impossible situation that I am not nearly savvy enough to handle.

"So, let me get this straight," the smirky shithead says, obviously enjoying the entertainment value of my emotional outburst. "Are you denying that this baggie, found right inside your purse, is yours?"

"Yes, officer," I spit, finding a wayward spark of defiance to spice up my sneer and wipe that surly smugness off his face. "I am completely, one-hundred percent, telling you that ... *stuff* ... is not mine."

Several seconds go by. We lock eyes, and I refuse to look away.

"In that case, Ms. Carmichael, get comfortable. This could be a long night."

As a group, they get up and leave. One cop hangs back. When they're gone, he puts both elbows on his knees. I blink at him several times, challenging him to break me some more.

Go ahead, asshole. Give it your best shot. Instead, his voice is more tender than condemning.

"I'll get you home tonight. Hang in there. You should have asked for a lawyer. And that phone call."

Then he's gone.

What the hell is happening now?

CHAPTER FOURTEEN

The sun is rising over the mountains. A thin layer of fog clings to the streets and the parking lot. My car is dewy, and my key slips out of the door lock on my first try. I shift the full weight of my sleeping son to my other shoulder while I try the key again. Bailey is dead weight, fully exhausted by spending the night on a pullout cot tucked away behind the front desk.

I have several papers fluttering from my other hand. Papers that are yellow and blue, that list court dates, an official explanation of the charges I will have to answer to at my arraignment next month, and a scribbled note from the bail commissioner. He told me to tack on an additional forty bucks because the state of New Hampshire can't hold someone even if she doesn't have the cash to leave, and surprise, I didn't.

I click Bailey into his seat. Climbing behind the wheel, I lace my fingers around my neck and squeeze. My head pounds with lack of sleep and shock. The events of the past several hours are dreamlike, almost as if they were happening to someone else and I just had the unfortunate assignment of bearing witness. Bailey stirs as I turn the ignition, asking in a near trance if he can have donuts for breakfast.

"Sure, buddy," I whisper back, encouraging him to nod back off. Bailey could have asked me for a new car right now, and I would have agreed. I am thoroughly ashamed of what this child has had to endure.

I lean my head into my hands along the upper curve of the steering wheel. An abrupt *knock-knock* on my window shakes me like a cheap shot to the temple. I look over to see one of last night's star players in my shakedown. He motions with his hand for me to roll down my window.

What now?

I slowly unroll the window, making him wait while I crank the handle. Imagine the irony, a drug dealer who can't afford electric windows. Once the glass is cracked, he leans in and checks that Bailey is asleep.

"You don't remember me, do you?" he asks.

"Yeah, of course I remember you. You're the guy who sat next to the guy who got the baggie. But I appreciate whatever you did to break me out," I tell him. He did keep his word, even though it wasn't exactly prompt. "What do you want now?"

"Bo," he sighs, exasperated with me, which is strange. "Had you simply called a lawyer like you're supposed to, but whatever … that's not the point. I could get into serious trouble right now. You need to listen carefully."

He checks the parking lot behind us, looking from side to side. What he tells me next is as explosive as a stick of dynamite with a short fuse.

"None of this adds up," he begins, leaning so close I can feel his hot breath.

"Go on."

"I have been working the drug scene around here for over fifteen years. I know every piece of shit two-bit player for three hundred miles. I carry Narcan even when I'm off duty. I know who's trafficking it in, and who's dishing it out on the streets. I know who's cooking meth in the basement, and who's sleeping off their stupors on park benches."

"Well, that's great for you. Nice work. What does any of that have to do with me?"

"That's exactly my point. None of it has anything to do with you. Someone like you does not just show up out of nowhere, with enough crank to supply an entire city block tucked in her purse, and some story about a buyer narc'ing you out."

He checks behind him again and then takes long strides to the other side of my car. He slides into the passenger seat and throws his head back. He makes sure he is low, under the line of sight if anyone is watching. I am too stunned to speak. My eyes strain the width of their sockets.

What the Christ?

"Bo, this is a very serious question, and I want you to think before you answer."

I can only nod. Blisteringly hot information floating through my car casts ghostly white streaks down the chilly glass windows, keeping our clandestine meeting on the down-low.

"Can you think of anyone who has it in for you? Anyone who would want to get you out of the way for a while?"

My face goes slack. The officer must have interpreted my silence as a lack of understanding. He tries to make it as clear-cut as possible.

"In other words ... have you pissed someone off lately? Somebody who may know people in high places?"

A heavy feeling of dread rocks my chest. I see the tan man glaring at me under the streetlight. Did he do this to me? Am I being setup by a future president?

Yes! No?

"Maybe." It's safely in the middle. Would this cop believe me if I told him what happened in the barn? Can I trust him?

Then he hits me with a paralyzing left hook. "Here's what I want you to do. Do you have a safe place you can go because you can't go home right now?"

"What? Why?"

"Because someone will be there waiting for you."

I didn't think it could, but it gets worse.

"Bo," he growls, leading me beneath the layers to explain how deep this goes. "That bag had *a lot* of crystal meth in it. Like, too much."

I stare blankly at him again. I am not up to speed on how much meth constitutes a lot, or too much.

"All right, let's try this. We're not Gotham City. Small towns hold no secrets. If you really were a dealer working this area here, I'd already know about you. Point one: you are not on my radar. Point two: the amount of ice that bag contained is a felony, a federal case. If you sold this shit on a regular basis, you'd live on the edge, streetwise and prepared for a cop encounter at any moment. You'd be cool, and sorry, you aren't. Point three: you sure as shit wouldn't waive rights and hand over your purse, and you'd *absolutely* carry two twenty dollar bills to make sure you could pay a bail commissioner. If, and that's another point in itself, *if* you were released on PR."

I stare dumbly, remembering how he had double-checked my file, grabbing one of the officers to ask him questions while he pointed to various notes inside. I tuned him out; his cop jargon didn't mean anything at the time. Now, I see why he wanted me out of there.

"There's one guy here that I've been watching for a while. He's the same guy who knew where you'd be, had the tip from the buyer, and grabbed your purse to search it. He told me he's been working you for a while. I think he's lying."

I gulp down the disgust; it hurts.

The officer looks behind him at my sleeping child. His mouth falls into a grim smile.

"I know you love this little guy, and I suspect you've stumbled into some serious shit." I nod as my eyes fill. "Find a place to take him," he instructs me. "A place no one knows about. Stay there and let me try to figure this all out."

Naturally, I protest such an insane command any law-abiding person would be uncomfortable with. He's telling me to bolt.

"But ... no, no, I can't. That's wrong. I have stuff at home that I need. Bailey's things. Not to mention, I have a job, you know. What do I do with my life?" My fragile composure unravels another notch.

"Do not go anywhere near your apartment. Do you hear me?"

"Yes, I hear you. But I don't get it. Why?"

"Because you'll lose him!"

"What? What do you mean by losing him?"

He pushes back the short hairs on the top of his forehead, struggling with himself over releasing confidential information.

"Bo, follow me here. You were kept much longer than normal, *hours* longer. This whole thing took way too long, just to make you good and tired and upset enough to go straight home once you were released. Of course, denying a lawyer played right into this, but they needed to make sure they knew exactly where you'd be this morning, and that he would be with you." He motions to Bailey again.

"Who are … *they?*"

"I don't know that yet. But whoever they are, they knew when you'd be at the doctor's office because the warrant was ready to go. You're aware of DCYF, yes?"

"Of course," I nod in affirmation that I'm well aware of the state agency charged to protect kids from neglect and abuse.

"Well, it's now hot on your trail, and I bet they're lining up his new family as we speak. Are you getting it yet?"

I feel like I'm drowning. I fight back to the surface, my mind scrambling to dissect an outrageous plot that feels as mushy as oatmeal.

How would they know where I was? How? If the tan man is the puppet master how is he working my strings? How does he know about my life?

Of course! It clicks. My missing phone. Someone *does* have it!

Dr. Fontaine's office probably called my cell phone reminding me of Bailey's appointment. They always leave a reminder message for forgetful parents like me. A message I never got, but whoever found my phone sure did.

"Someone is planting evidence …" I begin.

"Yes!" he exclaims, "but in such a way that your entire life will be ruined, that everything you care about will be taken away." His eyes are blazing as they move from Bailey back to me.

They want me dead. No, worse than dead. They want me completely and utterly destroyed.

They want to take my son away!

"Someone wants you to watch your child be snatched because you are an unfit mother found in possession of an illegal substance. They would claim you had drugs in the house you lived in with your child. Bo, the state will snap him up so fast your head will spin."

Don't worry, it's already spinning.

"I am the head of the narcotics unit. Granted, again, this is a small department, but we are in the midst of an opioid crisis of biblical proportions. Because of that, I personally carry out each and every search my team conducts. I did not search your purse yesterday. That bag of goodies came out of there like it was wrapped up in a big red bow for us to find. I know you have no idea how it got there, and the purse should have been marked as evidence. Yet, you got it back. See what I mean? Even the little details are all out of whack."

I nod, sniffling in.

"Get out of here. Don't worry about your stuff at home, don't even worry about your job right now. Expect things to get worse before they get better, and do not let them find you. Whoever they are, they mean business."

I notice that he does not ask me for names. He doesn't push me for information. At least not yet. He scans the parking lot one final time through a small hole in my fogged up windshield. He asks if I have a piece of paper and a pen. I find a gas receipt and a Magic Marker. I hand him both. He scrawls out a number, and a name.

"Call me from wherever you are. Don't tell anyone. Make sure the line would be untraceable."

Good God, I don't even know what that means. "You mean like a pay phone? Do those even exist anymore?"

"Yes, there are a few of them left near convenience stores especially. Find one. Just in case."

"All right. I guess I should thank you for trying to help. You have no reason to believe me."

"Yes, I do. I have every reason in the world to believe you. Good luck, Bo. Watch yourself and stay safe. I'll see you soon enough." He opens the car door and walks away.

I suck in quick, sharp bursts of air; my teeth rattle a ragged staccato.

Calm down, I tell myself. *Bailey needs you.*

I steady my hands and pull out of the parking lot. The streets are still quiet, only a lone light pops through the haze at a nearby coffee shop. I put my body on autopilot and my brain on rewind. I replay everything he just told me. I see the officer's blue eyes flashing. I listen to the deep pitch of his voice.

You don't remember me, do you?
Think. Come on. Remember.

* * * *

My foot does a quick punch on the accelerator as I get a flash from my past. Yes, that's it. Pull out the memory, make it clear, and focus in. I glance down at the scribble.

Detective Beckett Brady.

Yes, I can see him now.

It was one night just before we moved to Echo Valley. I was probably around thirteen. My father, more inebriated than usual thanks to an extra special batch of weed imported from Vermont had passed out with a cigarette in his hand and almost burned our house down. I called 9-1-1, gave the dispatcher our address and tried to haul buckets of water to the living room until they got there.

The fire department showed up to deal with the flames, the local drug detectives arrived to handle the drugs. My father almost wept as he watched his paper bag full of Vermont's finest grass being taken away by men in black jackets. As my parents were placed in the back of the cruiser, I stood on the porch, listening to the fire chief tell me I needed to vacate the premises because of smoke damage. Funny, I remember thinking. Where exactly did he think I should go?

One of the black jackets hung back, came over to me once the chief left.

"Hi," he began. I remember he had deep blue eyes. His face was young; his voice was tender.

"They'll be booked, but probably released."

"I know," I replied. I had been through the process before.

"Do you have somewhere to go? Who should we call? The state needs to make sure you're safe. We're supposed to take you into custody. You can't stay here alone."

"No, please. I'll go when they come. But, I'll be okay until then. Don't worry, I'll figure it out." I told him. He reached into his back pocket, pulled out a piece of paper burned slightly along the edges.

"I grabbed this for you. Thought you'd want to hang onto it." He handed over the commendation I had received from the principal of the junior high school. My mother had told me she'd put in on the fridge.

IN RECOGNITION OF OUTSTANDING EFFORT AND THE HIGHEST ACADEMIC ACHIEVEMENT: PRESENTED TO BO CARMICHAEL FOR MAINTAINING A 4.0 AVERAGE FOR EIGHT CONSECUTIVE SEMESTERS.

The principal had scrawled along the bottom … *"Congratulations, Bo. You will make a fine doctor someday. Keep up the good work."*

It never made it to the fridge. Instead, my father had been using it as a coaster for his booze-filled glass. The paper had a big wet circle right in the middle, but you could still make out what it said. I smiled up at the officer who was hauling my parents off yet again.

"Thank you," I said.

"You're welcome. You don't have to end up like them, you know."

"I know. I won't."

"I believe you. Good luck."

He had turned and walked off my front porch. Never did I expect to see him again. But there he had been, sitting right next to me in the front seat of my car, trying for the second time in my life to lead me along a better path.

CHAPTER FIFTEEN

I try to compartmentalize my situation, approach it one step at a time, so I don't lose my mind. I do not let myself think too far ahead of the possibilities, at the idea of losing my son to the state of New Hampshire's foster care system. It is such a hideous thought it actually makes me twitch.

Bailey is still out cold in the back seat, which buys me some time to think without having to explain anything yet. I will need access to a phone. I will also need to make sure I am not where anyone would expect me to be. Detective Brady's warning repeats itself in my head … *don't let them find you.*

They think they've concocted the perfect scenario to deal with me, destroy my credibility just in case I dare open my mouth about what I saw inside the barn. They think I'll crumble under pressure, maybe even confess to something I have not done simply because I am too stupid and intimidated to fight back. My tears are long gone, replaced by the fiercest rage I have ever felt. How *dare* they try to do this to me! Send me to prison; take away my child. Are these people so hungry for power and prestige they would actually orchestrate the decimation of another human being?

Well, two human beings if you count what's taken root in Mackenzie Mason's uterus.

I have to outsmart them. I have to take them by surprise. First, I have to get somewhere safe.

Only commuters heading into the city and bus drivers beginning their routes join me on the roads this early. Something about watching the slow rolling yellow school bus gives me the hint of a possibility. It takes me back in time. Where did I go when I was young? Where do I know my way around, but could be so inconspicuous no one would notice me?

I pull through the drive through of a Dunkin' Donuts, ordering a box of donuts and a large coffee. I pay with cash, because that's what all criminals on the run do, and take a right out of the lot heading toward the interstate. My wallet tells me I won't be able to do this much longer, but I can't risk a bank withdrawal that will leave evidence behind for the people I suspect are looking for it.

I need help. I need another brain on this. Someone who can think with logic and not emotion.

Someone who is not Peter Brenner.

I won't even consider involving him in this, even though I am certain by now he is going ballistic. He will be ticking off the hours until he can officially report us as missing, even though I'm sure he's already put his cop feelers out trying to figure out why we would stand him up and, no doubt, he's blowing up my missing cell phone. In order to keep Peter safe, I have to keep him entirely in the dark and pray no one traces the number back to him. They only want me, right?

Soon enough, Peter and everyone else will hear one side of the story. Given this is an active investigation the press won't get wind until I show up for my arraignment and the details become public knowledge. But this seedy shit spreads like wildfire. All it will take is one set of eyes in the parking lot to report to another and pretty soon I'll be wearing a giant "M" on my sweater that announces I've finally slid down the slope and become a meth head.

Some will say that it figures, a girl who would dis one good man, get pregnant by another, and torch her own future is a very likely candidate to wind up dealing potions and pills behind the local CVS.

On paper, they're right. But they don't know me. Few really do. Except Peter.

My chin quivers and my eyes swell again. I am about to crush the spirit of the only man who has ever truly loved me like I was his own. Peter has loved us unconditionally, taken care of us, planned a future with us. He had just begun to talk about taking Bailey down to the baseball field to teach him a few things about the game.

"It's time, Bo. This guy has all the makings of a natural."

I would only nod, not sure what exactly Bailey has the makings of, but willing to give it a try. It was to be a huge step for him. He would be returning to the place where he left his heart the moment his son stepped off the rubber mound for the last time.

The ball field will have to wait. I have some business to attend to first. If I can't have Peter, I'll have to find the next best thing. I need a razor sharp thinker who will trust that I'm not blowing smoke and stirring up conspiracy theories.

I move my car over a lane to take the next exit off. I haven't paid a bit of attention to where I have been driving, although I think subconsciously I knew where to go this whole time.

I don't have a choice, and I won't give him one, either. If he can't help me, I'm as screwed as Mackenzie Mason.

My stomach flips again as I imagine meeting him face to face after all this time.

I try to find the right words to say to the man who once wanted to be my husband, who promised he would cherish me forever.

And he did cherish me, right up to the day I told him I was pregnant with another man's baby.

CHAPTER SIXTEEN

The high school parking lot is already bustling. I pull up next to a middle-aged woman with a graying bun in her hair, and a pencil stuck through one side of it.

"Hi," I say, leaning out the window on my elbow.

"Student parking is on the other side of the gym," she begins, making a sweep with her arm to indicate the area beyond the big brick addition with a picture of an Indian chief near the door.

"Oh, no, I'm not a student. I'm just looking for someone. I thought maybe you'd know him." I am glad I put my sunglasses back on. This exchange is already way too long. She'd be someone who would remember me under police questioning.

"Well, I might." She walks closer to my car. I pull my hair over my cheek, trying to hide more of my face. Why I bother, I have no idea, because the biggest give-away of all chimes in from the back seat.

"Hi, hi, hi," Bailey waves his chocolate covered hand at her, fully awake now and chomping away on his donuts.

"Do you want a donut? Momma got me extra today."

"No, thank you, sir," she smiles back at him. "He yours?" she wants to know.

Dear God, why don't I just go ahead and tell her I'm a suspected drug lord on the run. "Yup, all mine. So, hey, would you happen to know Jackson Nichols?"

"Oh sure, Jackson works across the hall from me. He's a bit more enthusiastic than I in the morning, however."

She checks the slim silver watch on her left arm. "I'd say he's already inside, working on today's lesson plan. When you're young, you can rise with the sun. These days I need my trusty old alarm clock to pull me out of bed." On and on she tries to go about how each year adds another wrinkle and another fifteen minutes to the sleep cycle. I signal with my hand that I'm ready to go, much like Peter does with me when he wants me to stop talking.

"Thank you so much, I appreciate your help."

I pull around to the student parking lot.

"Where are we, Momma?" Bailey asks, licking donut residue from his fingers.

"At school. To visit an old friend, and I need a favor, pal." I catch his eye in my rearview mirror. He seems agreeable enough, given he's high as a kite on glucose and carbs.

"Okay, what you need?" he asks sincerely, ready to cooperate.

"My friend and I haven't seen each other in a long time, and he might be kind of mad at me for showing up at his work. I need you to be a big, brave kid and understand that we need his help right now."

"Will he keep those scary police guys away?"

"Well, hopefully, yes. He will help me keep them from taking us back with them again."

He digests this for a couple of seconds.

"Momma?"

"Yes, Bailey?"

"Do those guys do 9-1-1?"

"Who, honey? Who does 9-1-1?"

"Those guys, Momma, the ones who were mean to you."

"Well, technically, sweetheart, those officers were just doing their job. They are a little wrong about a few things, but yes, they would be the officers who helped people if they called 9-1-1."

"Hmmm," he replies quietly. "Momma?"

"What is it, honey? We have to hurry up now."

"I was just going to say that I would never call 9-1-1 again if those mean guys would answer."

Irony sure does sting. "Come on, Mr. B. Let's not worry about that right now, okay. Let's go see if my friend is inside." I exit my door, looking around for long black cars or cruisers with sirens blaring on the horizon.

"Okay, let's go." He thrusts his hand into mine, looks up and notices the big brick building for the first time.

"Ooooh," he says. "What's this place again?"

"This is a school, Bailey, where the teenagers go."

"Teenagers like Tucker?"

In Bailey's small frame of reference, Tucker is the only teenager he has ever known of.

"Yes, a place where kids like Tucker go to school."

"Only Tucker doesn't go to school anymore? 'Cause Tucker's in heaven?"

It makes me think of Peter again, and how he probably just spent a sleepless night calling old law enforcement buddies, maybe even hospital emergency rooms, looking for us. I try to change the subject.

"See here, Bailey," I walk him through heavy double doors that lead us into the gym that has shiny hardwood floors and bleachers that line both sides.

"This is where the big kids play basketball and volleyball. All those red flags around the ceiling are all the times they've won the state championship."

Bailey's eyes gaze up, and another "ooohh" of approval comes out.

This is New Hampshire's largest regional high school with a proven record of taking average kids from tiny towns and whipping them into college bound student athletes. They are routinely champions of just about everything. It doesn't surprise me that Jackson would find himself here. He and I used to joke that we would make the perfect team. He'd become Super-Teacher, raising up generations of quality societal contributors, while I'd be his personal physician who would make sure his body stayed up for the challenge.

My nerves run wild as we walk up a long corridor, past the cafeteria, to the door the woman in the parking lot told me was Jackson's room.

I knock. And I pray. And I hope to God he doesn't despise me as much as he has every right to.

CHAPTER SEVENTEEN

As I prepared to face the man I used to love, and just as I'd suspected he would, Peter Brenner was running recon, and he began at Gerry's Salon. The place went silent after he came storming through the door promptly as it opened for business.

"Gerry," he said, leading him to the back of the salon near the sinks, "a moment of your time, please."

Gerry was not used to moving so quickly. He took a second to let the burn in his lungs subside, cursing all those cigarettes that now made him feel like an out of breath senior citizen. "Chief, nice to see you again. Retirement agreeing with you?" He tried to begin with some light chitchat, though it fell as flat as a dead skunk on the side of the road.

"I need some information. Bo and Bailey are nowhere to be found. They didn't show up last night where they were supposed to. They aren't at her apartment. I'm trying to figure out what's going on."

Gerry shifts his weight and consults his watch. "Hmm," he says. "Bo's rarely late unless she's notified me in advance that Bailey's sick or something has come up. She has never *not* shown up for work."

Peter nods, taking mental notes, looking for the hint of a lead.

"Anything out of the ordinary yesterday? Did she leave on time? Was she early, late, anything at all?"

"Well," Gerry tries to think. "Actually, she seemed to forget that Bailey had a doctor's appointment yesterday. I had asked her to take a client for me around three o'clock or so. She told me she couldn't and left shortly after that."

"Was she upset? Did she mention anything else aside from a doctor's appointment?"

Gerry shakes his head back and forth. "I really can't think of anything out of the ordinary except that she didn't eat anything."

"Come again?"

"Well, as we all know, Bo doesn't exactly deprive herself when it comes to food. She's the only one around here who actually eats during her lunch break."

"Go on," Peter says.

"Well, yesterday was the perfect opportunity for her to stuff her face. Bo didn't touch a morsel, even though I had ordered a spread to celebrate."

"Celebrate?"

"Yeah, celebrate their weekend with Senator Anderson's family at the photo shoot. I was proud of them for doing a great job. It was just a little way of saying thank you."

Peter takes in the new information that to anyone else would sound like nothing. To him though, it is a strong start.

"So she wasn't hungry, which I agree is out of the norm for Bo. Anything else you can think of."

"No, I think that's it. Do you think something is wrong? Is Bo in some sort of trouble?"

"I'm not sure. Please let me know if you come up with anything else." He scribbles a number down on the back of a card, hands it over to Gerry.

"Call this number here on the back. It's my personal cell."

Gerry promises to call Peter immediately if something of note comes up. He detours over to the front desk while Peter makes his way back toward the front door. He is stopped by a hand on his elbow.

"Chief Brenner?" William asks him to hold up. "I know you and Bo are tight. I know she thinks you are *the man* and all that."

An impatient nod, as Peter cocks his head. William looks around to make sure no one else is listening.

"So, here's the thing. Bo's been off ever since the sex-ator ... I mean the *senator* ... sat down in her chair the other day. I mean, I never actually saw anything happen, and I assumed she was feeling all schleppy next to his glamazon wife who, by the way, is all fake boobs and bad attitude, and ..."

"William. Get to the point."

"Sorry. Anyway, Bo forgot her cell phone somewhere inside the barn. She went back in alone after we were all done, then came back out a few minutes later looking as scary as Lindsay Lohan after an all-nighter." William leans in closer, all conspiratorial. "You know, total haggs-ville."

Peter nods, letting William know he gets it.

"She said nothing was wrong, but she didn't find her cell phone, and then she like … totally barfed out the door."

Peter looks more intently at William, asks him to slow down and start with Bo leaving the car to go back into the barn for her phone.

"Okay," he begins. "We were all in Jessie's car getting ready to leave."

"Was Senator Anderson gone by then?" Peter asks.

"Umm, actually no. His cars were still there, but not in the same parking lot as us. Ours was full of swamp water, theirs was dry as a bone. Go figure …"

"Bo said she forgot her cell phone?"

"Yup. She told Jessie to wait a minute, hopped out and ran back inside. Maybe five minutes later she came running back, got in, and told Jessie to go. Her voice was a little shaky, and she really wanted to get the *fu* … sorry, the *heck* out of there. She looked awful."

"What did she say, William?"

"Not much. Only that she couldn't find the phone."

"Did you leave then?"

"Yeah, we left. But Senator Anderson was still there. He saw us leave, like … *watched* us leave, Chief."

"What do you mean he watched you leave?"

"Well I *think* he did. He and some other guy, I think his bodyguard or something, were standing near the door of their car, and I could have sworn I saw them watch us drive by. Bo saw them, too."

"Did they say anything to you as you drove by?"

"No, but ..."

"But what?"

"Something about the way they were staring at us. And granted Bo put away enough food for an entire African village ... but she wouldn't just regurgitate it for no reason."

"Huh?" Peter breaks in.

"Oh, well the Andersons didn't touch all the crap the caterer put out for them. We all helped ourselves to a little. Bo, to *a lot*."

"Okay, got it. Bo likes to eat. What's that got to do with anything?"

"Well, that's exactly it. She wouldn't waste all that good food."

"Waste it?"

"Yeah. 'Cause by the time we were back out onto the main road she told Jessie to pull over and threw it all back up. She was gagging and heaving and making a nasty old mess." William's lips purse in, like a phantom scent just wafted by.

"Why is this important?"

"Maybe it's not. But Bo has a stomach like a dog." William shrugs his narrow shoulders, "I just wanted you to know. Something spooked that girl. She was fine and dandy until she high-tailed it out of that barn like she was being chased by RuPaul. And, why would some guy who is all presidential and shit watch us drive away like we were any more important to him than the people who clean his toilet, or wash his underwear?"

Peter mulls it over, asks William if there's anything else he needs to know.

"No. But Chief?"

"Yes?"

"Bo doesn't have anyone in this world except that little kid. No family, no nothing, right?"

"Pretty much. Why do you ask?"

"Well, I only say that because she's been all hung up on making sure Bailey doesn't do his phone thing anymore. She respects the hell out of you, and never wanted to be a pain in your ass."

"I know that."

"What I'm trying to say here … is this. It would be *unlikely* for Bo to not show up for her job. But it would be *unheard of* … for her not to show up for you. You get what I'm saying?"

A slow nod, "Yes, I get what you're saying."

"If Bo is not showing up where *you* expect her to, then something just ain't right."

Peter thanks him for his time, and bolts for the door. The first few pieces of the puzzle were taking shape in his mind. He mutters to himself on the way out.

"Something ain't right, all right. Something is very, very wrong."

CHAPTER EIGHTEEN

After the second knock, I hear a muffled response from inside. "Come on, guys, first bell is still a half hour away. I'm working here, give me a break."

Just hearing his voice again makes my heart pound. I tap the door again, bracing myself as I hear a chair push back and footsteps move toward the hallway.

Toward me.

"All right, all right. I'm coming." He swings the door wide, thrusts his head out and says, "Can I help ..." before his mouth closes into a straight line. Still holding the knob with one hand, he leans against the door for support, as if seeing me standing there was like taking a two-by-four to the gut.

"Hi, Jackson," I begin, drinking in his face. I get a rush of warmth through my chest, yet I am fully aware that I am a stranger to him now. He is cordial, yet by the tone of his voice, closing in on annoyed. He doesn't waste time on pleasantries.

"What are you doing here?" he asks, looking past me down the hall to see if anyone else is coming, but stopping short when he sees Bailey. His voice turns soft, wistful. "Wow. This must be your son." He moves each hand roughly along the sides of his face like he's trying to wake himself from some strange nightmare.

"Yes. Bailey say hello to my friend, Mr. Nichols."

"Hi, Momma's friend, Mr. Nichols." He takes one hand, does a few quick waves under his chin.

"Oh my God, Bo. He's really great. Wow." He must be wondering if I've come here to torture him. Jackson always wanted a tribe of children.

"Thanks," I begin, resisting the urge to fall into a mortifyingly awkward silence. "I never would have come here if I wasn't ... um ... if I ..."

... hadn't kicked a bee's nest and am now trying to outrun its angry inhabitants.

"... if I had a choice."

"Are you okay? Is something wrong?"

"Yeah, you could say that. I realize what I'm asking here is ludicrous and totally insane and if you say no I will completely understand, but I'm praying to God you won't."

He cocks his chin down, but his head moves in the other direction. A tiny line forms between his eyes, one I've never seen before. With a quick look down at Bailey to make sure he won't hear everything that is about to rush out of my mouth, I start.

"Jackson, I need your help, there's no one else, and if I don't get out of here now I could ... *lose him.*" If I could sit on my hands right now, I would. They are fluttering as fast as my heart is beating.

"To who?"

"The state, the government, to strangers ... I don't know exactly to who ... but I've gotten mixed up in something bad."

"Okay. So call the police." Obvious reaction, if only it were that easy.

"I can't. They're part of the problem."

"What?"

"They think I'm a ... ummm ... I'm a ..." Oh just say it already! "A dealer." I push it out in a loud whisper.

"Like a blackjack dealer?"

"No. *No!* Like a drug dealer."

"What? Why? That's crazy. Right, Bo? That is *crazy*, right?" It's a fair question. Last he saw me I was pregnant and dumping him. I could have easily degraded from there.

"Yes, of course. It's completely crazy." I search his eyes for some hint of what he's feeling. Concern or disgust? "You have to believe me, Jackson. Because the first thing I need is for you to believe in me. The rest of this really hinges on that. Can you trust that I haven't completely lost my mind?" I can see his hesitation; I forgive him for it because I can't blame him. Every ounce of common sense would tell him to get the hell away from me. Along with the kid who isn't his.

I cut him off before he shuts me down.

"Before you answer, just hear me out." A subtle nod, he's willing to hear more.

"I'm a hairdresser now. I'm trying to pay my rent, and take care of him, and eat every once in a while on a paycheck that rivals what I used to make at the Dairy Queen. I had a big job last weekend, with some very important people. Long story short, I saw something I shouldn't have seen, and now I'm in serious trouble. I need help, and I don't have anybody else to turn to."

He levels a gaze that is part wince. "What is it that you need me to do?"

"I need you to come with me."

"Bo, come with you where? I can't just leave … I have students, classes to teach, papers to grade. I can't just … take off!" His face is clouding over; his voice rises with frustration.

My cheeks are on fire. This is wrong! I get an abrupt reality check that hurts like a third-degree sunburn. What was I thinking? I shouldn't be here. I have no right to ask Jackson for anything. Guilt feels like a wet blanket draping itself over my head, I can't breathe. I stumble backward, disgusted in myself for giving in to a weak moment. Showing up here and begging for help from the man I pushed away without explanation is a monumental mistake.

"I'm so sorry," I whisper, blinking back hot tears. "You owe me nothing, forget I was even here." I grab Bailey and pull him up sharply, eliciting a small whimper of surprise. We hustle down the hallway in shame. I hurry, heaving Bailey in next to my hip. Heavy, fast-moving footsteps catch up with us.

"Stop!" he grabs my elbow. "You can't just appear, after years go by, rattle off a personal crisis that sounds like life or death and then bolt. It's not fair, Bo. It's not fair to me. Not again." His cheeks are puffing out air.

"I know, you're right. None of this is fair, but I should never have come here."

Jackson sighs, his chin drops and he reaches for me. I melt into his arms but give myself only to the count of five to feel him. Then, I pull back. I have to get out of here.

"Forgive me. Please. For now, and for then. I'm sorry for everything I've ever done to hurt you, Jackson."

Instead of letting me leave, he leads me back down the hall, into his classroom and to a chair next to his desk. I'm as listless as cooked spaghetti, I melt into a chair with bones that splinter into sawdust.

Jackson checks his watch. "I have twenty minutes of privacy before an angry herd of teenagers storms through this door. I promise if there's something I can do to help, I'll do it. But my life is here now. I won't leave it."

I nod sadly. "Thank you. That's more than I probably deserve."

I unload just the pertinent details of my predicament, begging for his discretion. He thinks on it for a few minutes, asking me only a couple of questions. He reaches for a small square notepad and writes down a name and number.

"Well, I would listen to that detective," Jackson suggests, after I explained that there is one person who may be able to see through the smoke screen. "You have a friend here, Bo. Trust in it for once. Trust that not everything in this world is something you have to tackle all alone and with one hand tied behind your back. Let someone help you. It's just …" he looks down at his hands. "It's just not going to be me." He won't look me in the face.

A squishy rush of emotion deposits both sadness and regret. It could have been Jackson. For his protection, and my own, I don't share exactly who it is that's trailing me, and won't let on that it could be the scandal of the century. I stand up, reach for Bailey, and tell Jackson that it's time for me to go. I have to get out of here.

He hands me the piece of paper, it has a name and phone number scrawled across it. "My cousin is a local TV reporter. She's not the sharpest or the brightest, but she's a good girl, and I trust her. If you're ever ready to take this crazy story public, maybe she can help you. It's the best I can offer …" he trails off, but successfully delivers the message that this is as far as he goes.

I look around his room at the colorful posters and inspirational sayings to motivate his students. What a successful life he has created for himself.

Exactly what I had hoped for when I set him free.

"I can never thank you …"

He interrupts. "You don't have to. Just … stay safe, be smart. Work this out and have a good life, Bo. You deserve that," he smiles down at Bailey. "Both of you do."

I nod and put the slip of paper into my coat pocket. I reach for him one last time.

He whispers softly close to my ear, "And I do."

"You do what?" I ask, confused.

"I forgive you. For now. And for then."

I don't look back. I pull Jackson's door shut and lock onto Bailey's hand. I know I didn't get everything I came for, but I feel like I'm unloading the baggage of my actions once and for all.

Bailey and I walk briskly back to my car. I take my keys out, as two slips of paper fall into the passenger seat.

One has the name of Jackson's cousin the TV reporter on it, Sabrina Pressley. I fold that back up carefully and tuck it away. I reach for the other, the gas receipt with purple Magic Marker.

Detective Beckett Brady.

I pull out of student parking and back onto the highway. My next stop is an exit up, where I find a faded telephone booth concealed by trees next to a McDonalds. I pull the hood of my jacket over my head, drop in a quarter, and feel significant relief that I hear a dial tone. I punch in the number.

"Brady," says a gruff voice on the second ring.

"It's Bo. We're okay. So far, so good."

"Good. I'm making some progress here, but you need to stay away. Do you have a place to go?"

I get another flashback of a younger me standing on my parents' front porch, my shitty house burning down along with any shred of adolescent innocence I had left. My eyes finding the subaqueous blue of his, an authentic concern that wraps around me like a warm embrace. Even back then, my heart told me that Detective Beckett Brady truly cared about where I'd rest my head that night. I get the same sense now as he speaks those words to me again, *"Do you have a place to go?"*

"Yes," I reply. "I know exactly where I'm going."

Detective Brady instructs me to stay in touch. I click off, telling him I'll call again soon, not yet aware that the direction of his life, mine, and someone else we both know and love is about to change forever.

CHAPTER NINETEEN

The parking lot at Dr. Fontaine's office is shaped like a U. There's a breast center to the right and an orthopedic office to the left. Whether you're getting a flu shot for your kid, a mammogram, or a cast removed, you have to park in the same U. At the height of political season, visitors must also shuffle around various campaign signs poking up from the grassy squares as candidates seek to cover every inch of the landscape with their slogans and promises.

Peter left Gerry's Salon on a direct route to that parking lot about fifteen minutes away. He begins with Dr. Fontaine's receptionist.

"Well, hello there, Chief Brenner," Rosemary Nylan beams through the sliding glass door that separates her from the patients checking in. Rosemary knows Peter from way back. Much like everyone else around these parts.

"Hi, Rosemary, nice to see you again. Been awhile, huh?"

"Too long if you ask me. How's Emily? You two getting some time out on the links?" A rather strange question given that Chief Brenner loves to golf, but Emily Brenner prefers to shop.

"I sneak out from time to time. Emily is doing well. Thanks for asking."

"Good." Now that the niceties have passed, Rosemary wonders what he's doing there. She asks him as much.

"Actually, I was wondering if you might be able to help me out with something."

"Of course, if I can. You know that."

"Thanks. Bo Carmichael was here yesterday, right?"

"Bo? Yes. Yes, she was here. That little Bailey is just adorable. He had a check-up with Dan Fontaine."

"Was everything okay while they were here? Did Bo seem troubled at all to you?"

"Troubled? Well, no, not that I could tell. She is always very pleasant."

"I know you can't release medical information to me, but just from your perspective, did the appointment appear to go well?"

"Oh, well, yes I can't really give that to you. But since it's *you* and all, from what I saw, and what I know about Bailey, he's doing super. Growing like a weed, happy little guy, well-adjusted and well cared for. Bo may not have much in the way of family help, but she's doing a good job with that boy." She shuffles some paper around her desk, looks from side to side to make sure no one else was listening.

"Chief?"

"Yes?"

"Is Bo in some kind of trouble?"

"Honestly, I'm not sure yet. All I can say is that I'd like to find her. And soon."

"Do you think her car broke down or something?"

"I hadn't thought of that. Why do you ask?"

"Well, about five minutes after Bo had left a mother came in with her daughter who looked like she was covered in chicken pox. Imagine that? *Chicken pox*, these days! So, anyway, the mother asked if there was something going on in the parking lot."

"This parking lot?" Peter points out behind him.

"Yes. The one right out front. She said there was a police cruiser and four cops standing around a car. Sure enough, when I poked my head out, it was Bo's car. I could see her talking to them, but the next time I looked, she and the police were gone."

"Were they local cops, state cops?"

"Oh gosh, I wouldn't know that. A cop is a cop to someone like me."

"Thanks, Rosemary. That might help out a lot."

"Anything for you, and Bo for that matter. Sure, do hope she's okay. You let me know if you hear anything."

"Will do." Peter strides over to the door. He surveys the lot, trying to get a sense of what went down there. He quickly walks over to his car, turns the ignition, and heads out toward the main road. It's about a five-minute drive over to the Livingston Police barracks. There's a good chance it was Livingston police who responded to whatever unfolded in the parking lot.

Instead of calling ahead, Peter figures walking in might be an easier way to coax out some information, especially if he happens to run into his one-time protégé, Detective Beckett Brady. Beck owes him a few anyway.

* * * *

The lot at the barracks is half-full of empty cruisers either coming off the night shift or waiting to head out on patrol. Peter climbs out from his car and walks into the lobby. He reaches the bulletproof glass, gives it a knock and waves to the female officer punching something into a computer. After a buzz that unlocks the door from the inside, she walks over to Peter and throws her arms around him.

"Good Lord, look what the cat dragged off the golf course." She falls out of their embrace and into casual chatter.

"Hi, Jamie," Peter smiles back, "why does everyone think retirement is spent on the ninth hole?"

"Cause you're a guy, Chief. And for most guys, that's exactly where they wind up. Or sloshed by the 18th for sure. So, what brings you to these parts?"

"Oh, you know, just saying hello, making the rounds, reconnecting with some old friends. You've seen Beck around yet today?"

"Ha! You mean the sleep-at-your-desk, refuse-to-go-home-and-have-a-life, Detective Brady? Why yes, I have seen him. You want to know why? Because the man never leaves! When you start to think take-out from the Chinese place down the street is a home cooked meal, you have finally screwed the pooch. And Detective Brady, sorry to say, is head first into the dog house by now."

Peter nods and smiles, but it doesn't surprise him to hear Beck is a bit intense about his work. He learned from the master after all.

"Let me see if I can't shake the cobwebs off him a little. Find him for me, Jamie?"

"No prob, Chief. Come on in, I'll take you down to his office."

Jamie presses a key card to the door, waits for another buzz, and walks Peter down a narrow corridor to one of the doors deep in the belly of the department. This is where many of the undercover guys hang out, far enough removed from the lobby to stay hidden from sight. Peter breathes in the familiar smells of floor wax, burned coffee, and last night's dinner still clinging to the sides of the trashcans.

Jamie knocks twice on the heavy door.

"Hey, Beck. You got company." She taps Peter on the arm, tells him, "He's all yours," and heads back down the hall.

The door swings wide to reveal a tired looking detective still holding a small white cup of department brewed coffee. Beck's overtired and pinched expression dissolves into a grin when he sees the man standing in the doorway.

"If you tell me I'm late for my tee time, or ask me where I parked my cart, I will throttle you. Just sayin'," Peter's greeting accompanies a huge smile.

Beck stands a good inch or so taller than Peter Brenner, they look like two gladiators as they clap hands on each other's backs after a quick, but warm embrace. "Actually, I was going to give you a shout anyway, ask you how you're holding up. Retirement must be downright miserable, can't imagine it myself."

"Yeah, that's what I'm hearing. Are you trying to check out a little early, son? Spending too much time in this hellhole has a way of aging a man. I thought I taught you better than that, Beck. When was the last time you had a date?"

"I'm gonna have to plead the fifth on that one. I have the right not to incriminate myself, don't I?"

They are well-practiced at this good-natured ribbing. They've been doing it a long time.

"So really, now," Beck says, leaning against the edge of his notoriously unkempt desk. "Not that I don't welcome the distraction but what brings you by? It surely can't be to discuss my ... *ahhum,* love life, can it?"

Peter's eyes narrow. His tone grows serious. "I need your help on something."

"Of course, anything."

"You happen to be in on a little parking lot shindig yesterday, up at the doctor's plaza?"

Beck coughs on his coffee. Peter doesn't miss a beat. "You okay?" he asks, but the question is much deeper.

"I'm not sure," Beck says, wiping his mouth with the back of his rolled up sleeve. He shakes his head back and forth and mutters, "I know you're a regular on Satan's payroll, my friend, but this is bizarre." Beck always thought Peter had the kind of eerie sixth sense that would make some people put in a call to their local Catholic Diocese.

"Seriously, Pete. Before I answer that, I need to ask *you* something."

"Shoot." Peter's eyes begin to narrow. The cop in him readies for the play to be called in the huddle.

"As someone who has just exited the game, I need to know how deep you want to go on this."

As they lock eyes, Peter Brenner feels that old twitch in his gut whenever a hunch is confirmed.

"All the way, Beck. Start at the beginning, and tell me everything."

CHAPTER TWENTY

Peter and Beck stay locked behind the closed door of the department office, trying to piece together a feasible scenario using nothing but supposition. Peter uses the edge of his pen to make large circles around the name United States Senator Declan Anderson. Just one of several names the two detectives have jotted down on notepaper stained by their sloshing coffee cups or rolled into tight balls and deposited into the trash.

"She's a smart girl," Peter begins. "But she's desperate to do anything to protect Bailey. Doesn't surprise me they're using that. If someone wants Bo, he'll be working through the kid to draw her out. If you hadn't trusted your gut, he'd already be gone."

Beck nods into the heel of his palm, his elbow holding up one hand placed under his chin. It was a startling off-base accusation. Who would take such care to come up with a story that painted a girl—one paycheck away from bag lady status—as a danger to society who must be locked up?

"So much ice in that bag," he says with a sigh. "It was a ridiculous amount. And they really thought I wouldn't notice? Drove me nuts she didn't just call a lawyer. Or you…"

Peter nods. It's a moot point. Beckett Brady is the best at what he does and feels fury when the red line of protocol is smudged. His exceptional instincts first pricked Peter's ears over a decade ago when he plucked the then greener-than-a-shamrock rookie straight out of the academy. One of the best moves he ever made. Peter couldn't be more proud of the cop, and the man, Beckett has become. He trusts him implicitly. Beck had his own sixth sense and more connections to the underworld than The Prince of Darkness himself. If Bo was the crystal meth maven they were making her out to be, he would have disrupted her operation a long time ago. Beck does not swing and miss. Anyone who knows him knows that.

Beck shared with Peter his meticulous notes on this case, starting with the minute he got wind of a warrant. The Livingston Police Chief had come by his office, asking what he knew about the girl who was high enough in the pipeline to get caught, yet crafty enough to go unnoticed for so long. Not thrilled that Beck was completely unaware of her, their conversation was laced with disappointment; the chief flustered that his point man had let something this big slip through his fingers. As a final word on the case, he insisted Beck assist on the arrest. Otherwise, he never would have been there for the parking lot ambush.

"Jesus Christ, Pete. The smoke from this fire is making me fucking choke."

Peter reaches again for the copy of the warrant sitting on the desk. They know it's as bogus as the argument that men buy Playboy just for the articles.

The officer who had submitted the written affidavit knew he was doing it under oath, and yet the information it contained was ludicrous. Officer Spencer Diaz was new to the Livingston Police Department, a sketchy guy who didn't make eye contact or friends. He preferred a cordial yet distant relationship with whoever shared a patrol car with him and gave off the distinct impression that he had better places to be. Everyone else had already shrugged him off, but something about him really bothered Beck.

Both he and Peter also knew the judge who had signed off on it. Judge Stanley Nelson was an equal opportunity offender who made both prosecutors and defense attorneys cringe to see him behind the bench. A portly, balding man with a temper as fiery as a coiled cobra, Nelson had signed the warrant at 12:36 a.m. the morning of Bo's arrest. Unusual for a couple reasons. No cop worth his salt ever presents an affidavit to Judge Nelson if there is any other judge within a thousand-mile radius who is drawing breath at the time. There would be no way in hell he would answer a phone call past dinnertime, let alone in the middle of the night. Yet, somehow, the officer with the personality of a surly repo man had purposely sought out the tyrant with the legal conscience of a mosquito to issue an arrest warrant for a single mother who was supposedly the modern day version of Don Corleone. It didn't take long for Peter and Beck to realize they were unraveling a pretty disturbing case of quid pro quo. What would Nelson be willing to do in exchange for a phony warrant on a perfectly innocent young woman? Is he knee-deep in this charade, or was he simply being bamboozled by someone?

The other officers assigned to Bo's arrest were just figureheads, acting on orders, pure and simple. They joked that she was hot but were totally fine with chalking her up to just another druggie skank. Officer Diaz, however, had an inordinately strong connection to all this. When Beck had cornered him, demanding details on a suspect that had come out of nowhere, Diaz had been aloof and condescending. He hadn't wanted Beck anywhere near this case, objecting to the chief that he wanted to handle it on his own. After muscling his way in, Beck had to swallow the shock of watching Diaz throw the bag full of junk onto the table. That much crystal meth would guarantee prison time even for someone with a clean record. So, not only was she an anomaly in the drug world—a lovely looking, gainfully employed single parent with no priors—she had been catapulted to a federal level. And on his watch to boot!

Why the fuck was Diaz trying so hard to wrap his greasy fingers around this to keep Beck's off?

"Have you heard from Sloan yet?" Peter asks, his voice breaking the tension like the snap of a thick twig.

"No, but I will." Beck says.

Sloan Tennison was an old flame who had flickered pretty hot a few years back. She and Beck dated for several months, and then cooled off when she realized there would always be something more important in his life than her. Beck understood. Work came first, and no woman alive would come in second to a mistress like that.

Sloan still had a soft spot for Beck, which was why she had agreed to do him a favor. As Executive Assistant to the head of the New Hampshire Division of Child, Youth, and Family Services, she had access to just about everything.

She told Beck she would check on Bo's file for him. It's not unusual for anyone suspected of a crime to receive a visit from DCYF if a minor lived under the same roof. In Bo's case, the visit was imminent, and just as Beck suspected, about to happen without her knowledge. The information was available in her police file, but the explanation for the immediate action was not. He asked Sloan to dig a little and find out why.

According to law, DCYF is required to inform parents of their rights at the outset of an investigation. Technically, if Bo had been on Diaz's radar screen long enough for him to secure a warrant, he should have notified DCYF, and there would be a record of that. Bo would have the right to refuse entry to a DCYF worker knocking on her door. But if she had no idea they were coming, or someone fooled the agency into thinking she was in the process of slitting her child's throat, they could storm right in. Beck already knew what would have happened if he had allowed her to return to her apartment. She would have done what most innocent parents do, thrown the door right open and let them in. Bo would have no reason to be on guard.

Someone was banking on that.

Still making long, lazy circles around the name of Senator Declan Anderson, Peter speaks without looking up.

"Talk to me, Beck. Tell me why you want to go ahead and destroy a perfectly good woman."

Becks nods, taking on the role of whoever is so royally pissed off at Bo Carmichael right now.

"Because I think she's fucked me. Somehow, she is in the way. I plant some shit on her that I know will put her away for a while, but more importantly, shut her up."

"Okay. So you remove the woman. Fine. Why do you still want to get to the kid?"

Beckett slides back forcefully into his chair, throws his arms wide on the suddenly obvious explanation.

"Because I want to kick her while she's down. I don't just want to put her away, I want to rip out her guts. I want to tear apart the only thing she can still feel. I want to make sure she'll be destroyed. If she's lost it all, she will *never* fight back."

The two men stare at each other, lost for a moment in the scenario that now seems to fit perfectly. Peter doesn't even notice his thick fingers have pushed the tip of the pen so violently onto the notepaper the plastic tip has snapped clean off.

"You remember when you told me about the monsters we'll hunt in this job, Pete?"

"Yuh," confirmation comes on a grunt. "I told you some of them would have a ton of slimy tentacles reaching out in all kinds of directions."

"What else? What else about those monsters?"

"I also told you that every monster, no matter how big, will only have one head. One brain, calling all the shots."

"Exactly."

"What are you working, Beck?"

"Following the tentacles. I'm starting to think they may lead us straight to him."

Beck motions with his chin down at Peter's fingers still wrapped about the broken pen. The ragged tip remains planted in place, right on top of the name he had scribbled down hours ago and refused to cross off his list.

The name of United States Senator Declan Anderson.

CHAPTER TWENTY-ONE

I head north along I-93, trying to forget Jackson's final embrace and return my attention to saving my own hide. I put the radio on an all-news station, listening for any mention of a young mother on the run.

Once we are past the gold dome of the Capitol building I pick a random exit around Canterbury and get off the highway. Bailey is chirping about all the colorful leaves, and a flock of wild turkeys near the road. I pull into a business plaza and park. I spot another pay phone behind a 7/11, exactly what Beck said about convenience stores. I know I'm damn lucky to have found two functioning pay phones in an era of handheld communication devices. The old relics are saving my ass right now.

Bailey is still unfazed by our sudden departure, although he has begun to ask for his stuffed monkey, and wants to call Peter to tell him all about the mean officers we met. "Wait until Peter hears about them," he says. "He sure gonna be mad."

Yes, he will be mad, but mostly at me for running for the hills when I should stay and fight. I can hear him now. "Why didn't you call me, Bo?"

How do I explain that there are forces at work that just might follow a phone call all the way to Peter's front door? Who knows what would happen after that. I have to trust my instincts, which are telling me the further away I can get myself the better. I won't make Peter a target.

"Come on, Mr. B. We're going to give my car a little rest here and make a quick call."

I pull my hood back over my head, tuck away long strands of my hair, and stroll through the door of the convenience store. I grab some snacks for Bailey, a soda for myself, and give in when his huge eyes find a happy pink rack of Blow-Pops. As we exit and walk toward the pay phone, I unwrap one and hand it over.

"It's sticky, be careful."

"Got it!" he reaches for this new treat.

Detective Brady grabs the phone again on the first ring. He asks me where I am, and I tell him I know where to go. I get about halfway through my grandfather's address before he shuts me down cold. This man is not one for wasting time or his own breath.

"I'll be right there. Stay put, Bo, I mean it. From here, we go together." The line goes dead.

"What the heck ..." I stare at the phone.

We go together ...

We do?

"What's a matter," Bailey lisps through lips shiny with Blow-Pop residue.

My hand is still gripping the plastic receiver. I hang it up and pull Bailey back toward my parked car. "Nothing's the matter, honey," I say, squeezing his hand and telling him lightly that we need to wait for someone. Bailey is all over it.

"Peter?" he says, excitement building in his voice.

"No, buddy, not Peter. Another officer, a good guy, a friend." I watch him carefully. Bailey may be four, but he is no slouch in picking up on subtleties.

"No, Momma, not one of those guys from before?" His eyes well with confusion as to why his mother would let any of those scary men near him again. Bailey doesn't know yet that Detective Brady says he is on our side.

I'm still trying to figure that out myself.

CHAPTER TWENTY-TWO

As they dart out of Beck's underground office, the two men travel in different directions. Peter is heading to the apple orchard, site of the weekend's big photo shoot and the last place Bo had been before she became public enemy number one.

They decided that Beck would go to Bo. Peter insisted. So did Beck. Once he learned that Peter actually knew Bo and Bailey, he tried to further jostle an explanation on why she wouldn't have called him right away.

"Makes no sense, Pete. She's got you ..."

"No," Peter cut him off. "She doesn't want me anywhere near this. She's trying to watch out for *me* here, imagine that." His face broke into a melancholy half-smile loaded with both affection and worry. Beck shook his hand and held it tight. He looked his mentor straight in the eye.

"I will protect them with my life, Pete. I promise."

"I know you will." Theirs was a bond built on mutual trust and admiration, so the obvious question came with the utmost of respect. Beck hadn't probed too deeply into this mysterious relationship. But he needed to. He had already told Peter about the night he first met Bo. When her parents were being hauled away in the back of a cruiser and her dumpy home was ablaze. The last time he had seen her, Bo was pocketing a crumpled piece of stained paper that had proven to Beck she was so much more than what she was surrounded by. When he mentioned the address way up north that Bo started to give him over the phone, Peter knew exactly where she was heading.

"She's got nowhere else to go," he muttered.

Beck felt like he was climbing scaffolding. Strange connections in this case were everywhere, but it was difficult to establish his footing. He needed to know where and how Peter fit in.

"Pete. Tell me to fuck off if you want, and I'm not trying to pry, but …"

Peter held up his palm, his bold habit of breaking off a difficult topic. Beck sensed he was trying to formulate a respectable response. Something that would give substance to a relationship that had no familial place in his life yet existed there solely because he wanted it to.

It reminded Beck of the National Geographic lion specials he sometimes watches when he's coming in late off an arrest, and he's too wound up to go to bed. The voiceover with the uppity English accent describes the alpha male lion as being responsible for protecting the entire pride from outside males. That especially meant the females and their cubs. Peter was protecting his pride.

"Emily doesn't understand," Peter began. "This whole Bo, Bailey situation. She doesn't think it's right."

Beck understood that. Emily would very likely be hurt by Peter's heartfelt interest in a family that wasn't his. Or hers.

"What … is … the situation?"

Peter's explanation began with an admission.

"Beck, I was dead inside. I lost interest. In my job, in my life, I guess in some ways, in my marriage, too. Nothing mattered to me. I went through the motions but I was empty, a shell. That probably hurt Emily the most. She was falling apart, and I was incapable of doing anything but watch it happen."

Beck already knew that Peter Brenner's nature was to fall on the sword for far less that went wrong. If Emily's award-winning tomato plants failed to yield a giant orb for the state fair, Peter would tell everyone it was because he spread the lawn fertilizer a little too close to their roots. If dispatch accidentally reported the wrong address to the EMTs responding to a 9-1-1 call, Pete would make a notation on the report that it was his fault for not updating the system when the new housing development went in. The buck always stopped with him. He made damn sure of it. But this time, Beck wasn't entirely sure Peter deserved it.

"Pete, you lost your kid. You were grieving ..."

Peter cut him off. "Yeah, I get that, Beck. That's not what I mean. What I'm saying is that I never expected to ... *feel* again. I thought that was gone forever."

Beck felt a moment of deep anger that a man like Peter would face such unspeakable loss. He saw far-lesser human beings routinely enjoying more of life's rewards than they were due. How was it that a man built to do such good in this world would receive its harshest punishment?

"That little guy, Bailey, he makes me feel. He makes me *want* to feel."

Of course, Beck knew Peter was suffering. His child had died; his entire world had crumbled. But not long after he buried his boy Pete was back on the job. Beck had respected him enough to take that at face value, assuming he needed his work to force him to get on with his life. Now, he realized that he should have done more. He had let his friend down by not understanding exactly how much of him had evaporated.

"It's not like I think he's Tucker, Beck. Don't go working your psychoanalytical angles on me, now."

Beck stifled a mild chuckle. "Wasn't doing that at all. I'm just thinking that all in all, I've been a pretty lousy friend."

Peter shook his head. "No. Don't do that to yourself. Trust me, I'm the first one to admit that when life pulls the rug out from under you, there's no *right* way to try and find your footing. You either do, or you don't. There's nothing you could have done."

Beck had the feeling Peter was working through emotions he'd never shared with a single person.

"For a while, I stayed in his room at night," Peter said, his face soft. "Emily would tell me it wasn't healthy, but I couldn't help myself. I needed to be in a place that was all his." Peter looks down at his hands before he continues to unload his most sacred memory. "The night he died we had a long talk, man to man. Maybe it was because he was getting ready to leave for college and I realized there were important things I may have said to him only in passing. I wanted him to hear me, to really hear how I felt about him."

"Sure," Beck said gently. "But Tucker knew that all along."

"That night was different. These kids fly through life with one finger on a cell phone at all times. They're virtually stuck in a social media whirlwind. I wanted Tucker to shut it all off and listen to me. And he did. That night I had him right here." Peter cupped his hand. "It was the best talk I'd ever had with my son. I told him how proud Emily and I were, not about all that baseball stuff, I didn't mean that. I wanted him to know that I loved the person he had become. How honored I was to be his dad." Peter's voice fell on a small quiver. "It hit me that my boy was becoming a man. I know lots of parents say kids grow up so fast that one day you look at your own, and it's like you don't recognize him anymore, but that wasn't it. I knew exactly who he was, and it was the best feeling I've ever had."

Beck swallowed hard. "You raised a good boy, Pete."

"He was a *great* boy."

The two men let the heavy moment settle. When Peter spoke again, his voice was back to full strength, and it was pissed. "She reminds me of him. So strong and good. At her core, you know?"

"Yup, I agree. This sucks."

"Anyway, one night, Bailey got a hold of the phone and dialed up 9-1-1. I was covering an overnight shift and went to check things out. After I left, I couldn't stop thinking about them. I knew Bo had come back to town and had to drop out of school when she found out she was pregnant. I also knew that everyone was talking about what a shame it was that she had messed things up. I think there's more to it. Bo was so driven to escape, to succeed. It just never added up to me."

"What exactly are you saying here?" Beck pressed.

Peter shook his head. "I don't know what I'm saying. Forget it."

Forget that, Beck thought. He mulled it over. He had seen Bo only in crisis mode, and even when it seemed like the walls were closing in on her, she came off as stable and alert, using her mind to pick up the pieces before the dust had even settled. Could Peter be suggesting there was something much more sinister to blame for Bo's sudden reversal of fortune when she was just an undergrad?

Holy shit, what was he saying? Beck felt his muscles suddenly tense with anger. "You think someone *hurt her*? You think that, don't you?"

The two locked eyes. "More like deserted her. Ignored her. Cut her loose to figure everything out on her own. Just a theory, but it doesn't really matter because she loves that boy with her entire being. You have to get to her quickly and don't tell her you and I are on this together. Not yet. She'll be worried about me, and that would muddy the waters."

He pointed a finger toward his one-time apprentice and expelled an order.

"Keep her safe, Beck. There's absolutely no one else who cares. About her …" what Peter said next struck Beck as one of the saddest things he had ever heard.

"… or Bailey."

CHAPTER TWENTY-THREE

Sloan came through big time. Beck took her call on his way over to the crime lab at State Police Headquarters in Concord. He needed one more piece of hard evidence before he met up with Bo. He was ready to wager his firstborn that someone had been by the vault recently. Someone who hadn't left empty-handed.

Beck immediately called Peter to fill him in on Sloan's mother lode. Once the DCYF director left for a meeting, she was able to pull up Bo's file.

"Sloan says she's listed as an "imminent danger," Beck tells Pete.

"Meaning someone reported seeing or hearing her hurting her child?" Peter asks.

"Yes, or threatening to hurt him, or even engaging in dangerous behavior that would put his well-being at risk."

"Who called it in?"

"Here's where the noose tightens on Diaz. Little fucker is all over this."

"Tell me," Pete says, his voice low.

"So the report reads that a neighbor called the police to say Bo was behaving erratically, and strange men were seen coming and going from her apartment. The neighbor suspected drug activity."

"Go on."

"Well, it gets a little weird here. Bo's apartment would fall under the jurisdiction of Echo Valley. The, *ahem,* officer who filed is from my department, surprise, surprise."

"Wouldn't that be a red flag?" Peter poses the question but already knows the answer.

"Well, yes," Beck confirms, "but only if you're looking for it. Otherwise, the report follows protocol."

"Huh," Peter grunts. "The report wouldn't happen to include a name now, would it?"

"Funny you ask, indeed it does. I had to promise Sloan that if I leaked this out I'd be forced to marry her and support her in a lifestyle my paycheck will never cover."

"What's the name, Beck?"

You could almost feel the turbulence flow right through the phone.

"Officer Spencer Diaz of the Livingston P.D."

CHAPTER TWENTY-FOUR

Peter hung up with Beck and then detoured home. He had complete faith that Beck would get to Bo and Bailey and fortress them away from harm. He roamed his silent house for a while, sat in deep thought behind his desk in the study, and went over the clues he and Beck had assembled and the ones they were still missing. He made some calls, reconnecting with an old friend he thought he might be needing soon and making plans to drop by to chat.

Peter's thoughts kept racing back to the Carmichael farm. Bo's safe house. The old man she'd told him about would roll over in his grave at the thought of his cherished girl in trouble. Peter could barely stay away himself, but he wanted Bo to think he wasn't involved for as long as possible. It would only bring her more stress.

Finally, he couldn't fight it any longer. In police work, there was a lot to be said for having a finger on the pulse of the action. Instead, Peter wanted his finger on the people he loved.

* * * *

Emily Brenner was just pulling into the driveway as Peter was heading back out. She asked him where the fire was, he told her he was just working on a project for a friend and that he'd call her later. A quick peck on the cheek, and he was gone.

Emily Brenner was a wise woman who had seen Peter in the trenches of a hot investigation too many times to count. She watched him back the car out with narrowed eyes. Something was going on. With a bad feeling sinking in she climbed up the front steps of the porch, adjusted her overnight bag on her shoulder, and opened the door. Everything looked pretty much as she had left it, save for the spilled coffee near the sink that Peter hadn't bothered to clean up. She grabbed a paper towel and wiped it away, thinking that her husband had suddenly developed a bad case of restless life syndrome.

Retirement felt about as comfortable to Peter as a vegan walking into a butcher shop. Emily had no doubt that whatever he was doing it had something to do with police work.

Or, perhaps more likely, something to do *with Bo*.

Emily sighed to herself as she carried her bag into the laundry room. After depositing her dirty clothes into the washing machine, she added some detergent and turned the knob. Her fingers gripped the dial too tightly, and it popped right off in her hand.

Damn it, she thought as she wrestled with the plastic, trying to stuff it back into the hole. *What was it about that girl?* She had loved the man she married for three-quarters of her entire life. He was the most honorable, upstanding, do-the-right-thing person she had ever known. But his fascination with the young mother and her child was perplexing, maddening even. Peter would only say that they needed him, they had no one else.

Well, what about me she had begun to wonder. What about your wife, Peter? You know, the woman who shares your bed every night. Do you even notice she is still so grief-stricken she talks to her dead son like he's standing right next to her? When did her husband stop caring about her?

Feeling supremely deflated after a buoyant weekend with her sister, Emily wandered back into the kitchen to pour herself a cup of the leftover coffee. She then sauntered over to Peter's office where the computer was. She figured she'd catch up on email from the library, and set her volunteer schedule for the next few weeks. She slid carefully into Peter's leather chair, trying to hold her arm out steady in front of her as she sank into the deep cushion to avoid spilling.

Damn it, she muttered as warm liquid rushed over the top of the mug and landed on the corner of Peter's ancient blotter. Emily reached for a tissue next to the desk and ran it lightly over the top of the spill trying to soak up the coffee without smudging what Peter had written beneath it. The blotter had been here longer than she can remember. It was so old it still had Tucker's crayon scribbles near the top right-hand corner. Emily would often run her finger softly over the green and yellow markings, wishing her son could still feel her touch.

She wasn't looking at the top right-hand corner. Something else on Peter's blotter caught Emily's eye. She would never have noticed the fresh pen had the coffee not hit directly above it. She recognized the familiar swish of Peter's tight cursive, but the blue ink looked fresh. She leaned in over the notes and began to read them.

Beck-Neighbor-DCYF-Orchard-Bo-Farm.

Damn it! So this *was* all about Bo. But what did the rest of it mean? Why would Peter involve Beckett Brady in something that involved Bo? When was the last time he had even spoken to Beck? What about DCYF? Is the boy hurt?

Emily Brenner forgot all about the library and her schedule and even her dead son's crayon lines that usually haunted her for days. She left her coffee cup on the blotter and reached for the lowest drawer on the left side of the desk. She didn't know why, but something was telling her it would be wise to grab what was inside of it as she set out to find her husband and figure out once and for all how Bo Carmichael had managed to wrap him around her little finger.

What are you up to, Peter Brenner?

Damn it!

CHAPTER TWENTY-FIVE

The crime lab that held the drug evidence at State Police Headquarters ran like a tight ship. If, however, you were a cop, even a dirty one, you could get in with some extra effort. Beck pulled his car into the parking lot and entered the building through a side entrance.

He knew that the arresting officer on a seizure case that included a good chunk of crystal meth would have signed the evidence in. This was the new protocol demanded once federal funds had begun to roll into New Hampshire to deal specifically with the growing methamphetamine, and now, opioid problem. The feds had an easier time of keeping track of how much was being taken off the streets.

Once evidence was secured after a suspect was arrested and interrogated, it was stored until it would be brought out during the suspect's trial. But historically speaking, crime labs are, simply by nature, prone to leak items out into thin air. Often enough, evidence in cases of convictions will be destroyed only after the window of appeals has passed. Yet sometimes the junk sticks around indefinitely, only because there aren't enough bodies on staff to deal with it. If no one needs it anymore, it becomes that much easier to forget about.

Or, as Beck suspected, use it to set someone up.

Officers were encouraged to keep an electronic evidence file. If there was evidence seized, they could enter it, and a special server would save it. Beck was hoping that the answers he needed might be just a few clicks away. He walked in, stopping to shake hands with colleagues who were more like old friends.

"Beck," they were saying good-naturedly, "What brings you by? Did we lock up one of your pals this weekend?"

"Nah, most of my friends are out of town at the moment." Beck grinned at the group forming around him. They all knew Beckett Brady was one of the good guys who would do all he could to make sure their sons and daughters didn't have unfettered access to the substances that existed solely to destroy them.

They were asking him about various cases, when he was up for testimony, who he was trailing; a solid, natural exchange that wouldn't raise a single eyebrow. Beck had every right to pop in here unannounced. He had a million excuses ready to go, and any number of them would check out. He shook a few more hands before he took a series of right-hand turns and climbed up several flights of stairs to the third floor. He was praying that someone would have left a scrap of evidence behind when he walked out the door with the juju he would use to come down on Bo with the burning fury of a hundred suns.

Beck notices an unfamiliar uniform talking into a cell phone just outside the foyer. He motions with his hand that he needs to speak to him, and then leans against the wall to check his own phone. No new calls from Bo, but he needs to make this quick.

The dark-haired man with early signs of a desk paunch around the middle greets Beck with an outstretched hand. "Hi," he says with a grin. "What can I help you with?"

"Detective Beckett Brady, Livingston P.D." Beck gives him a firm handshake.

"Ah, yes. Detective Brady, nice to finally meet you. I've heard a lot about your work. I'm Shaun Davidson, just transferred here from Vermont, figured it would be just a matter of time before I crossed your path. I guess time's up." He had a genuine smile that fit nicely in his round face. On another day, Beck would spend more time trying to get to know him.

"Any shot of having you check on something for me?" Beck asks, cutting off the chatter but respecting his authority not to let him breeze right into secure space.

"Sure, in here?" Shaun motions behind him to the counter space. Beyond the counter was where the goods were stored. You had to get by the counter to get inside. "I'm happy to, but it's slightly disorganized right now. Part of why I came here was to make sense of this black hole. Had some trouble here not too long ago with swinging doors letting too many people in."

Swinging Doors. Beck's eyes narrow, exactly what he'd thought.

"Tell me, Shaun," he says, "about that trouble."

"Well, let's just say things weren't as locked down as they should have been. You still had to sign in and out of course, but for a while, nothing was being cleaned out, and too many people were signing in. All the shit no one needed anymore was just stacking up. We're just now getting around to dumping it."

"So there's no way to tell if any of it just walked out on its own, then?"

"No, not that I can tell. All the crap logged for trial is still in place, but as for the expired stuff, no one was keeping track."

"Do me a favor?" Beck looks beyond Shaun into the evidence locker. He moves toward the computer on the desk. "Check the computer for me?"

"Sure. What do you need?" Officer Davidson had no reason not to help Detective Brady. In fact, he was hoping that one day he could buy him a beer, listen to his war stories.

"Doing some work offline, a little research to follow how much ice has been stored here recently."

A slow nod as Davidson gives the computer some cues. "Yup, got it right here. Some is on hold waiting for cases to hit the courts, shit load of pot, and heroin, but one big seize came in a while back." Davidson leans closer to the screen, pointing something out to Beck. "Looks like it was a big one, which is the most we've seen here recently. Want me to print this out for your records?"

This was not the time. Beck just wanted to solidify for himself the way they set her up.

"No, but can you check one more thing? I'm wondering if anyone from my department has been by. I'm working a few cases, but I can't quite remember who I asked to sign some junk in for me. It could be as recently as a day or two ago."

Beck would never have a subordinate sign any evidence in for him. If it was his case, it was his responsibility—start to finish—though it was not unusual to ask a proxy to drop something off if he happened to be passing by.

"No problem, I can search Livingston or a specific name." Officer Davidson pauses with his hands poised again over the keyboard, waiting for Beck to instruct him further.

Beck plays it cool. He asks him to begin with a search of the department. A few hits come up, and Beck maintains his nonchalance as he asks Davidson to check a specific name. He keeps his voice light, even though it takes substantial effort.

"What about Diaz. You got a Spencer Diaz signed in anywhere?" He feels his gut pull because he can visualize him wrapping his slimy fingers around a bag of evidence that no one would know was gone until they went looking for it. Instead of being thrown into the incinerator like it should have been, it was tossed at a blameless girl brought in on a fabricated story of unrestrained greed and lawlessness.

"Let me check," Davidson mutters as he punches in the name, and hits enter. Almost instantaneously, it pops up. "Uh-huh, you got a hit. Says he's been here a few times, no specific dates, but he did sign in as "evidence check" only. Can't say for sure if he got through those swinging doors like I mentioned," Davidson looks at Beck and rolls his eyes. "It doesn't say if he dropped anything off or took custody of anything for trial. Want me to search another name for you?"

"Nope, that's all I need to know. Thanks, Davidson, I owe you one."

"My pleasure. Hope to see …" Officer Davidson never does finish his farewell, because no sooner had he pushed back the metal legs of his plastic chair, he noticed Detective Beckett Brady was halfway to the door.

CHAPTER TWENTY-SIX

Beck makes quick time back into his Jeep, calls Peter again and confirms his findings. He then calls the P.D. to let everyone know he's out of the office working a case. He shoves his fingers roughly through his hair, thinking that the edges of this puzzle are taking shape, but the middle still sits empty.

Drugs, politics, ambition, greed; all of that swirling around an innocent girl who had already had the kitchen sink thrown at her when she was forced to grow up in a household not fit for a cat. Peter's right. A girl like Bo doesn't deserve the repeated backhands karma seems intent on delivering.

Beck roars the engine to life and pulls out of the lot, his mind spinning out in different directions, yet all of them connected to her. He recalls her eyes, a bright blend of blue and gray, popping with a potent combination of alarm and distrust when she's confronted with danger. He imagines them mellowing into a docile glow when she's at ease.

What?

It's his job, right? Beck stares at the highway and cuts across the road to enter the onramp. His tries to let himself off the hook by insisting it's all part of how he solves crimes. He notices a person's habits, ticks, facial expressions, and body language. When he picks up on high cheekbones, swaying eyelashes, and full lips, it's because he's a detective. Only because he's a detective.

Bullshit.

He could see it even when she was a teenager. The proud features have blossomed from adolescent delicacy to adult elegance. She is a total knockout but in an off-handed way. Her skin is flawless, yet naked of sparkles and shine, her style modern but understated. Wickedly smart, she wouldn't bother trying to tease a man with her body because she'd be too busy breaking them down in her head.

Bo Carmichael is getting no credit. Someone is assuming she's soft, flimsy and ineffective, her skills powerless to escape the trap they've set. Beck punches the accelerator hard. He listens to the wind whipping past his window, getting more and more pissed that no one except him and Peter has her back.

Why has a beautiful, intelligent woman like Bo been left all alone in this world to raise a child and fend for herself? Beck races up I-93, blowing by other cars in a mad dash to get to her, determined not to just be another guy who lets her down.

* * * *

After what feels like forever and with each stranger looking like a possible specter of the tan man, I see him behind the wheel of an approaching Jeep. Watching him from a distance, my jumbled nerves fire off mixed signals in my head. Part of me is leery of his brooding intensity; he is all muscle and brawn, a formidable presence that makes me a little light-headed.

Bailey is also peering at the tall man now exiting his Jeep with hooded eyes and a fast foot. He wasn't sure what to make of Jackson, and now he has to come to terms with the fact that his mother is telling him the officer who hauled her away really isn't the Boogie Man.

"Are you two okay?" Detective Brady moves with fluid determination, making me take note of long, muscled legs and a broad chest beneath a light coat. He is one jacked dude.

"We're fine." I try to smile at him. I fail. "I'm sorry, this is just weird for me. And for Bailey," I motion over to him, slumped down in the seat, afraid to look at this larger-than-life police detective.

"Don't apologize, I get it. Get your stuff together, I'll drive the rest of the way. Bailey, I'm Beck. You hungry?" He leans over my window and smiles broadly at Bailey, making the entire dynamic of his face change. When he smiles, his eyes dance. I wonder why I notice.

"A lil' bit," Bailey says, willing to offer this once menacing person a slight grin because he'll usually accept anyone willing to feed him.

"Come on, then. Let's load up on some good stuff while your mom hooks up your seat. Okay?" He pulls my door open and holds out his hand. Bailey climbs over me and skips away toward the convenience store at the other end of the plaza. Through the rays of morning sun bouncing off the pavement, I can see their figures: one large, one small, joined in the middle by clasped hands.

Am I prepared to tell him everything? Should I? This man says he believes in me now, just like he did when I was only a kid living with two people who had never grown up themselves. But will he still believe in me once I spill the sordid details about my lost cell phone, the shock of seeing Mackenzie Mason's prescription tumble from her bag, the not-so-subtly veiled threats from Senator Anderson, and the tan man's two-fingered salute from under the street lamp? When my story leads him straight into the swamp, will he cut bait or tread water?

I stumble over to his Jeep, throwing my purse and Bailey's leftover donuts in the back. I lean in to attach his car seat. When I'm done, I see them exit the convenience store with a paper bag stuffed full to the top. Beck shifts the bag to make sure he has a free hand to grab Bailey's as they walk back to where I'm waiting. Bailey's hand glides easily into his, and I notice another red lollipop popping out of the fingers on the other hand. He is giggling about something, looking up at Beck with both curiosity and fascination. I bite the inside of my cheek to keep another strong rush of incertitude at bay.

They cross the last few feet over to the Jeep, as Beck releases Bailey's hand so he can run to me. He jumps up against my chest while holding his lollipop up near my nose. I get a strong whiff of cherry Blow-Pop.

"Look what Beck bought me!"

He does a few quick hops up and down, making Beck laugh out loud.

"He's funny, Bo. What a happy little guy. You're doing a good job with him."

Before I can answer, Bailey does first.

"Momma is doing a good job, Beck. And Peter helps, too. We were supposed to have pizza with Peter. Right, Momma?"

The avalanche of sudden information throws Beck into stunned silence. I see a muscle work along his jaw, but he only smiles. "Tell you what, Bailey. If it's okay with your mom, I'll make sure we find a place with the best pizza in the entire state. Sound good?"

"Sounds great!"

I wait for the question that doesn't come. I wonder why this detective isn't grilling me about the name-drop, asking who Peter is, and what his connection to us is. Maybe that will come later.

What the hell do I tell him then?

I wipe at my eyes. They have started to sting under a crushing exhaustion that begins at my head and ends around my knees. They quake. I lean against the Jeep and take a deep breath.

"You all right?" fingers wrap around my elbow. How did he get here so fast? His grip is holding me up, but I feel myself sink lower, falling into two arms. "Get in the car. Close your eyes."

I can only nod. I allow him to steer me toward the passenger side, letting Bailey's chatter descend into background noise. I smell mint and some warm cologne that reminds me of long walks through deep, mossy woods.

One breath. Two … three … I count slowly to twenty-five and climb back up.

"It's okay. Everything will be okay now. I promise." Beck says, taking my keys and locking my car before he climbs behind the wheel and we take off. Bailey is humming to himself, boosted up on excitement and his second Blow-Pop of the morning.

"Momma?" he asks, too absorbed in his own adventure to have concern for my crack-up.

"Yes, bud?"

"Is Beck going to be my new daddy?"

There is no way he didn't hear it even though he doesn't react. Beck's hands stay firmly on the steering wheel and his eyes on the road.

I explain quietly to Bailey that Beck is just our new friend, and we'll talk about it later. He stuffs his lollipop into his mouth and shrugs me off, noticing Beck's eyes in the rearview mirror. He waves toward the front seat, and in between licks, sinks my battleship.

"I don't have a daddy," he says nonchalantly, like it's just a simple fact of life and not the sum of all my failures. "Don't worry, Beck. Momma says Peter can't be my daddy, either."

My shoulders slump again in defeat as I wish I could shrink down to the size of a dust ball and just float away on the wind.

CHAPTER TWENTY-SEVEN

"Feel free to turn the heat on if you're cold."

They are Beck's first words to me in over fifteen minutes. Other than a steady stream of babble from Bailey in the back, we have been sitting in silence.

"Thanks. I'm good."

After another few minutes of Bailey jabbering about the leaves, the clouds, and the gum he hasn't yet gotten to in the center of his lollipop, Beck begins.

"There's a lot we need to talk about, but I'm beginning to figure a few things out. It's a total inside job."

His deep voice is like the water in a hot tub, making my muscles melt with relief that he is still keeping the faith that I'm innocent. Half of me wonders if this is just his way of reeling me back in and taking me straight to the crowbar hotel. Instead, he gets right back on the highway, heading north to the only place in the world I can think of that should provide safe shelter until this is over. Bailey's voice grows weaker until he finally gives in to the magical lull of rubber wheels on the road. He's out cold, snoring softly.

I feel my shoulders release a tiny bit of the tension that feels like bricks stacked behind my neck. I look sideways at Beck's profile, perplexed at why I imagine what his skin would feel like under my fingertip.

When I speak again, my voice is heavy, steeped in deep sadness that I have stifled for so long.

"I can't believe this is happening. I have messed up my life so badly. I feel like I'm disappointing you." I can't look at him.

"Disappointing me, how?"

"I do remember you, Beck. That night. My house. You told me that I didn't have to end up like them. Thing is, I'm even *worse* than my parents. I'm, I'm … failing at everything …" my hands cover my lips to stop them from shaking.

"No, you're not," he says with finality. "You're going to get through this, Bo, just like you got through the instability of a miserable childhood." One hand leaves the steering wheel and squeezes mine, almost touching my face. It makes my body jolt.

I look over at him, noticing the wave of a longish sideburn that is overdue for a trim, a strong, straight nose, and at least a few days' worth of dark growth along his chin. The tips of his hair are lighter, sun bleached. What women will pay me a bundle to do with chemicals, nature has done naturally for Beck. When he smiles at me, even if it's merely to comfort me, his face becomes soft, but with a firm thrust of his chin, I can see he's probably respected by many on that alone.

"You had wise eyes, even for a kid," he continues, sharing his own thoughts from that night so long ago. "I remember thinking that you were the only responsible one in that house."

"They weren't evil, just immature and selfish. Two people who never should have had a child. They've only seen their grandson a few times over the past four years." I look behind me to make sure Bailey is still asleep.

"It's a shame. For them and for him."

"I know, but I can't torture myself with what could be. I have to accept what is, and then give Bailey the best life I can. That's why all of this just … it just sucks. He doesn't have anyone else who would take care of him, nowhere else to go … it makes me … really mad to think someone would exploit that."

Really mad? More like fucking bullshit, but I won't lose control like that in front of this man. I need him to believe I can think like a rational person and not a frenzied momma Grizzly bear.

I-93 stretches out in front of us for miles. I used to drive this route all the time, heading to a place where the rest of the world faded away. Tucked away between majestic snowy peaked mountains and miles of serene, undisturbed forest, our farm shut everything out. It was just us, my grandfather and me, along with a barn full of animals he nurtured from birth to death.

"It's a bit beyond just exploiting the fact that you're a single parent," he says sharply. "You should be aware that this is deep and serious and we need to fire back with both barrels. I need to know everything. From the moment you woke up that morning, until the moment you walked Bailey out to the car in the doctor's parking lot. All of it. It's critically important you are completely honest with me. You have to trust me, Bo. You don't have a choice this time." Beck is staring straight ahead, speaking quietly so Bailey isn't disturbed.

Do I just blurt it out? *Yes, do it*. Just blurt it out and then worry about doubling back to pick up the pieces. I feel that rage rising again as I remember how the senator's arm flew out to grab Mackenzie Mason, hissing at her with the ferocity of a rabid dog.

"You stupid bitch. Who the fuck do you think you're messing with?"

I remember the look of utter shock on her face as she choked on the horror of watching the man she loved turn on her. I think of the tan man's quickly laid plan to ruin me, take my child away and then spit on my grave.

Bailey stirs in the back. The story will have to wait.

CHAPTER TWENTY-EIGHT

Peter found the owner of the apple orchard about sixteen rows in. All by himself, and flirting with seventy-five years old, the old man was as firmly connected to his apples as their stems were. He spoke in low tones, mostly about nothing, but he was convinced the branches thrived on their conversations.

He heard Peter approaching long before he saw him, muttering, "*Who there!*" as Peter turned down a row of trees that looked exactly like all the rows before, and after.

"Mr. Bloomfield. Come to ask you a couple questions."

"Well, we're setting to close up for the season soon, afraid I might not have the answers you're looking for."

"Actually, I'm thinking you might be able to help me out quite a bit. Thing is, I'm looking for someone who was here not long ago."

Mr. Bloomfield straightened back up, put aside his rakes and buckets full of fallen fruit, and approached Peter with an outstretched hand. No more talking would be done until he greeted this visitor like the gentleman he was. "Don't believe I caught your name, young man."

"Peter. Peter Brenner. I'm a good friend of a young lady who spent some time here last weekend."

"Uh-huh. Had myself a full house. Lots of im-*po*-tant people milling about. Silly, if you ask me, but I'm not one to turn down some free advertising. Which lady you looking for. As I recall, we had quite a few of those here."

"Her name is Bo. She was one of the hairdressers."

Mr. Bloomfield nodded slowly, trying to entice a memory to pop through the haze of his aging brain.

"What she look like?"

"Bo is tall, around here." Peter raised his hand and with his palm flat, placed it near his nose. "She's on the thin side, with light brown hair and bluish eyes. Very pretty. She might have had her hair in a ponytail, and was probably wearing black pants."

"Well then, that certainly don't fit with the princess who left my barn smelling like the inside of a brothel. 'Course her perfume probably cost more than my television set, but *Jesus Christ* she stunk up the whole place."

Peter chuckled softly, appreciating the simple and honest manner in which some folks live their lives.

"No, that's not Bo. That may have been Mrs. Anderson. The wife."

"Yup, probably. Anyway, tell me more about this Bo. I'm trying to find her in my mind."

"So, pretty girl with light-ish hair, bluish eyes, tall, thin. She was probably carrying a big, black bag for her supplies. You getting anything?"

Mr. Bloomfield was shaking his head. "Nope," he said, "nothin' yet. Keep going though."

"Okay," Peter said patiently. His gut was telling him this apple farmer could be a vital cog in the wheels that were churning. He describes Bo once again, explains the purpose of the photo shoot, why the salon people were there. Mr. Bloomfield interrupts.

"Did she do the kids?" he blurts.

"Ah, yes, good point. She was actually the one doing Senator Anderson's hair."

"Hmmm," he began, stroking the gray stubble on his cheek. "That guy," he says with as much subtlety as a gunshot, "thinks his own shit don't stink. Was grateful and all, said thank you, but there's just something about him that don't sit too well with me. Especially when I saw him grab at that girl of his."

Peter pounces. "What girl, Mr. Bloomfield? What did he do to her?"

"Well, I saw him get all up near her face, then clamp his paw on her elbow. Just too close for my liking. If she's working for him and all, he shouldn't be touching her. It's just not right if you ask me."

"Did that girl look like Bo? Like I've described her to you?"

"Nah, not that girl. She was, ah, how do you say? Fancy? Yeah, she was pretty fancy, and she came in from a big SUV. She didn't look like she did hair, that's for sure."

"When did you see this, Mr. Bloomfield?"

"When they were all leaving, just before their cars pulled out but after the hairdressers and makeup people had packed up. I was coming in from the field to make sure they got off okay when I heard them fighting. I didn't pay much attention until I saw through a window him grabbing at her. That girl was all upset, crying even. She tried to hightail it right out of there, but ... *hey, wait a minute*. Tell me about your girl again?"

Peter sighed heavily, this was taking far too much of his precious time. He trusted his instincts and pressed on with yet another description.

"Ah-huh. I think I remember seeing her now, Pete. I think she was the one who slammed into the other one as she was trying to get away from the creep."

"Hold up. Let me get this straight here. You think you remember seeing Bo, but you said all the hairdressers had left, right?" Peter needed this to be fact, not a phantom recall cooked up by a declining mind.

"Well, yeah, I thought they'd left. But she was there all right, I can see it clear as day now. She was standing there when that gal plowed into her, almost knocked her right over. Now, I try never to mess with another man's problems. I got a wife, and an ex-wife, so this ain't nothing I want a part of, you hear me, Pete?"

"Yes, sir, I understand. I'm just trying to figure out what Bo might have seen here. Who plowed into her? Was it his wife, or someone else?"

The old man pushed back against a stubborn curve along his spine, putting two calloused palms aside worn hipbones to stand straight. "Lord only knows," he begins, his nose wrinkling up in disdain. "I walked away after that, Pete. None of my damn business when a man thinks he can corral two females at the same time. It's worse than two pigs fightin' for space at the trough."

Peter's fingers were twitching. If what this weathered old man was saying was true, it confirmed his initial hunch. He *knew i*t. Bo had seen something they hadn't wanted her to. Peter had done a few presidential details in his career, dealing directly with the staffers who devote their entire lives to someone else's pursuit of public office. They were driven, single-minded, and entirely steadfast in protecting the future of their chosen one. They would do just about anything to preserve the image of the candidate.

Especially if that candidate was running for the highest office in the land.

Especially if some *nobody* had stumbled onto their carefully laid path, and was threatening to muddy it up.

Peter muttered a stilted thank you to the well-meaning apple farmer, and made a hasty retreat, making sure his walk back to his parked car took him right by the red barn with the shuttered wooden door. He stood just outside, closed his eyes, and forced his breathing to slow.

"Talk to me, Bo," he whispered, "Tell me what you see." It was an old habit that Peter had first developed working a murder scene. He would close his eyes and picture the victim in life, in motion. He would breathe the air deep into his lungs to smell what he had smelled. He would look up, down, behind corners, and under stairs. He would picture the crime, he would see the weapon, feel the icy chill of fear, follow the movement of the killer until he could envision the end of a life. He forced himself to feel it, remember it, and then solve it. He walked over to the barn door, running his fingertips lightly down the wood, then around the metal hook of the handle. He gripped it, squeezed it, and imagined Bo's hand pulling it shut as she raced from the barn to escape the horror of what had just happened inside.

Peter's eyes were still closed, but the images behind them were darting back and forth. He felt Bo rush by; he smelled her fear, her wild need to break away from the fancy girl and the presidential candidate. She was in shock, her brain trying to send so many messages at the same time it was misfiring. She was running, but he'd bet his last breath she was fighting back.

Peter's eyes snap back open, and he releases the door handle to find his keys. He needs to get out of there; time is running out. Bo has somehow made herself a liability. She has seen what's behind the mask, awakened the beast and he was hungry. Hungry for the power he felt he was owed, the place in history he deemed was his own, and the adoration he believed he had already earned.

He would not let some *nobody* fuck it all up.

He heads back to his car, ready to have that drink with the old friend he'd already put a call in to. Once Bo was safe, she would need his help most of all.

CHAPTER TWENTY-NINE

"Momma, look at me. I'm wearing braces on my teeth!"

"Dude, guys don't wear pink braces," Beck playfully responds from the front seat.

Bailey finally got to the good stuff in the center of his lollipop and has been entertaining us with all the things a four-year-old can make gum do. He stretches it between two fingers, tilts his head back, and sticks it to his upper lip.

"Now look, I have a big giant booger hanging from my nose." He giggles himself into a stupor, as does Beck who reaches behind for some skin.

"The best way to make girls like you, my man, is to make them laugh. Although boogers usually won't do the trick."

They slap palms loudly and then laugh some more until I tell Bailey to hand over the gum before it gets caught in his hair, or in Beck's seat, or some other place it's not supposed to be.

"Oh, Momma, you ruin all the fun. Peter says Momma is so serious because she is trying to take good care of me."

Here we go again.

"Your Momma is too serious?" Beck plays along, looking into the rearview mirror to find Bailey's face.

"Well, not all the time. Sometimes Momma is silly, like when she dances in front of the mirror while she's drying her hair."

"Really," he smirks. "Momma dances in the mirror, huh?"

"Yeah, but she's not good. She can't sing good, either."

"Sing *well*, Bailey. Use proper English to insult your mother, please."

"Are you sure you're just four years old, Bailey? You're smarter than most of the guys I work with."

"Momma says it's important to be smart. She tells me to use all the words I know, even the ones that I can't say the right way. She's a good Momma."

"I'll bet she is, buddy." Beck looks over at me. He waits until Bailey finds something to distract him.

"Is it hard, Bo?" he asks me. "Raising him, I mean. Is it hard work?"

"Yes. And no. The love is easy; it's instant, and it's constant. All the other stuff buries me, though."

I watch Beck look up into the mirror, to make sure Bailey can't hear us. He is now fully engrossed in an ESPN magazine he dug up from under the backseat.

"Is it okay if he's got your magazine?" I ask because pretty soon Bailey will have it in tatters.

"Of course, he can have whatever he finds back there. Tell me about the other stuff. The stuff that is hard for you."

We have agreed to hold off on the heavy details of my circumstances until Bailey is distracted or asleep. I don't want my son hearing about the men who want to take him away from me.

"Oh, well, I just meant the life stuff. How worrying about him hurts like a shark attack, and trying to make sure my paycheck covers as much as I need it to, and then figuring out what to cut when it doesn't. I struggle with all the usual things most parents do unless you're a Hollywood A-lister and you have enough dough to adopt an entire third world country."

Beck ponders this for a moment. "You don't have to answer this if you don't want to, but …"

"Go ahead. Ask me anything. I promised I'd be honest with you."

"Well, it just seems wrong that you're all alone with him. Again, it's none of my business, but…"

"Beck, just spit it out."

"Is his father, uhh, helping? At all?"

I think of Riley. How my son looks exactly like him, but will probably never even meet him. How he would spot me on campus in the days after our drunken encounter and walk right by. How he demanded an abortion and then verbally decapitated me after I refused.

Riley O'Roarke helping? Not quite.

Only recently have I felt my feelings for him move from high flame to simmer. I realize now that I don't entirely hate him anymore. A part of me is at peace with what happened that night, only because it gave me the biggest gift of my life.

"He's not really, uh … equipped … to handle a child."

Beck only nods, but I drag my eyes away, feeling small and ashamed. I know the real deal about Bailey, but it must sound awful to someone who doesn't. "I know. My life is like an episode of Teen Mom."

Beck laughs. "Hardly," he says, smiling over at me. "You're a good mother."

"I'm trying." I look back to make sure Bailey is busy and distracted. He is pointing out pictures of things he recognizes from a baseball article.

"Baseball bat. Pitcher's glove. Dugout ..." on and on he goes, being more of a good sport than he can possibly realize. I turn back to Beck, feeling an inexplicable urge to explain more of why I returned to Echo Valley, pregnant and alone.

"There was a time when I had big dreams and high expectations for myself," I say. "Before Bailey, I wanted to be a doctor. I had a full scholarship. I loved the idea of using my brain to help someone else. Make a difference, you know?"

"Yes, I know."

"I studied really hard. In spite of no one caring whether I got "A's" or flunked out of school, it mattered to me. I never expected to come back here."

"Sometimes plans don't work out," Beck says, looking sideways at me in a way that suggests he knows more about my life than I think he does. But how could he? "Things happen. What I admire most is that you were able to take an unexpected U-turn, and still make it work."

"Hmm," I mutter, unsure of how much I should reveal. "I never had a choice. Bailey is my entire world now. I can't imagine not being his mom. Although, at one point in my life I couldn't imagine not being a doctor. Funny how perspectives change, huh?"

Beck is quiet. He merely nods. I ask him if he has any children.

"No," Beck's mouth falls on the word. Any more detail on that subject is cut off by a high-pitched plea from the back seat.

"Momma, can I have these?" He holds up an extra-large bag of M&M's.

"How about after lunch."

"Okay. Momma?"

"Yes, Bailey."

"Can I have lunch?"

I check my watch. We're approaching late morning, but not quite lunchtime. Not that it makes a difference; Bailey could eat twenty-four hours a day if I let him. Much like I used to, until fear took over the space inside my stomach where my appetite used to be. I can't even remember the last time I ate.

We come up upon the next exit. We're deep in the North Country now with just a few more exits to go.

CHAPTER THIRTY

Beck cuts the Jeep over a lane and tells Bailey we're heading for the best pizza joint in the entire Northeast. The word "joint" prompts happy giggles.

"That's a silly word! How do they cook pizza in a joint? Peter says pizza has all kinds of good stuff in it that will make me grow up and be strong enough to lift Momma over my head. Peter says I need to take care of Momma when she's old."

"Sounds like Peter's a wise man. And I'll bet you're going to take very good care of your mom. I think you already do."

"Yup, me and Momma take care of each other, only she won't let me drive yet, or use the oven, or touch bad chemicals or smoke cigarettes …or …"

"That's enough, Bailey. I think he gets the point. Just so you know," I tell Beck. "I call Windex and Tide chemicals … so he doesn't try to drink them. And he's seen my boss smoking a few times. I've told him if he smokes, he'll die, or get all nasty and wrinkly like Gerry."

We chuckle together.

"Gerry is your boss?" Beck asks.

"Yes, he owns the salon where I work. He's a good man, he's just a little extreme."

We are turning into what probably started out as a business plaza, but has since emptied out almost completely. Storefronts are dark, parking spaces empty, except for a few cars taking up the area directly in front of a giant slice of plastic pizza hanging from the roofline of the last door on the row. Yellowish strands of cheese drip off the sides, stretching over the tops of the windows on either side. I suspect the red blinking lights scattered over the yellow are meant to depict slices of pepperoni.

"Oohhh, Momma. Look at that. That's so cool." Bailey is transfixed by the cartoonish appearance of the pizza shop. He is already unbuckling himself and sliding over to grab for the door handle before I can get there. I scramble to get to him first, but quickly realize that Beck is already there. They are again hand in hand walking the short distance to the front door. Beck lifts his arm up so Bailey can hop over the curb, giggling as the strong hand gives him a bigger lift than the one he's used to with me.

"Up you go, buddy." Beck uses his right arm to swing the door open, never letting go of Bailey with his left. I enter behind them; taking the door from Beck but feeling our fingers brush during the hand-off. If he felt it, he doesn't let on. He is looking only at Bailey, picking him up and plopping him butt first onto the counter so he can look at the menu posted above the cash registers.

"What'll it be, Bailey? Gooey-cheese, extra gooey-cheese, or disgustingly gooey-cheese?"

"Dis-gust-teen cheese, please." Bailey laughs, as he breaks out in that broad grin that still makes my heart skip a beat. How I adore this child. How wonderfully he fits into a "normal" life, how eager he is to love the few men he has encountered.

How he deserves a father.

"Disgusting cheese it is, then. Why don't you hop down and go pick out a table with your mom, okay?"

"Yup." Bailey scurries off to find an empty booth. I slide into it first, facing away from the television hanging from the ceiling, just in case it is about to advertise my face as a "Most Wanted" suspect who has absconded with a child who is now a ward of the state. My appetite is squashed again on that thought, even though it had started to resurge on the sweet, familiar smell of bubbling dough and cheese. Peter was right; pizza is my comfort food that usually makes all the evils of the world fade away on each stringy bite. Today, I think I might choke on it.

I rub my eyes with the outside of each pointer finger, trying again to take away the strong burn I've felt ever since I squared off with the officers—including Beck—in the parking lot. The thought of Peter suffering on the unknown brings up the swig of Diet Coke I just swallowed.

"Where are we going? Did you take the day off to play with me?" Bailey asks, breaking through my gloom.

"Um, sort of."

How much do I tell him? How much can he handle?

Bailey reaches over for the salt shaker, which is usually forbidden because he ends up with salt in his hair, salt in his eyes, salt down the full length of his shirt. I don't have the energy to take away the tiny glass dome. I watch him dump it all out in front of him. He looks up at me as if to say, "You watching this?"

I try to speak, to protest, to use this as another teachable moment, but I have no voice. All I want to do is put my head down right on this old plastic seat, and fade to black.

Beck sits down next to me on my side of the booth, facing Bailey. He takes a pinch of the scattered salt and throws it over his shoulder.

"For luck," he says.

"What you mean?" Bailey copies him. I cringe at the handful of tiny pellets hitting the bald-headed man sitting directly behind us. I mouth "sorry" to him as he turns his head in annoyance.

"Gotta be careful Bailey, you cancel out your good luck if you hit someone with your salt."

"Oops," Bailey giggles, covering his mouth.

"I'm sorry, sir. I didn't mean to hit you with my salt."

The bald man waves his hand and returns to his Greek salad. Along with the teacher, I stopped in the parking lot of Jackson's school, we have just added another potential witness to worry about. Under police questioning, this man will undoubtedly remember the salt boy who sat behind him at the pizza shop. More breadcrumbs fall around us. I am a horrible criminal; I am leaving clues everywhere I turn.

"You okay?" Beck asks, noticing my pained expression.

"Yes."

"You sure about that?"

"No."

Bailey is making salt swirls, softly singing to himself about gooey pizza. Beck and I watch him quietly, not even attempting conversation. In less than ten minutes, the teenager at the counter yells over that our pizza is ready. Bailey takes one-sleeved arm and wipes the remaining salt off the table and onto the floor. I would normally react to that. I don't react at all. I just stare dumbly at the wisp of white on the black tile square next to my shoe.

"Mmm, mmm! Yummy pizza, Momma. Can I have three pieces?"

"How 'bout we start with one, okay?"

"But after one comes two, and then three, four and five," he says to himself. "Peter says I have to be five to play T-ball at Tucker's old field."

Beck plops the pizza between us on the table, sliding one piece off the metal plate and handing it over to Bailey.

"Careful, that's really hot," he tells him. "So what's this about T-ball?"

"Peter's going to coach me. He says I'm going to be a pitcher just like his boy was before he went to heaven," Bailey tells him in between hard blows on the cheesy tip of his pizza.

I watch as Beck's jaw tightens but he doesn't push for more information about our buddy, Peter. This is starting to get weird. I thought he wanted to know everything?

He loads a second paper plate with a slice of pizza and puts it in front of me. I should be famished, but I barely have the strength to reach for it.

"Thanks," I mutter.

"I used to play first base when I was a little older than you, Bailey. One year we won the championship."

"Ohh, that's cool! Peter says I'm going to be really strong when I grow up and he's going to catch all my home runs."

"So Peter is your buddy, huh?" Finally! Here it comes. I brace myself.

"He's my best friend. He used to take me to his work, and I played on his desk, and he lets me ride in his cruiser." He looks at me as he carefully pronounces the word we've worked on for months.

"Nice job, honey." I smile at him.

"Peter's going to worry about me, Momma."

"I know. We'll tell him we're sorry as soon as we get home."

"When are we going home?"

"I don't know yet, sweetheart."

Bailey stuffs an oversized bite into his mouth, drops half of the cheese onto the table, then picks it back up with two fingers and shoves it back in.

"Eww, that's gross. Try to use a fork." I hand him a plastic spork-type thing that looks more spoon than fork. Beck bats my hand away.

"Please, Bo. Real men do not use *sporks* any more than they wear pink braces, right Bailey?"

"Right!" he says, in between chuckles and cheese.

"How did you become a hairdresser?" Beck suddenly asks.

"Momma cuts my hair all the time. And she cuts Peter's hair, but not Emily. She goes to someone else."

I feel myself stiffen on her name. I wonder if she knows we're missing. How relieved she'd be if we never came back.

"Emily. Peter's wife. She's not exactly a fan."

"Hmm."

"Peter says Emily is busy, that's why she never comes with us when we get pizza or ice cream."

Beck is quiet, building the mystery of why he is not pushing me on this.

Bailey finishes off slice number one, asks for number two. He licks the grease off his fingers as Beck breaks off another slice for him.

"Here ya go, pal."

"Thanks. Beck?"

"Yup?"

"Do you have any boys?"

"You mean, as in sons?"

"Yup, do you have any sons? Do you have a wife or a dog?"

"No," Beck smiles through the chewy, thick pizza crust. "It's just me. No sons or daughters or wives or girlfriends. But I do know a lot of people who drive me crazy sometimes."

"Momma says I make her crazy, too." Bailey takes his shiny finger and rolls it next to his head, just like Peter does when they share a joke together about me.

I smile as I watch them float easily through this happy chat. Bailey is, by nature, a chatterbox who would talk to Freddy Kruger if he happened to sit down next to him. He could be jaded, even at four, disgruntled and angry that he only has me. Instead, he is a joyful little creature who has limitless potential and a loving heart.

How could anyone want to hurt this boy!

My boy!

"Momma, *momma*!"

"What, honey?"

"Why are you crying?"

I am? He is right, even though I hadn't even noticed. I look down at the table under my chin to see several fat splats of liquid that must be my tears. I wipe them away and try to move on without an explanation. Suddenly, I am the world's biggest crybaby. Mercifully, Beck lets it pass.

"Finish up, Bailey, it's time to go."

"Go where? Where are we going?"

"We're going to a farm, honey. A farm with a huge barn and lots of trees, and a big fireplace in the living room."

Bailey's eyes go wide with the thought. "Who owns the farm?" he asks.

I know who used to own the farm, but now I have no idea. Or do I?

"Actually, I think in some ways, we do." It makes my heart swell with pride.

"Will Peter meet us at the farm?"

"No." I smile at Bailey, but try to shut him up for now, glancing over to confirm that Beck heard yet another mention of this arcane person. The elephant in the room stomping so loudly it's deafening. We grab our stuff, deposit the greasy paper plates and unused sporks into the trash by the door and settle back into the Jeep.

I get Bailey buckled in, and haul the seatbelt back across my shoulder, keeping my eyes on my lap. Beck starts the Jeep and pulls back onto the highway. I can't let it go, this is crazy.

"Beck, Peter is a good friend to us … he's …"

Beck drapes his arm along the back seat. Gently touching the back of my hair, he softly tells me something I am completely unprepared to hear.

"I know, Bo. I know exactly who Peter is."

CHAPTER THIRTY-ONE

The sun throws red hues across the roofline of the old colonial. It reminds me of the moment Scarlett O'Hara returns to Tara to find it pillaged by the Yankees, but still standing. My grandfather's home—not quite as battered—is also still standing. I breathe in the crisp air that still smells of him.

"Momma, where are we?"

"This is your great-grandfather's home. And all his animals used to live right out there."

"Can I pet them?"

"No honey, they're gone now. No one lives here anymore."

"Why?"

"Because there's no one left." It was true. Even in the sporadic contact I've had with my parents since Bailey was born, I have never brought up the topic of this farm. I don't want them anywhere near this place. They would tarnish everything it meant to my grandfather, and to me.

Perhaps, someday, Bailey will bring this place back to life.

Beck moves the steering wheel sharply to the right to avoid a savage looking pothole.

"So it's just abandoned now?" he asks me.

"Pretty much."

"Didn't anyone contact you about the house? The property? Any of that stuff?"

"Well, no. My grandfather wasn't much of a legal eagle. If he even had a will, I'm certain he would have left everything to my father. In spite of a mountain of reasons not to, I think he held onto some hope his son would come to his senses one day."

"I admit I'm not entirely up to speed with property laws, but wouldn't the state do something to claim the land if your father never did?"

I had asked myself this many times in the years after my grandfather's death. I certainly pay taxes to the State of New Hampshire, so it knew perfectly well how to find me. My parents on the other hand, took more than they ever paid back, so who knows what their file looks like. There was the possibility the state had claimed the residence and the land to settle up the Carmichael tab, but if that had happened, I had not been notified about it.

"I don't know. I really don't. I haven't been back up here since he died. I guess that's a terrible thing, isn't it?"

"Don't beat yourself up. Sounds like you've been busy."

"Yeah."

Bailey is pointing out things he's only seen so far in books.

"There's a barn, a wagon, and a giant red crayon over there!"

"A *what*?"

"A giant red crayon. See? Right there, you're looking right at it."

I follow his pointed finger past my head and out into the distance. Just behind the barn, toward the edge of the now sterile cornfield sits a four-year-old's version of a giant red crayon.

"Honey, that's called a silo. It's where farmers store their grain."

"Oh," he says. "Si-*low*," he repeats the two syllables on lips formed into the shape of a circle.

Beck follows the overgrown imprint of a trail leading behind the house and parks the Jeep. As we pull around, I look back toward the street in search of headlights following us. As far as I can tell, we are alone. As he hops out, Bailey is hot on his heels. Even though we are in a strange new place, my son doesn't even look for me. He feels completely at ease by Beck's side. I grab my purse, reaching a hand inside to double check that I have the paper with Jackson's cousin's number on it. I still don't know what I'll do with it, but I don't want to lose it.

I think of Peter again. Beck had shocked the hell out of me by revealing that he and Peter somehow know one another, but I can't tell if it's beyond the normal I'm-a-cop-you're-a-cop connection. He promised he would explain but this is getting more bizarre at each turn, and the day's not over yet.

Fantastic. Thanks a lot, Senator Shithead.

Listlessly, I rifle through Beck's supplies in the back of the Jeep, not surprised to find that he has enough camping gear to get him through a week on top of Mt. Everest.

"Jeesh, you are quite the macho mountain man. This stuff must have cost you a fortune."

"Yeah, I guess. It's an investment when you live in a place like this. If you buy the good stuff, it's supposed to last awhile."

"That's what Momma calls me, an in-ve-ta-ment. She says I'll pay off some day." Bailey says, his juvenile mouth struggling with the word, yet completely serious.

"You said it. You're my ticket out of here." I grin at him, as Beck laughs.

"Smart and funny, you are an interesting little man, Bailey."

"Yup, except when I call Peter on the phone. Then Momma says I'm not funny or interesting at all, I'm just bad."

"Not bad, honey. Just wrong. There's a difference." I stare at Beck, making a strong effort with my expression to remind him that he still owes me an explanation of how Peter fits into his world.

Bailey launches into a passionate explanation of why he won't call the new Echo Valley Chief of Police. He says he's short, wears funny glasses, and won't beep his horn at the kids getting off the bus. At the very least, if I make it out of here alive with my small family intact, it appears my son's 9-1-1 days are over.

Beck loads up Bailey's arms with a long, flat camping pillow and a box of bottled water sitting precariously on top. He tells him to take slow steps up the back porch and then wait for us. I find the key exactly where I last left it, under an old metal watering can just below the first step. I brush off the cobwebs and dirt then fit it carefully into the hole under the rusted doorknob. With a push to the right, I hear a click, then another one. The bolt lets go, as the swollen wood groans at me for disturbing its slumber.

Bailey giggles at the sound, but watches the door inch open like we're on the precipice of an amazing discovery.

"Push, Momma, push. I want to go inside. Hurry, hurry!"

Beck pulls my elbow back so that he can enter first. Last afternoon dusk is now falling, casting long shadows through the threshold of the front door. The kitchen is silent, but we pause for a few seconds to listen for any scurrying going on inside. Beck looks around, opening cabinets and drawers to check for critters. I can hear his long legs move toward the living room off to the left, and the sitting room to the right. Eventually, I hear him climbing the enfeebled stairs up to the bedrooms. His footsteps echo along the beams of the front porch.

"He's going to break the roof!" Bailey gasps.

"No, he won't. Your great-grandfather built this house to last. It may need some TLC, but it will never fall down." How hard my grandfather had toiled here. Right up until his last day on earth. I wonder if he worked twice as hard, trying to make up for the drag on society his son had become. Did he live his life trying to erase a deficit he believed he was responsible for?

"All clear, come on in," Beck calls from the living room. In the distance, I can see him set down his supplies in the middle of a couch. I take Bailey's hand to prevent him from running full bore through the dark rooms.

"Bailey," I say firmly. "Wait."

"Momma, no! I want to go in!"

"Yes, I know that. But listen first. You listening?" I reach for Bailey's chin to direct his eyes on me. "Eyes on who?"

"Eyes on you," he mutters, reluctantly forcing himself to slow down.

"We need to be very careful inside. We can't throw things, or break things, or even turn on the water or use the toilet. Do you understand?"

"Eww, where do I go potty?"

"Outside, buddy. Just for now. Okay?"

"Okay. Can I go in now?"

"Yes, go ahead. Just go slow."

Despite my warning, Bailey races off to find Beck. He dumps the pillow and the water just inside the door, and is off like a shot.

I step inside and take a deep breath. My eyes close on the memory of apple pie baking in the oven, and the smell of hay blowing in on the wind. How happy my days had been here and how strange it feels to come back at a time when my life is falling apart. I feel guilty for bringing trouble to a place where I had felt the most peace.

I clear my throat to loosen what feels like fingers closing around my windpipe. In my mind, I can see my grandfather rising from his recliner to meet me at the door.

"Ah, there's my girl," he would say, taking my bag and leading me by the hand into his kitchen. He would have brewed fresh coffee, and put out two mugs. One was a generic ceramic thing you'd find in any store, but the other was reserved strictly for his use.

"Never underestimate the power of school-bought clay." I would laugh, as he filled the lopsided mug with the steaming liquid.

"Or the hands that made it." He would wink at me, smacking his lips together in approval.

Sixth grade pottery class had produced a few items, including a bird that lost a wing when I dropped it on the bus, a butterfly that looked more like a splat with antennae, and a coffee mug that had been my grandfather's Christmas present that year. He had unwrapped it carefully, marveled at it from several different angles, and then told me it was the best mug he'd ever seen. Every now and again, when just the perfect sunflower grew outside his front window, he would snip it off and plunk it into the crooked lip.

In spite of the creaky old floorboards giving me advanced notice of his approach, I don't hear Beck until he is standing directly behind me.

"Oh, sorry," he says, as I jump sideways, "didn't mean to scare you."

"You didn't. I guess I'm just remembering what it felt like here."

Beck gives me some space, backing up toward the door. "I'm going to go grab some food. The upstairs is clear, but lock the door again when I leave. Okay?"

"Yes, okay."

"When I get back, after Bailey goes to sleep, you're going to tell me what happened. Everything. The whole story."

"Of course. And you are too, right?" He knows I mean the details about Peter.

"Yes." He starts to leave just as Bailey comes tearing toward us.

"Momma! This house has such good stuff inside!"

"Your great-grandfather made a lot of that furniture, honey. With his own two hands." I hold out the palms of my own hands to make a visual connection for Bailey.

"Wow," he says softly. He notices Beck at the front door.

"Where you going?" he demands to know.

"To the store, buddy. Be right back."

"You're really coming back, right?" he asks, making me wonder if my child already expects all men to leave him.

"Promise. But I need you to stay here and watch over your mom." Beck reaches out a hand and ruffles Bailey's hair.

Just like Peter does to him. Just like my grandfather used to do to me.

I watch as his Jeep rolls down the driveway and takes a right onto the street. As his headlights fade in the distance, I look out over the tree line and across the hills. Nightfall is pushing in. It was always my favorite time here, listening to the crickets playing in the field and the rock of the wooden chair my grandfather would settle into to leaf through the well-worn pages of his Bible. I'll bet it's still safely tucked away in the first drawer of the nightstand he made as a gift to his wife when they were first married. He would tell me stories of a woman I had never met, who taught him how to darn a sock, peel an entire apple without stopping, and love without condition. Somehow, these two extraordinarily good people had created just one offspring who was all take and no give. The wonder of genetics had backfired on both of them.

Her name had been Lydia Bailey Carmichael. It is written in delicate calligraphy right there on the first page of my grandfather's leather bound family Bible.

As I peer out of the wooden windowpane of their home, I close my eyes and quietly ask them both to watch over us.

Please, I whisper. *Protect my child. Protect Beckett Brady. Protect Peter Brenner.*

They are all I have.

Please, help me keep them safe.

CHAPTER THIRTY-TWO

Beck returned with subs, sodas, chips, even ice cream. He said he had stood beneath the television mounted on the wall near the cashier to watch for any news of my disappearance, and had checked in at work. There was nothing new to report.

Bailey unwraps his sub with such savagery it would seem that he hadn't eaten in days. "This is yummy in my tummy," he gushes, opening his mouth wide to take the first bite. I look down at my own eggplant sub, toasted with extra cheese dripping off the sides. I can barely stand the smell of it.

Beck and Bailey are sharing pieces of each other's sandwiches, comparing the taste, and then laughing when Bailey's face scrunches as he hits the sharp tang of an onion. I take a small bite, because both of them will ask me why I'm not eating. They fill the air with silly chitchat that covers my silence nicely. As I watch them from my old seat at my grandfather's kitchen table, I move my finger against the crusty part of the bread. I can feel the pointy edges of the spot I just bit off, but my mind is racing. How do I make sure that no matter what happens to me, Bailey is safe? If I should get thrown into some dark dungeon at the hands of the tan man, or some other surrogate they pull out to do the dirty work, who would raise my child? Would it be Peter, who has no blood ties to us but loves us like we share the same genetic code? Would Emily curse me for bringing a child into her home that would disturb the memory of the one who left it?

No. None of that will happen, because I am a woman who lives on the edge, who doesn't have a will, or a life plan, or even a cushion to break my fall if I suddenly catapult myself from the side of a mountain. Bailey will be bounced from one foster home to the next, never knowing what it feels like to be part of a family that would fight to the death to protect him.

Bailey is pulling on my sleeve. "Why you crying again, silly Momma?" He is right. I have started up again with the waterworks.

"Oh, gosh, honey, I don't know. I'm sorry. What were you saying?" I look straight at Bailey, avoiding the urge to meet Beck's eyes.

"I was telling Beck that Peter makes an "s" look like a snake when we practice letters. Beck says "s" is for sub. And for silly. And for super-cali-fragilistic-expi-all-a-dosh-us!"

"Wow, that word is bigger than you are."

"Not for long. I'm growing up. I'm going to be big like Beck and Peter," Bailey chews for a couple of seconds before blurting out, "and Tucker. Even though he's in heaven, Peter says he was big and strong."

"Yes, you will be big and strong one day, Bailey. You will be smart, and kind, and …" I fall apart some more as I think there's a good chance I won't be here to see him grow into everything I know he will be.

"… and goofy, with giant teeth and big ears, and humongous feet," Beck picks it up, careful to divert Bailey from my emotional breakdown.

I watch Beck and my son go back to kidding with each other, until the final scraps of food are finished off, and Bailey scoffs up a few sloppy bites of ice cream. I tell him it's time to think about getting some sleep. I know that just beneath all the intrigue of his new friend and this new place, is sheer exhaustion. He barely puts up a fight.

"Where am I going to sleep?" he asks, opening wide on a huge yawn.

"Down here with me. I think that nice, long couch will feel just like your bed at home."

Bailey walks from the kitchen, then plops himself down on the cushion closest to the armrest. He lays his head on that, curls his body into a tight ball, and asks me for a blanket. I grab one of Beck's camping blankets. By the time I return, he is snoring softly. I cover him up, pulling the downy edges over his chin, and kiss his forehead.

"Love you, Mr. B. See you in the morning."

Darkness spills in through the windows. Noiselessness follows right behind. Bailey's steady breathing is the only thing I can hear. Even Beck's rustling in the kitchen seems drowned out by the power of the country quiet. When there is nothing man-made to disturb it, it can calm a restless soul. I wait for it to work on me. It doesn't. I am as nervous and anxious as a guard dog. If anything, I hope the quiet will serve as my guide, giving me ample warning of approaching danger. I know it is coming.

Beck comes to stand next to me, looking down at my sleeping son. "He's exhausted."

"He doesn't know it, but he's been through a lot these past couple days. It's all catching up with him."

"Come on, I made some coffee. Granted it's instant and more lukewarm than hot, but it's still coffee." Beck walks back to the kitchen, pulls out the same chair he sat in to eat dinner. "Sit down, Bo. Time to talk."

I detour over to the kitchen door, turning the heavy doorknob to make sure it's locked from the inside. I cup my hand around my eye to peer out into the night. Stars sprinkle the black of the sky, throwing off enough light to give me assurance that, for now, we are alone here.

I sit back down at my seat and wrap my fingers around the coffee mug. Taking a small sip my hand flutters and liquid surges up and out. Beck reaches over to stop me from jumping to find a towel.

"Leave it, no one cares about the coffee. Talk to me."

I settle my rear end back down, run my sleeve over the wet spot, and nod. "You're right. No one cares."

Beck's stare is expectant. This story must start with me. Here I go.

Filling my lungs with a long, deep breath, I peer down into the dark liquid inside my mug, feeling like a diver on the high board, risking a triple back flip. I push off and pray that the water waiting for me down below is not as icy cold as I fear it will be.

"I'm in big trouble. You were right. There are very powerful people who are very mad at me."

"I could do without the encryption."

"Sorry, it's just so *messed up*. Like, who in the world gets hired to do someone's hair and ends up being a moving target? That's what I am, I am somebody's reward. Wanted dead or alive, but either will do."

He is quiet, not quite patient but willing to wait me out.

"The drugs are completely bogus. You believe me about that, don't you?"

"Yes, of course. I already told you that's why I'm here. I know it was planted. In fact, I'm pretty sure who planted it. What I don't know yet is why."

"It was planted, all right. Planted as a way to get rid of me. Get me out of the way because of something I now know about someone else. But who are *you* talking about? That squirrely guy at work?"

"We'll get to that, you go first." Beck sips his coffee, nodding. "Go on," he prompts again. He's read my report, after all, I'm not sure how much of this he already knows, and I'm really anxious to hear about the origin of the baggie. In due time. I know Beck wants my side first and then he can plug in the rest.

"We've covered the fact I'm a hairdresser. I work at Gerry's Salon. It's decent, and I put in long days with mostly a regular clientele. I know I'm not giving Bailey a Norman Rockwell childhood experience, but I'm trying to do right by him."

"I would never think otherwise."

"So when my boss told me about a job last weekend, I knew that I had to take it."

"Of course. Why would you not?"

"Well, I really had no choice. He gave me what he thought was the best assignment of all, which in retrospect turns out to be the exact thing that could ruin me."

"Here's where you need to just ... *say* it!"

My hands wring together in frustration. "Okay, okay, please just try to bear with me here. I'm trying to make sure I don't skip anything. So, the job was at an apple orchard. I was working in the barn at an apple orchard."

"Got it, an apple orchard. Big job. Move on to the part when your life suddenly became an episode of 24."

"Well, we were hired to get a family ready for a picture. Only this family, is ... ummm," I struggle to find the right word, "... special." I guess that covers it.

"Special how?"

"Special, as in they could soon be the First Family."

Beck's eyes narrow as a slight grimace crinkles his chin. I get the feeling he was prepared to hear exactly what I just told him.

"This *is* about Senator Declan Anderson, isn't it?"

I nod. "Entirely."

"Tell me. Tell me exactly what happened to you inside that barn?"

I pour out the details, thick and gravely at times, but I don't gloss over a single thing. I tell him about Mrs. Anderson and her imperious attitude, the kids getting carte blanche, the weird feeling I had meeting Senator Anderson for the first time. I tell him about Mackenzie Mason and the terrible burden she will be forced to carry with her the rest of her life. I tell him what I saw fall out of her expensive purse, and how Anderson came at me with more venom in him than the rattlers my grandfather used to stab at with his pitchfork. I tell him about the tan man; how he made damn sure I knew they were coming for me.

I blurt it all out. Everything. I hold nothing back until I realize I have been talking for so long my voice is fading out and my coffee has gone cold.

At one point, Beck reaches for my hand, absently moving his thumb in wide circles near my wrist. He nods at times, shakes his head at others, but does not speak again until we pass officially into the deep dark of night. Eventually, the story is finished.

* * * *

"You have to beat them at their own game," he tells me, after thinking hard on this for a long while. "This can't be a straight-up legal exercise. You have to be underhanded, clever, and ready to play dirty."

"How? How do I do that when I don't even know what game we're playing? And I don't think I know how to be underhanded and I'm so *not* clever."

"Then you'll have to be. Come on, Bo. This is your life you're fighting for. Your kid! You don't have a choice." Beck pushes his chair back from the table, leans over the rounded wooden back of it. He is thinking; the wheels are turning. I am so weary it feels like a fruit fly could take me down, even though I know I would bleed out in battle if it meant protecting Bailey.

"We expose them first," he mutters. "It's what they fear the most. That's why you're so dangerous, and they moved so fast. You could call him out on his dark side. Even the hint of impropriety can bring a guy like Anderson down. Or below the margin of error, which when you're running for president, is even worse."

"I agree. But I'm a no one, and he's ... well ... he's beloved. You know it and I know it, no one is going to believe me over him. It's pointless, he'd win, especially if I'm claiming all of this from a jail cell which is exactly what they're trying to ensure happens."

Beck nods. I am right, after all. I am a total unknown who has the kind of background that would support exactly what they're accusing me of doing. It would be more than logical given the gene pool from which I evolved. He does a slow turn away from the chair and starts pacing back and forth on the stained wood floor. I watch him. An idea takes shape, slowly gelling as I focus on Beck's stature. I'm seated, he's standing tall in front of me. Like a candidate would before a crowd. I absently reach into the pocket of my sweatshirt I've been in for too long and rub together the edges of the paper Jackson gave me. The phone number of his cousin.

His cousin the TV reporter.

That's it!

"I've got it!" I shout, throwing myself upward with such force the old wood groans.

"What is … *it?*"

"The perfect way to expose this asshole for exactly what he is."

"Tell me," Beck says, intrigued.

"Think about it," I squirm with sudden energy. "You're running for president, and you're in a state like this one, how do you get your message out? How do you reach the people?"

It clicks for him, too. He does several slow, deep nods. "You do interviews," he confirms rigidly. "You take it directly to the voters."

I feel my hands go up as I rush at him with wild eyes. I am so close to his face I notice a small scar under his right eyebrow as it pulls up with curiosity.

"Exactly! That's *exactly* what you do. You do as many interviews as you can until you find yourself facing a question you're totally unprepared for. I know he's got a bunch of public events coming up. I heard his campaign people talking about interviews, press conferences, all of that crap."

Mackenzie Mason telling me to hurry the hell up because her guy had an incredibly important schedule to keep.

"Right!" Beck affirms. "We get him where he doesn't expect us to be, which also happens to be the exact place he needs to be right now." Beck and I are together on the same thought. Then he takes it a step beyond by suggesting something that sounds deliciously vengeful if we can pull it off.

"Better yet, we get the whole thing on tape. His public implosion will guarantee the only thing people would be willing to vote for after that … is his nomination for loser-of-the-month-club. Only thing we need now is to find someone on our side willing to infiltrate a public campaign event and then—"

I can't resist the forward motion of my body. I press myself against him so abruptly a stupefied breath shuts him up. This is not meant to be an expression of physical temptation, although his body curves around mine so perfectly he must feel it, too.

Tucked here under his chin, I feel warm and safe, the first time in a while I've been able to see through the brume of my current predicament to make out the distinct possibility of a future.

It's suddenly become slightly less horrifying.

My fingers leave his shoulders to clutch the paper in my pocket again.

And they squeeze.

"I need your phone," I say, sending a silent plea to the gods of cell phone service in rural areas. "If I can get through, I think I may already have someone in mind."

CHAPTER THIRTY-THREE

It had already been an excruciatingly long day, and Sabrina Pressley spent most of it thinking of a hundred other places she'd rather be. This was all wrong. She never wanted to break *news*; she only wanted to break bread. While other enterprising young reporters were following leads on robberies, purse snatchings, or stabbings, she was following Martha Stewart on Twitter, and staying up past her bedtime to watch the judges trash the contestants on Bravo's Top Chef.

She also knew her news director, Alex, only put up with her because his best friend was Sabrina's uncle. He was doing him a favor that had fallen out of *his* favor a long time ago.

She held in a long sigh as noises skittered all around her. This was *so* not cool. Beating the pavement on the cruel streets of New Hampshire was supposed to be her quick and easy ticket out, emphasis on the quick. Sabrina had been determined to shove her stiletto heel through Alex's office door and refuse to let him close it until she had the job. She didn't count on the fact that once she had gotten the job, she decided she didn't want it anymore. Who the hell *wants* to stand out in the rain all night, or knock on the door of a family that's just lost their kid in a freak skiing accident, or sit in court all day for the ten-minute arraignment of the scumbag who stabbed his wife because she spent his booze money on diapers?

She had about as much patience as it took to wait out her soufflé, or to allow a marinade to permeate the marbled layers of her London broil, but not nearly enough for the next phase of her life to begin. If only Paula Dean would retire, or Rachel Ray lose her voice once and for all, or The Barefoot Contessa stub a toe, suddenly there would be an opening and Sabrina would take her rightful place as ruler of the daytime TV kitchen wars.

All this news nonsense was just a way to build a resume tape. Once she could prove that she wouldn't freeze into a mindless Cindy Brady on live TV, the convection oven on the fancy overpriced New York set would be all hers. After six agonizing months of doing story after story on humans behaving badly, Sabrina's soufflé was damn near falling flat.

She wanted out!

She sipped delicately on her grande mocha half-skim with no sugar latte, waiting to hear that she was finally free to go home. As she heard more mumblings over the scanner, she tried to move to the far end of the newsroom to avoid being sent back out on the building fire the station was doing live breaking news cut-ins on. It had been burning for hours, demanding overtime duty for the entire newsroom. Sabrina glanced down at her Stuart Weitzman's, feeling a rush of guilt for raking their gleaming tips through a sea of ash and grime. If it meant salvaging her snake skins, Sabrina would happily volunteer to cover anything else besides fire scenes, even if that meant *politics*.

If she hated chasing public defenders for soundbites, she flat out *despised* covering politics. Alex had told her how fortunate she had been to arrive at the station just in time for the presidential primary.

"The *what*?" she had spat out through the cherry blossom lip-gloss that made her lips shine as brightly as her new Coach purse.

She never meant to sound like an airhead. She had just never given much thought to the idea of trailing presidential candidates across the Granite State. She had no interest in trailing anyone anywhere, unless it was to the front door of Williams-Sonoma during a clearance sale. Her innocuous question was met with two steely eyes and a firmly set jaw. No sooner had she left his office that first day than Alex had dialed up the friend he had the unfortunate obligation of owing a favor to, and roared into the mouthpiece.

"Jesus H. Christ! You didn't tell me she was a fucking moron."

"I wouldn't say she's a moron," her uncle had tried to explain. "She's just … ah … really pretty."

"They're all really pretty, asshole. This is TV news. Most of them are former Miss Something-Or-Other."

"Give her a year, Alex. Let her make a tape. Then she'll be out of your hair and onto the Food Network. Please … for me."

The news director had hung up on his friend, but he had yet to fire Sabrina. He knew Sabrina needed a solid collection of live shots to get her big break in the world of three-egg omeletes and buttercream cupcakes, so he threw her out there every day with just enough rope to hang herself. Miraculously, she hadn't so far. Once this girl buckled down on a story, she was actually decent at telling it. Not that he wasn't eagerly awaiting the day he could finally plan her going away party, but he was partially comfortable in knowing she could get through a live hit without fainting, puking, or saying something that would get him sued.

Corporate was tightening the belt this year, preventing him from stocking up on extra talent to get through the primary. When there were multiple presidential candidates coming and going almost on a daily basis, Sabrina was going to have to jump into the deep end of the pool. He had taken her into his office recently and advised her to start reading more than just *O* Magazine, and *Bon Appetite*.

"Try the *Post*, the *Times*. Get to know the candidates, the issues, whether they're Republican or Democrat." He wasn't sure she knew there was a difference.

"Okay," she had said, in between snaps of her sugar-free Dentyne Ice that promised to freshen her breath *and* whiten her teeth. "I'll try."

She had left his office in a cloud of citrus perfume and haughty indifference.

As the entire newsroom was running in circles trying to cover this breaking news, Alex watched Sabrina take a call on her cell and disappear. That's why you could have knocked him over with a pizzelle when she came running into his office imploring him to let her cover the Anderson campaign's press conference the station was planning to carry live the following afternoon. He wasn't shocked that she had no interest in the blazing fire tearing down an entire city block.

"Please, Alex. I'm *this close* to begging you right now," she was saying, leaning forward onto his desk and holding her thumb and pointer finger inches from his face.

"Like ... this close."

Alex had intended on putting his senior ranking political reporter on it. Declan Anderson was the front-runner, he was spending a fortune on ad buys, and the national media would be crawling on this like maggots on rotten burgers in an alley dumpster. Alex needed to be well represented. His general manager would pop an aneurysm if Sabrina dropped the ball. He might even fire her on the spot.

Exactly what Alex had been hoping for.

He quickly considered his options. This just might be a perfect way to get Little Miss Blueberry Muffin the hell out of his newsroom. The sooner she skipped on out of here, the sooner Alex could work on rebuilding his reputation as a true talent builder in the industry. This apple tart had done some serious damage to his street cred.

He looked at the blonde wonder that was Sabrina Pressley. Maybe it was cruel to set her up like this, but wouldn't he be doing her a favor in the long run? They both knew her time would be better spent preheating an oven somewhere, or discovering new and exciting ways to sauté root vegetables. At least this way Sabrina would be sealing her own fate, taking it out of his hands completely, closing the lid on her own coffin.

Hopefully, God wasn't watching as he cashed in a chip he had been hanging on to, figuring he still had more time on earth to make up for what he was about to do.

Sabrina was impatiently rolling her fingernails on the polished wood of his desk. She was completely oblivious to the chaos breaking out on the other side of the glass wall of Alex's office, as weary assignment editors tried to figure out how to rotate already overworked crews to cover the stubborn inferno that was chewing through buildings at an alarming rate.

Jesus H. Christ. How clueless can one girl be?

Alex's phone began to buzz, as reporters knocked loudly on the glass to get his attention. Breaking news would not allow him to ponder this any longer. He went with his gut, which had not failed him yet, and gave Sabrina exactly what she wanted.

"Fine. It's yours. Be here at eight o'clock sharp. You'll be live at noon to set the scene, you'll toss live to the presser, then package it for the five and six."

She clapped her hands together like a third grader getting the lead role in the school play.

Dear God, what was he thinking? Alex stood up quickly to go tend to the world falling apart outside his office.

"Sabrina," he said sharply before he dismissed her. "Do not ... I mean ... *do not* ... make a fool out of me. Understand?"

"Perfectly," she said, taking off from his office and making a beeline to her desk, where she quickly reached for her cell phone again and punched in a series of numbers. Alex felt his eyes narrow as he watched her speak to whoever was on the other end. She seemed serious, concerned even. He never thought she could be either.

What was going on here?

Alex pushed Sabrina from his mind as he walked over to the assignment desk and asked the closest person for an update.

"What do we know?" he demanded, thankful to regain a small portion of the self-importance Sabrina Pressley had just ripped to shreds.

CHAPTER THIRTY-FOUR

Spencer Diaz gave the woman a shove that was way above gentle.

"Move it," he muttered. The woman huffed as she awoke, but something about this man's eyes, even in the darkness of the bar she met him in the night before, had sparked a concern for her own well-being that she could not ignore.

"All right, all ready. I'm going." She edged herself to the side of the bed, felt around for her clothes and asked if she could use the bathroom.

"I'd prefer you didn't," he replied ungenerously. He was already done with this woman; she'd given him everything she was worth. Now, he just wanted her to get the fuck out of his house. Diaz threw the covers off and exited from the other side of his bed.

"Time to go."

The words themselves weren't threatening, but the tone was unmistakably ominous. Brenda Dwyer was the original good-time girl, but even she got the message that her company was no longer desired. She barely allowed her ego to feel the bitch slap because this encounter was sharply different from what she was used to. Apprehension trickled through her stomach as she half expected him to drop her into a hole in his basement with a bucket of lotion and a barking poodle named Precious.

Only when she pulled the front door shut behind her did she realize her car was still parked at the bar across town. This shithead had driven her here and now wasn't as much as offering her cab fare home.

"Asshole," she spat out, looking around to get her bearings even though the sun wasn't even up yet. Through the fog of a dull hangover, she pushed her stiletto back onto her foot, walked down his front steps, and began to trudge her way home.

Spencer Diaz watched the woman from his bedroom window. It wasn't because he had any concern for how she would get herself home, he just wanted to make sure she got the hell out and didn't feel the need to turn back. Once she crossed the corner at the end of his street and disappeared from sight, he let the shade close and sauntered over to the shower. He was nursing a bad feeling, and the warm body he'd allowed to accompany him home last night hadn't done much to take it away. His back molars were throbbing, sending waves of pinching pain up into his eyes and around to where his neck connected to his shoulders. If he could name his headache, it would be called Beckett Brady.

Diaz couldn't stand the guy long before he was shoved down his throat on the arrest and interrogation of the girl. He was like the straight A student you sat behind in high school. No matter what Diaz did, he would never reach the level of awesomeness Brady seemed to ride upon like a magic carpet.

Not that he had the patience or demeanor to actually earn it, no Diaz wasn't interested in paying his dues. Fuck this whole serve-and-protect mentality, Diaz had no interest in being a small town hero. He wanted a cushy job catering to the security needs of society's supremely over-privileged. He fancied himself the sharply dressed man riding in limos, and boarding private Gulf Stream jets that shuttle the asses of the uber rich to places on the globe mere mortals aren't allowed to venture to.

Being stuck up here in the frozen tundra, working stupid cases against stupid people was getting old. If he had to buy one more pair of boots with plastic non-skid heels, he'd take his department-issued Glock 9mm and remove himself from his own misery.

It was that haste to escape that had Diaz holding up one end of a bargain that was starting to feel like the edge of a slippery slope. It had sounded simple enough, with the tantalizing possibility of a return that promised a destination almost as golden as The Valley of the Dolls. His role would be risky, but the reward well worth the trouble. It was supposed to be his ticket out.

Suddenly, he was wondering if the ticket had expired.

Diaz rushed through his shower. He wanted to get in early, swing by Brady's office to see for himself that he had moved on to the next case awaiting his attention. Diaz had done his level best to keep Brady far away from Bo Carmichael, but the Captain had insisted Brady go along. Diaz had practically fallen to his knees, begging the Captain to let him have a moment to make a name for himself on the force, trying to spin this case into something it clearly wasn't. It needed to be inconspicuous, swift, with predetermined players all assuming their predetermined roles. Instead, Diaz was now playing on a team he didn't put together and worse yet, he'd lost his place in the batting order.

Fucking Brady!

Technically, his part in this shady production was already over. He'd done what he'd been brought in to do. The only thing he should be worried about was how soon the call would come to signal he was on track to begin his new life. He had already written out a suitable resignation letter and was itching to hand it off to the captain with a big grin and a thank you very much. He was also prepared to give them all the finger once this Podunk town was in the rearview mirror of his brand new BMW.

It had been relatively simple to set up the total eradication of Bo Carmichael. Diaz had done some homework, learning there would be no family to rush in and provide her with anything beyond the freebie lawyer that would see her case as nothing more than a good learning experience. Her parents were a joke, and that would only help reinforce the state's argument that Bo was nothing more than a continuation of a garden full of bad seeds. Her kid would suffer through foster care for a while, but if Diaz felt the hint of guilt at taking a child away from his mother, he certainly didn't allow it to overshadow the glee of what his dirty deed was about to bring him.

Sacrifices had to be made, right? Diaz was chasing a certain lifestyle and sometimes that required tough choices. It was all part of his get-rich-quick plan. He became a cop after hearing of six-figure jobs in law enforcement. He got through college and applied to a few local departments across the Northeast, where cops made some decent dough. When the job at the Livingston, New Hampshire Police Department opened up, he took it. Most of his college friends were struggling to keep their heads above the economic tidal wave that had washed away all opportunity for his generation. They were already turning into the nation's newest entitlement recipients, and Diaz—doing pretty well for himself—barely had the energy to return any of their emails anymore.

He had nothing in common with anyone at the P.D. either. Diaz was shuffling through partners at such a rate the captain had taken him aside and warned him that a day would come when he would need someone next to him that would have his back.

The Cap was wrong; Diaz didn't need anyone. He watched his own back.

That's why he knew that something was wrong.

He drove straight to work and looked around. No one was stirring yet, the night shift was wrapping up and the morning shift had yet to come in. He took off in the direction of Detective Brady's office. He hoped the dumb asshole hadn't spent another night curled up on his disgusting desk going through his endless cases. The man had no life; he had allowed this scummy job to take up every ounce of space inside him.

What a loser.

The hallway was dark. Diaz breathed in, trying to detect the smell of freshly, or at least recently, brewed coffee. Nothing. He walked toward Brady's door. It was closed. He tried the knob. It was open. He knocked softly, yelled, "Brady, you here?" and waited for a response. None came. He pushed the door wider and stepped inside the office. He pulled the door shut behind him and turned the lock. He looked around. The office was in shambles. Discarded mounds of crumpled paper littered the floor. Paper cups lined the desk, some of them still filled almost to the top with old coffee that looked like shoe polish.

Disgusted, Diaz bent down to retrieve one of the balls of paper and pulled it open. He squinted his eyes and stared at the random scribbles. To any other person what was written inside wouldn't make a bit of sense. To him, however, it meant quite a lot. As saliva began to build in his throat, he gagged down last night's beer trying to fly out of him as fast as it had gone in.

With shaky fingers, he made the call that felt like he was signing his own death certificate. Through clenched teeth, he dialed up his old pal, the only college friend he had deemed worthy enough to stay in touch with. He had been instructed to lay low for a while and avoid unnecessary contact while the moving parts of this operation were still in motion. He was not expecting his friend to greet him warmly on the other end of the phone.

He didn't.

"What the fuck are you doing calling me?"

Diaz did not mince words. He got right to the point, which was as sharp as an arrow aimed straight at his heart.

"Because we've got trouble."

"What kind of trouble?"

"Ah, the kind that tells me you better come up with a Plan B. And fast."

A loud sigh, a muttered *fuck*, and a "Go on," from the voice, in a tone that hadn't melted one iota.

"They're onto you. And I think they're helping her."

Diaz knew he was fucked as he rattled off the one final tidbit of information he'd found inside the crumpled paper. With his headache exploding now from the inside out, he clicked off, shoved his phone back into his pocket, and rushed out of the office. He took long, quick steps out into the parking lot. He never went back to his apartment. He just hit the interstate and kept on driving.

CHAPTER THIRTY-FIVE

The deep ache in Troy Olander's left thumb made him realize he was on the verge of smashing it right through his cell phone. He very quickly deleted Spencer Diaz from his call history and contact list. He wouldn't be needing him anymore. Now he had to figure out a way to clean up his mess.

Goddamn it! This had been going so well. They were almost ready to pull out of this state with enough confidence to believe the next time they came back it would be as the presumed nominee. The general election was a foregone conclusion as far as Troy was concerned. His guy was almost in. Troy thought he had sufficiently brushed the barn calamity right back under the wretched rug from which it came. It would seem he missed a few pieces.

"What was that all about?" The question cut through the air inside the campaign bus headed north along New Hampshire's most traveled highway. They had gotten an early start this morning to make sure they could get from the northern half of the state back down again in time for an event at noon. It was a near-frantic pace, and all eyes, including Troy's, were tinged with sleep; as the tiny kitchen coffee maker was pushing out its fifth pot of the young day.

Troy's typically hermetic avidity was deteriorating under all the bullshit. He hadn't signed up for this. He had been picking up this bonehead's pieces for too long, desperate to preserve the image of what he needed the rest of the country to see. The man's unabashed lust for anything with boobs and two legs was getting to the point where it could cost them everything. If Anderson had just kept it tucked away, he wouldn't be dealing with Diaz's complete failure to perform the simple task he had been given.

Fuck, what was he supposed to do now?

Troy's jaw clenched at the thought of watching his entire future get flushed down the toilet by an irrelevant, witless single mother hairdresser who probably wasn't even registered to vote.

Fucking Anderson! Fucking Diaz!

Troy's fingers wrapped themselves around his lower biceps as he thought of the cop who had assured him all would go as planned. He cursed himself for thinking anyone but he could do it right. Even back in college, Diaz could never follow through. He was lazy, sloppy, and thought his golden goose was just a day or two away from landing in his backyard. Why did Troy think this would be any different?

"Nothing, sir," he said, struggling to hide the bold hatred he had for this man. "It is nothing you need to worry about. I will take care of everything."

Like I always do, you asshole.

"I would expect that you would," Senator Anderson states, without even looking at him. He had given Troy a quick synopsis of the altercation with the girl and instructions to "deal with it." Anderson didn't want to know how because it reduced culpability that way. His image was to remain clean and presidential. Troy's, however, was expendable.

The bus bounced on a pothole the size of Lake Winnipesaukee, sending the coffee Senator Anderson had been drinking straight onto the pleated front of his pants, just below the zipper. A fitting spot, Troy thought as he watched his boss leap up and look around for some subordinate to snap to it and help him. Preferably, some fine young staffer whose tender fingers could brush the extra liquid away while getting a little too close to the sweet spot. Troy watched it happen all the time. The man was insatiable, controlled by urges so strong he was at risk of literally carving up his own legacy with his bare hands.

Declan Anderson didn't see it that way. He thought he was perfectly within his right to exorcise the stress from his life the only way real men were supposed to. When Troy had once innocently asked why he didn't just enjoy the company of his lovely wife, Anderson had practically ripped his head off. It was never spoken of again.

His dalliances are tightly wrapped little secrets. He pays his staff well to hide the fact that he goes through more women than an entire hockey team. To his credit, he did manage to make sure his women were of a certain caliber, with just as much to lose if word ever got out. As he watched the curvy intern attend to Anderson's nether region with a paper towel, Troy thought again of the beautiful Mrs. Anderson, already home with their children at their thirty-two-acre estate on rolling green hills. He wondered if love had ever lived within the Anderson's four walls. And if it had, when exactly it had pulled up stakes and taken off.

Troy suffered through all of their disgusting family drama, trading in his morals for a front row seat to the big show. The headiness of presidential politics had been consuming his conscience for so long now he barely remembered what it felt like to have one.

There had been a time when he believed, *truly believed,* that every now and again, one great man can come along and infuse back into society all the goodness, wonderment, and inspiration that gets chipped away by the rigors of life. Troy felt that familiar sense of self-loathing—as constant as his own shadow—reminding him how askew his instinct had been when he signed onto something that had systematically taken away every ounce of his dignity. He had reached an uneasy peace with the notion that he was spending his days foreclosing on his own soul. There was virtually nothing left he hadn't already done or wouldn't do to get this campaign bus across the threshold and onto the victory lap.

Troy first met Declan Anderson when he was a starry-eyed politico looking to attach himself to the right ticket. Anderson's look was Kennedy-esque, while his resume boasted an acceptable mix of capitalistic success, appointments to all the right committees, and charitable servitude. His wife was gorgeous, his kids born healthy and adorable, and even his dog was trained not to bite the reporters who stopped by for a soundbite. If Troy considered himself the idol maker, he had finally found the man who would become his king. He hadn't known at the time that theirs would be a union born deep in the belly of Hades. He wasn't sure that would have mattered, either.

When the time was right, the crowd assembled, and the media outlets ready to roll, they formally announced his candidacy. It was the best day of Troy's entire life. He was boarding an elevator that would take him straight to the penthouse with the million-dollar view.

As he watched from just behind the podium, he almost lost himself in the moment of grandeur, as the resplendent man wielded his mystically emotive power like a scythe, making political hyperbole sound simplistic and genuine. He made every person in that room forget that their lives really weren't that bad by stirring a lust for gratuitous things none of them needed but suddenly felt they were owed. He was their blessing. He was their future. Troy has been so caught up in the rapturous delivery of Anderson's speech he almost forgot he'd written it himself. He was floating on air that was so overripe with parasitical affection he allowed himself to let it waft him away.

He had exited the stage behind Anderson, accepting handshakes and kisses on the cheek. He had helped load the Anderson family into one limo and then climbed into the one behind it with the candidate. It was just Troy and Declan Anderson, alone. Buoyed by his own sense of imperiousness for a job well done, Anderson was full of bravado and zeal.

"This is it, Troy ... this is *IT!*" he gushed, reaching over the middle to clasp Troy's knee and shake him back and forth. Exuberance filled the space between them.

"You are everything they need right now, sir. You are all they will think about tonight. You have just guaranteed yourself every vote in that room." The words had come from Troy's heart. He meant them; he *felt them*.

"I need to celebrate ... do something to remember this moment ..." Anderson said, as his fingers flexed and his eyes narrowed.

Troy had expected Anderson to ask him to book a fancy table at a special restaurant, or send out an email to his team and invite everyone over for the party they should've been having that night. He should have rallied the troops, whispered to his wife how he could never have come this far without her, and then kissed his children good night with a heartfelt missive that he was doing all of this to make the world a better place for them. Instead, he delivered to Troy the first of many crushing statements that would reveal the true reptile he was.

"I need ... to ..."

Troy waited. He inhaled the expensive leather of the seats, the subtle twinge of nervous sweat, and the unmistakably sweet incense of success. He allowed himself to imagine, how years in the future when some production house was putting together a biopic on President Declan Anderson, he would be asked to describe this night. How the candidate and his closest advisor marked their moment of triumph with hopes and dreams of all they would achieve for the people of their great land.

"I ... need ... to ..." Anderson's fingers were still twitching, kneading a ball of imaginary dough.

Pray, Troy thought. Eat a steak? Throw back a shot of whiskey? What could he so desperately need?

"I need to ... *fuck!*" he said finally, setting off a cacophony in Troy's head that felt like a marching band had just moved in.

"Ex ... *cuse* me, sir?" Troy's voice was breathless, a full octave higher than normal. He sounded like a fourteen-year-old who was still in the process of becoming a man.

"You heard me."

Declan Anderson then demanded Troy hand over his cell phone. He always held on to his candidate's devices during a speech. With fingers that felt frozen, Troy reached into his coat pocket and extracted Anderson's cell, handing it over to the senator in what felt like a trance. He watched him punch in a number he apparently knew quite well, one that clearly wasn't the simple button that connected him to "Home" *and his wife* ... and then ask whoever answered to join him for a few hours at their usual spot. When he clicked off, he looked Troy in the eye and spoke with acidity so potent it could melt skin.

"So tell me, Troy," he started, his drawl making Troy's muscles stiffen.

"Yes, sir?" His voice felt caked in sadness.

"You like sausage?"

"Sausage, sir?"

"Yes, boy, sausage. You ever eat it?"

"Ah, sometimes. Why do you ask?"

"So, would you say you like sausage, then?"

"Yes, sir. I would say that sometimes I like sausage."

"You ever heard the old saying that if you like sausage don't watch it being made, Troy?"

Their eyes held. The warm celebratory mood was replaced by a chill so deep inside Troy's chest he found it hard to breathe.

"I think I may have heard that, sir."

"Well, consider my life a little bit like making sausage. You may not like all the things that go into it, but you're sure going to love how it feels sliding down your throat. You understand what I'm saying here?"

Troy understood. It was a shocking tutorial on how quickly the human spirit can replace devotion with repulsion, and yet keep people fused together just the same. If there ever was a biopic made about Declan Anderson, Troy would not appear in it, and he certainly would never talk about what happened that night in the limo.

He continued to watch the lovely young woman spin herself into a tizzy trying to clean the spilled coffee from Anderson's lap while he made some half-assed attempt to tell her not to bother. Troy felt abomination pull his mouth downward as the senator's southern twang became husky with longing. What a disgusting cad this man is. What a challenge it is to mop up his messes.

Speaking of that, he needed to call Mackenzie. She was staying back in Concord to make sure the live presser at the New Hampshire Statehouse would go off without a hitch. She would finalize media credentials, spend some time with the governor going over his introductory remarks, and then work some contacts to make sure Anderson's appearance hit the network news that night. She was also trying to make sure the local station carried most of it live during the noon newscast. Mac wouldn't let him down, she always got the job done.

He shook his head, wondering yet again what the fuck she was thinking crawling into Anderson's harem. Troy felt a tug of culpability over Mackenzie Mason. He had personally brought her in, luring her out of the upscale Dupont Circle law firm that had been prepping her for a plum lobbyist position on the Hill. She was sharp, classy, and ambitious, a key player on his team. He had hoped Anderson would consider her more of a daughter. Now, she was just another plaything that was threatening to derail the entire train. Once they left New Hampshire, she was scheduled to reroute to her apartment in Virginia, where she would swallow the pills prescribed to her by a staff physician and wait out what followed. Anderson had coldly told her to take a weekend. Troy amended that by telling her to take the whole week, especially after the fiasco in the goddamn barn. Mackenzie had been so desperately unsettled that an interloper had breached the precious circle of secrets that she nearly passed out on the barn floor. Fortuitously for Troy, as she dropped down on one knee, she landed near a tiny silver cell phone lodged in between two planks of the wide pine floor. He gently scooped her back up and through her sweaty hair, shushed her to calm down. He also pocketed the phone just in case it came in handy later.

And it had.

Senator Anderson was settling back into his seat across from Troy, moving right then left on the cushion in search of a spot that hadn't been defiled by coffee. "Troy," he says abruptly. "Scoot on over here, switch sides with me."

In other words, you take the wet spot. Troy didn't argue. His entire life had become one giant wet spot.

"How much longer," Anderson asked him once they had swapped out seats.

"About two hours. Enough time for you to go over the notes I wrote up for you. You'll be speaking to a Mr. Smitherson, he's the owner of the mill we're touring. Make a point to bring up the cost of exporting to Canada, and why expanding trade will be an important piece of your agenda."

"Uh, hummm," Anderson mutters, throwing on his reading glasses and accepting a file of papers from Troy across the top of the table.

Troy watched him for a couple of seconds before looking back out the window of the moving bus. He felt as empty as the tree limbs as they traveled north toward an economically trodden mill city that Troy already knew would vote their way.

He rolled his thumb back over the end icon on his phone. He wasn't allowing himself to become alarmed by Diaz's failure to secure the threat of the girl. He had already considered the very real possibility that he would have to employ a solution of his own. His psychiatrist had already warned him he was skirting dangerously close to being fully absorbed into his narcissistic and unyielding ambition. It was then, she warned, that a desire to be one's best can override rationality and if he sailed that far off course, she couldn't be certain he wouldn't hurt himself.

Or another.

If narcissistic ambition was a drug, it had Troy so strung out he wasn't certain of that himself. Since he figured he'd already damaged himself enough, and because he still needed to restrain his unabashed longing to throttle his lascivious boss, there was only one sacrificial lamb left.

CHAPTER THIRTY-SIX

Jackson Nichols had always been Sabrina's most favorite second cousin. Or was he a third cousin, twice removed? She couldn't remember exactly how they shared a branch on the family tree, but she had happily talked to a friend of his after her phone rang late the night before, just as she had been trying to separate herself, *and her shoes*, from the hysteria of that stupid fire.

It didn't take any prodding for Jackson's friend to get to the point of the call, and once she started listening, Sabrina's entire world shifted off its axis. Her family member's friend was in crisis, and if there was anything that troubled Sabrina more than using nutmeg past its expiration date, it was someone messing with her people. She wouldn't stand for it.

About twenty minutes later, Sabrina made a direct route to Alex's office. She dismissed his attempt to reroute her right back out, and plopped her hands down on the highly polished wooden edge of his desk, leaning in just over his head.

"I want you to know that I will be covering Senator Anderson's press conference tomorrow. It's time, Alex, and I'm ready. I won't take no for an answer."

Eventually, Alex had relented. He sent her out of his office with the stern warning that in no uncertain terms was she to allow herself to fuck up.

Sabrina had called Jackson's friend right back to confirm she was in. She didn't allow herself to ponder it any further until she was eventually dismissed from fire duty and on her way home. Then, the weight of her assignment fell on her like a sequoia tree. As she fumbled around her apartment, she had no direction. She absently tugged off her suit, tossed her dirty heels into the closet, and wandered into her favorite place in the world—her kitchen. If she were to find any peace right now, it would be there. Despite the late hour, she pulled out pots and pans, turned on a burner, measured out some water, butter, and salt. As she waited for the rumble of bubbles to take hold, she tried to quell her nerves with a glass of room temperature Shiraz. She broiled herself a medium-rare filet then topped it with bacon béarnaise sauce, giving herself props that even though her brain was on overload, she had properly emulsified the delicate liquid so that it showed no sign of breaking.

A few bites into her exquisite meal and her appetite got up and left the table. She had hoped the meat would settle the spin cycle her stomach was stuck in, and the wine would galvanize her dormant courage. She piled everything into the sink and fell into a troubled sleep thinking that neither had done the trick.

Her alarm clock went off while her eyes were already wide open. She kept the shower spray on her back for an extra five minutes, going over what she would say and do to ensure she didn't let a friend of her cherished cousin down. Jackson had been the one to entice a mutual uncle to get her this TV job, for God's sake. It was the least she could do to return the favor, even though she was thinking she could end up getting fired in the process.

Maybe even thrown in jail!

Sabrina had always done pretty well on instinct alone. She tended to sabotage herself when she put too much thought into anything. Typically, that meant going with her gut when a recipe called for a *heaping* tablespoon and she knew in her heart of hearts it really should only be a *level* one, at the most. Or, when all the other female reporters were telling her that no one was wearing frosted lipstick anymore, she listened to the voice in her head that told her she could still pull off her favorite shade of Sorbet Sunset. She even ignored Alex when he asked her to stay away from nail polish that looked like blood. Didn't any of them know that OPI's Cocktail Waitress Red was the leading seller at any spa worth its salt scrub?

Whatever.

Nobody thought she could hack it. They thought her idea of the real world was the version she grew up watching on MTV. She knew they all made fun of her behind her back; some of them did it to her face. She put up with it because most of the time they were right. In this pressure cooker environment of hard news, she was nothing more than a joke in a designer jacket. She had considered telling Jackson's friend as much, but she hadn't given her the chance.

Sabrina had to find that *uumph* from somewhere deep inside her to get this done, even though the instinct that had always guided her was backfiring like the jalopy she used to drive in high school.

Her breakfast oatmeal tasted like beach sand. She half listened to the morning news on TV, which was full of updates on the now smoldering fire. She waited for mention of Senator Declan Anderson's lunchtime press conference and then felt herself recoil as her own publicity picture popped up as the anchor teased the station's upcoming coverage. The audience was told—or more likely warned—that Sabrina Pressley would be reporting live from the statehouse during the noon newscast. Her spoon fell against the side of the glass bowl as Sabrina raced to the bathroom and gagged up every last bite of her fiber-enriched blueberry-flavored Quaker Oats.

Forget it, she thought, *I can't do this. I'll mess it up. Worse yet, I will have that Cindy Brady moment Alex is so worried about and get myself booted right off the air.*

Just as she was considering how her mug shot would compare to Paris Hilton's, she realized that all the mortifying possibilities of public failure and humiliation paled in comparison to what Sabrina was most worried about. She felt tears well up as she saw Jackson's face. He needs her. He trusts her enough to have her help someone in need. Disappointing Jackson would be worse than serving up a scone with the unmistakable and very unwelcome crunch of a wayward eggshell. It just couldn't happen! Her entire being ached with foreboding.

Her cell phone buzzed on the kitchen counter. She hurried to grab it, thinking Jackson's friend had just come to the same realization and was wisely calling to retract her request for help. Only it wasn't her at all, and it wasn't Alex telling her he had decided that putting her on this presser was probably as wise as having his six-year-old drive him to work this morning. It wasn't any of that, but it was something that made Sabrina slow her breathing to a level just under what a hyperventilating lunatic would consider overextended.

She brought the phone closer to her face to read a tweet that had just come in. It was from her master--Martha Stewart--and it seemed to be meant just for her.

The Queen had issued an invitation to her followers on this day: Do Something Different and Grand. Of course, what she likely meant was to challenge her minions to exchange their light brown sugar for the dark variety, or perhaps reorganize their utensil drawer. Whatever the intention really was, Sabrina used it to confirm that it was indeed time for her to venture beyond her comfort zone of Bundt cakes and chocolate ganache.

This was her one chance to do just that—do something different and grand! She would not let her cousin's friend down; she would not let *Martha* down! Just like her favorite brand of baking yeast, she would force herself to rise to the occasion.

Sabrina headed for her closet. She poked through bright oranges and pinks, brushing them aside in search of something serious, more professional. She remembered a gray cardigan her mother bought her last year for Christmas. Granted, it was cashmere and nicely tailored, but Sabrina loathed gray, it made her feel like a corpse. She cocked her head to the side and fingered the soft fabric, rolling her finger over the tiny buttons while thinking that if somehow, all the planets aligned and she managed to pull this off, she'd better not look like a candy apple or a circus clown. She decided the gray sweater would be perfect.

After all, if she was going to take down a presidential candidate on live television, she had damn well better dress for it.

CHAPTER THIRTY-SEVEN

The air is warm as it blows across my cheeks. I am sitting in the corner of my grandfather's creaky chair, my feet dangling off the side. I have an errant thought that my feet should be able to touch the ground, but I dismiss it as I watch him make his way over to me from across the yard. I recognize his crooked gait, how his gnarled hands always find their way to the small of his back to lend support. He sees me sitting there on the porch and gives me a wave, his wrist hitching with arthritis. Stopping with a foot on the stone step, he points up to the sun. It is so bright I wonder how he's not squinting, but his eyes are clear and wide open. As he speaks, his voice is tinny.

"Grandpa, I don't know what you're saying …" I ask him to slow down, but he doesn't hear me. "Grandpa, stop … stop… I can't hear…"

He's shaking me. Why is he grabbing at me like this? I try to move away and feel like I'm falling off the chair that is still too big for me to sit in. I'm falling … falling …

"… warm enough, Bo?"

His plaid shirt is wiping at my cheek. Soft and warm, I reach up to grab hold of my grandfather's arm. It moves away, and he backs up, just out of my grasp.

"No, wait … don't go yet. Stay, talk to me. Stay with me, Grandpa."

"Bo. Wake up … it's me."

I shake myself awake. I look around at the dim light coming in through the living room window. I look for

Bailey, who is still asleep on the couch, tucked up against the same pillow he fell asleep holding.

It was just a dream.

What I thought was my grandfather's shirt is really Beck's camping blanket, now wrapped around me from chin to knee. I see him settling back into a chair across from me.

"You were talking in your sleep. I think you were cold, I figured you might want my blanket."

"Oh, thank you. I was dreaming about ... well, just about being here, only it wasn't now, it was when I was little, and my grandfather was here with me."

The dream is starting to fade, seeping back into the air the same way dry ice evaporates around your legs as you walk through its fog. Still, I can feel him. He is here, all around me, even in the tiny dust particles floating through the rays of light pouring through the window. The sun is beginning its orange descent up over the horizon. I tuck Beck's blanket under my nose and breathe in. It smells like a man.

"I'm sure in many ways he is here with you."

We are whispering, careful not to wake Bailey. I pull my knees toward my hips and shift into a sitting position. Beck looks exactly like he did when I finally gave in to the downward pull of my eyelids last night. He doesn't look disheveled, or sleep-deprived, or even remotely out of sorts.

"Did you sleep at all?" I ask.

"Not really," he says, as his hand comes around to support his chin.

I gaze at my sleeping boy. He will wake up soon wanting to know when we will go home and have pizza with Peter. Before I can remind Beck that I still need to know the truth about his own link to Chief Peter Brenner, Bailey stirs on the couch. He isn't ready to get up just yet. He rolls over to face the back of the couch, shutting out the pesky light trying to rouse him. We both watch him moving.

"He's a lot like you," Beck says, smiling at me, but putting off the curious topic of Peter.

"Maybe. I think he's just being himself."

"Are you going to tell him about any of this?" Beck asks.

"No, not for a long, long time. I think Bailey has started out with enough stacked against him already."

"What does that mean?"

"Well, he has me for a mother and some *ass-* ..." I clamp my mouth shut before I let the rest of it fly. Beck advances like the consummate inquisitor he is.

"Some asshole for a father? Is that what you were going to say?"

"I shouldn't say that."

I have made it a habit not to throw Riley under the bus because it reflects poorly on me. I've gone to ridiculous lengths to keep details about him tucked away from public consumption. I've lied to Jackson, been vague to everyone else, and completely dishonest with myself and Bailey.

Even members of my extended family have stopped asking. My friends simply know he's not around and I prefer it that way.

"It doesn't matter …" I cower in shame.

"I think it does. It does matter. Even if it didn't happen as you had planned it would, he's here. So, yes, it still matters."

My eyes have burned through the tired haze and are watching Beck's face go tight. This is getting too intense. "No, don't," I begin, putting a hand up. He discards the warning.

"Don't dismiss the events of your life, Bo. It's important for you to realize that all of this matters. A lot."

"Beck, stop. I'm telling you to stop …"

"And I'm telling *you* to stop."

"Uh, you're impossible. And I'm too tired right now to take you on, too."

He's relentless. He digs at me some more, pushing me to a place I have refused to go. Just past the guilt, fury awaits. Riley O'Roarke—combined with a temporary yet immense lapse in judgment—completely stole my future! I am still slaving to put it back together. Even though my heart is now sustained solely by love for my son, it has been deeply and irreparably damaged.

If Beck is suggesting I'm aloof, then that's just a bucket of malarkey.

"All right, all right. Enough already! You are totally right, Beck, it does matter. There, happy? Do I need to remind you that I spent my entire childhood not mattering?

I get how that feels, you know, because I had it shoveled at me every goddamn day of my life!"

I can't look at him. I wring my hands beneath the thick blanket, but I know Beck has earned an explanation for my choices. For dropping his life to help save mine, and almost blindly believing in my innocence, I owe him at least that.

"Sorry," I try to return to a steady voice. "But you're wrong. First of all, don't suggest my son doesn't matter—"

"I didn't … don't put words in my mouth."

"Well, saying something like that isn't right."

"Of course it's not. That's why I didn't say it."

I sigh loudly. "God, are you ever not a cop? You spin more than Senator Anderson."

"Not more, just better. Go on …" he winks at me.

"Beck, my life hasn't been smooth or even pretty most of the time. I'm independent because I've always had to be. I don't want your sympathy but just try to understand how that shapes who you become."

"I can see that."

"So, I don't have a safety net. I know I haven't done right by Bailey in many ways and that includes not being honest about how he came to be. When you throw in this insane drama at the apple orchard, you shouldn't be surprised that I feel like a shitty mom. So I'm defensive, shoot me. It's only because I love him so …"

He moves toward me; his strong body is so surprisingly fleet that I freeze. He scoops the chair by its neck and plops it down to my right, stretching out a hand to touch my cheek. He means to bring empathy, but all I feel are his knees pressing into me, feeding a fiery attraction that idles between allure and annoyance.

"I just don't want that kid to ever think he doesn't matter. I don't want you to think that either." Beck's hand brushes back my hair. I cringe, thinking that it's been awhile since I gave it a good wash. I pull sideways, but he slides two fingers downward to grip my chin gently below my jaw.

"You both deserve to know that someone out there will cherish you. Not for a night that never should have happened, but forever."

Say what? "Jesus, Beck. That's a little too deep for my liking. I prefer to tread water in the shallow end." My mouth twists into an ironic grin. Such an endearment strikes a shocking discord with his brusque physique. "Seriously," I continue. "I know I have messed everything up. But what happened to me ... to us ... isn't completely my fault. Well, it is ... and it isn't. I made a mistake. But when I look at my little boy, how can I say that?"

He just shakes his head at what is obviously my emotional paradox. While one side roils with regret, the other rejoices with unexpected treasure. While I knew I didn't have it in me to shave away the result of that one night, I never expected it to morph into my life's biggest joy. Sure, there are tough days with many more to come, but the limitless potential I see in Bailey sustains me even when I'm failing, floundering or totally incapable of securing a positive outcome for him.

Kind of like right now.

I'm usually pretty good at cutting men off before they can get cute, or overly obnoxious, so maybe it's immature to think I need validation from this one. But with Beck, there's this odd, intangible tug. Even with Peter, I tuck away all my insecurities about Bailey because they're way too heavy a burden for a man already saddled with so much of his own. Beck acts like I'm committing a capital offense by *not* asking him to pick up my slack. It's like an alien landing a spaceship on my front lawn and then wondering why I don't ask him to fertilize the grass while he's at it.

We sit in the quiet for a few minutes. I watch the blanket rise and fall on each breath Bailey takes.

"You're right," I say finally.

"Yup, I'm right a lot," he jokes. "But what part do you mean?"

"I had that kind of love once," I admit sadly. "Not to get all gushy and unproductive on you, but I know what it feels like to be cherished. I had to let him go because it was the right thing to do." I work up that old, protective shield because the ending to my love story doesn't fit the formula and it still pisses me off. In romance novels, you always end up with the poor slob who loved you even though you screwed him over every which way to Tuesday and then back again. I wanted to be better than that, but it's a difficult concept to explain. Especially to a guy.

"When is that ever the right thing to do?" Beck counters, elbows extending to his sides. I resist the cord drawing me closer, leaning more toward angry again: at

Beck, at Riley, at myself. Beck gets the hatchet because he's the closest.

"What would you know about love, Beck? You're not married, you don't have kids. And besides," I blast indignantly, "when something bad happens to you, but shouldn't happen to someone you love, you have to make a *choice*. That's what I did, and what I would still do." Frustration and raw pain clamp together, making my brain scream the words that never stop rattling around in my subconscious. I narrow my gaze with this sarcastic reminder. "And, hello, you seem to keep forgetting the fact that I didn't exactly grow up with homemade beef stew on the stove and good night kisses. I may be predisposed to messing up my own relationships—"

"Bullshit," he interrupts. "Don't play that game with me, Bo, it won't fly. You're too smart for an excuse like that, and … *hello* … if anyone has indisputable proof of that, it's me."

Beck is intent on going deeper, almost sensing that he is scratching the surface of my long-held secret and he's withholding permission for me to take refuge in it.

"So you made a choice," he continues softly. "Okay, I can respect that. But did you give the guy who cared about you a choice or did you just shut him out because you thought you knew best? Because if that's the case, then you gave up, not him."

Any ego I have left is shouting at him to shut the fuck up, but my mouth won't let it out. I feel my fingers make clutching fists to rage at the unjustness of his uninvited intrusion. "I don't have the energy to discuss this with you … it's irrelevant to what's going on right now anyway."

He won't be dismissed. His blue eyes dart around the room in frustration, veins pop along his forearm and on either side of his bulky neck. He absently rolls his knuckles until they pop to release his internal tension.

"No, it's not. Jesus Christ, Bo, you're raising a kid here, and you're smacking away the people who are willing to help you do it. That's a problem. You should be building an army of allies instead of a fortress to keep us out."

"Ugh, stop! You have no right …"

I taste the embarrassing admission punching holes through my stubborn facade; threatening to push up from my gut. His job is to seek out the truth. He wants it from me. He wants to hear the unspoken reason for my drastic U-turn from brilliant physician to struggling single mother.

Okay, fine, Beck. Let's go! You want to dip your pole into this lake, then get ready for the big fish to bite. Let's discuss the pathetic crawl I made back to the hometown that held no sentimental place for me even after I had sworn I would never return. I brace, ready to unload.

I was drunk! I was stupid! I was a typical kid for a moment in my life, and it bit me right in the ass!

The screaming stays in my head. We hear a sudden noise on the couch, followed by one word that redirects everything.

"Momma?"

I swallow hard, pulling away from Beck and his hardscrabble session of self-discovery. My son is awake and deserves my full attention.

"Hi there, sleepyhead. I'm right here with you." I tap soft kisses along his forehead. "You are okay, buddy. We are still at your great-grandpa's house, and it's pretty early. Go back to sleep."

"No, Momma. Where's Beck? Did Beck leave?"

"No way, my friend. I am still right here." Beck is beside me, tousling the messy spikes of Bailey's hair.

We won't look at each other. Like two boxers on the verge of a resounding knockout, we retreat to our own sides of the ring, physically drained, wondering who the hell just won the round.

CHAPTER THIRTY-EIGHT

Troy is watching the man about four rows deep, with at least a day's growth of beard on his face, and thick arms doing their best to cross over an equally thick belly. He hasn't smiled once.

As the owner of the plant prepares to escort Senator Anderson to the next section of his warehouse deep inside a renovated brick mill building, Troy steps between them. "Sir, you need a break for a glass of water," he says, giving Anderson a sharp look with his eyes.

"Ah, yes. Mr. Smitherson, give me a second now, won't you?"

"Oh, of course, Senator. Folks, let's give Senator Anderson a moment to whet his whistle. We'll continue on in just a couple of minutes." The man saunters off to fetch a cold bottle of water. Troy quickly pulls Anderson off to the side. "Sir, someone is not a fan. Not yet."

Troy's eyes are trained to find people just like this burly factory worker who aren't fully caught up in Anderson's allure, and then convert them.

"Work him. Otherwise, he's going to go tell everyone within earshot at the bar tonight that you're an asshole who doesn't understand what it's like to be a working stiff like him."

"Which one?"

"Fat guy, blue checkered shirt, receding hairline—right over there."

"All right, thanks," Anderson says quietly. He throws a big grin at the plant owner who is back to deliver a generic brand of water that his wife wouldn't see fit to wash the house pets with.

They move back toward a small opening in the circle of employees waiting for the chance to touch him, joke with him, or have him acknowledge their existence. Most of them will finish out their day like they were walking on air, eager to run straight home to the wife and kids to tell them they had just chatted about next year's Red Sox bullpen with the guy who's going to be president of the United States. Only one or two, including the paunchy plaid shirt guy, aren't sold yet. While Anderson promises job security and increased benefits, an inevitable few will be wondering if he is aware that three-quarters of the staff here are at constant risk of getting laid off. To them, job security is the pleasant surprise they feel each morning when their key card still gets them past the locked front door.

Troy watches the retreating back of Declan Anderson, willing him under his breath to move in and attack. "Good boy," he mutters to himself when he sees Anderson walk up to the plaid shirt and place a hand on his shoulder. Before long, and probably to his own shock, the man breaks down and smiles. He and Anderson exchange a few comments and a friendly handshake before Anderson moves on. Troy's eyes linger on that man.

Wait for it. Wait for it.

Troy has played this game long enough to know what comes next. Once the lower middle-class man feels properly recognized and appreciated, he will give in. His stiffly held shoulders will relax and soon he will be telling his buddies that Anderson is his man. Anderson gets him. He understands his story. He wants to make it all better.

Troy gives quiet props to Anderson for being such a solid closer. He shakes his watch down below the cuff of his sleeve and checks the time. He catches Anderson's eye just before he disappears down a new aisle in this cavernous plant, and gives him a small salute with his right hand. Anderson returns a half wave back.

Troy explained that he had some business to take care of and won't be joining him for the presser in Concord. Anderson never asks for details, nor does Troy provide them. Safe distance achieved.

Mac will be the one to escort Anderson to the stage, monitor the crowds and the media before she exits the party temporarily to take care of her own business. Troy grabs the arm of one of the campaign aides and tells him he'll meet him later. He also asks who among their group drove his own personal vehicle.

"Who wasn't on the bus with us," Troy wants to know.

"Uh, we got a few. Skippy, over there, and Johnny Walker, and Greasy Bob, for sure. I think at least one of them drove up."

They know them only by the nicknames they've earned on the campaign trail. Skippy is a skinny kid, probably not out of college yet, who is so jumpy he looks like he's skipping an invisible jump rope all the time. Johnny Walker stinks like whiskey, no matter what time of day it is. Greasy Bob always has at least one blotchy stain on his shirt. They hang back, like the young political junkie misfits that they are, just behind the Anderson crew actually getting paid to be here.

"Hey, Skip," Troy starts with the one closest to him.

"Ah, yes, sir, Troy. What do you need?"

"A car," Troy says, pulling him aside.

"Uh, sir. I don't understand. You're on the bus." He says it with a noticeable measure of reverence, like the word *bus* is code for paradise.

"I have to run some errands. I need a car. You got one?"

Troy sees his beady eyes getting all squinty and nervous. His parents' Buick is off limits to anyone else but him. His father had warned him about this. "Son, no one but you is on my insurance." His father's voice runs through this young man's head just before the devil on his other shoulder shouts back at him.

If he let Troy borrow his car, well, then, perhaps he'd be owed a favor. And maybe that would get him a seat onboard the bus. Hell, he'd even settle for the one closest to the bathroom.

"Uh, yeah. I mean, yes, sir. I have a car. It's not mine, but it's uh, here."

"Good enough. Give me the keys." Troy's patience is thin.

He takes the kid by the bony elbow and leads him back through the factory doors and into the parking lot. He feels the kid starting to hesitate, his legs falling behind Troy's quick gait.

"Come on, Skip." His voice is rigid enough to make sure that whatever excuse this kid is about to kick up will bounce right back off.

"Troy, I, uh, I don't know about this. It's my folks' car, and I'm really not supposed to let …"

Troy turns on his heel, putting himself inches away from the young man's face, which grows so red you almost can't see his cystic acne scars anymore.

"Tell me, Skip?" he begins, in a tone that suddenly becomes as endearing as a best friend's. Poor old Skip just melts.

"Yes, sir?" he says, feeling like he is on the precipice of being welcomed in to the most exclusive club known to man.

"You like sausage?"

CHAPTER THIRTY-NINE

Now that Bailey is awake, he goes immediately into search mode for something to eat. Given the few choices we have this morning I figure the remnants of the donut box will suffice.

"Um, mmm, good!" Bailey declares with relish, licking the sticky remains of his day-old donut from his fingers. "Donuts sure are yummy," he tells Beck, who nods and makes him a most generous offer.

"Someday, I'll take you to my favorite donut shop where you can watch the bakers make them from scratch."

"Can we go right now?"

"Not today," I interject before Bailey pushes too far. "Today we are going to do some exploring. I want to show you all the neat things that you can see only on a farm." I know that I have to keep Bailey here for just awhile longer, while Jackson's cousin carries out our covert operation. She assured me over a choppy cell phone connection that she would be in position by noon. We carefully came up with a script—which she insisted was easy to memorize because it was like a recipe—and we hung up. I can only hope she doesn't forget any of the ingredients.

Bailey tells me he has other ideas that don't include barns or fields.

"No thanks, I want to do the donuts instead." His little face registers frustration with me. Beck's invitation is so much more tantalizing than walking through old hay or overgrown grass.

"Not today, Bailey. End of discussion."

"Uh, Momma. You're no fun!"

"Nope. I'm not. No fun at all."

Bailey takes a powdery finger and points it at me, whispering, "You a stupid head."

Even though his back is turned to us, I can hear Beck stifle a laugh.

"Bailey Carmichael, did I just hear you say something to your mother that is entirely inappropriate and unacceptable?" Of course, that's *exactly* what I just heard him say and under normal circumstances I would march him straight to his room for this very fresh outburst. Here, I have nowhere to send him, so I give him an easy out. For both our sakes, I am really hoping he takes it.

Bailey sighs so soundly it seems like he is wobbling under the weight of the world. But when he looks back up at me standing there with my hands on my hips trying to look stern, he shakes his head.

"No, Momma. No, I didn't say anything."

I kneel down and take him gently by the shoulders. I brush back the hair matted to his forehead. Once I get my life back, *if I get my life back*, this child badly needs a bath.

"Come on, snap out of it for me, okay? I need you to be good, and helpful, and not … mean to me. Can you help me out, be my big boy?"

Bailey thinks for a few seconds, shoves his finger back into his mouth, and then touches my nose with it. I scrunch up my face, which makes him laugh. *Thank you, Jesus*, for blessing our children with luxuriously short attention spans.

"Gotcha! You got a donut nose now!"

I straighten back up and grab him under his armpits. I give him what I call a Snuffleupagus kiss. I hold his little body until he is twitching with giggles. Instead of degrading into tantrum territory, we laugh together even though I get the thought that I always do when I throw some Snuffleupagus kisses his way. They would be so much better if there were a dad around to add some whiskers to the mix.

"Stop! Stop! Can't breathe! No more Snuffel-op-o-tiss kisses!"

I pull him around, so I am holding him to me with his legs wrapped around my waist. I whisper into his ear, "I promise we'll have some fun today. This place is special, and I want you to like being here."

Still choking on giggles, Bailey lets go of my neck and pulls himself around. He takes one little hand and puts it on the side of my cheek. "Okay, Momma. I promise I will try to like this place. Because it is special to you, I will make it special to me."

I feel my eyes fill. I don't want him to see my cry, not again. I put him down and watch him run off into the living room and jump onto the couch. Beck follows him. I hear loud conversation broken by regular bursts of Bailey's high-pitched laugh.

There is so much still left unspoken between Beck and me. We put a quick halt to the conversation we had been having just before Bailey woke up. Now that I've chilled back down a few degrees, I suppose I owe him another apology for getting edgy. He shouldn't suffer the brunt of my pent up remorse.

He gives Bailey a notebook and a pen, asking him to draw his favorite animal, and that he'll be right back. Bailey is fascinated with giraffes right now and will happily craft one for Beck that has a neck as long as a tether holding a hot air balloon. We draw giraffes together all the time, although mine usually look more like lopsided mules.

The floor moans as Beck returns to me in the kitchen. In my grandfather's house, there is no stealthy approach. After looking back over his shoulder to make sure Bailey is distracted, he asks me if I'm ready for what this day will bring.

"Are you sure you're comfortable with everything that's about to happen?" he doesn't seem to be holding a grudge.

"No," I begin, shuddering at the thought of someone I don't even know taking a risk on my behalf that could be life-altering. "I'm not comfortable with any of it. I'm just not sure I have a choice."

"It's the *best* choice, Bo. It's the only thing that gets the ball rolling for us to clear you. Give this a shot to work, and then we'll move on to all the police formalities. I told you we can't follow blueprints on this one."

A golden hue surrounds him as he shifts from one foot to the other and the sun builds in from the back. The angelic image is not lost on me, and it makes me smile.

"What?" he asks, moving his hand up to his hair. He tries to smooth down pieces that don't need any help at all. "Are you mocking my look?"

"Not at all. I'm actually admiring you. You look like you've been … bedazzled."

"Yeah, I get that all the time." We smile at each other, but we are so preoccupied with our own thoughts it feels forced. "Look, I know you're worried, and you have every right to be. Please, try to have some faith. Tell me what else is on your mind. Besides the obvious. Obviously." He grins, but his eyes look as tired as mine feel.

"I owe you an apology, Beck," I try, but he holds up a hand and insists that I don't. It's not enough. "No, look, I do. I didn't mean to say something that insulting. I have no idea about your life. I only know that I would be lost right now without you. I probably could have made my way here, gotten through a couple of days with rainwater to drink, but I'd never have come up with a way out of this. I would have crumbled eventually, turned myself in." I hear Bailey yell something about his giraffe almost done, and I swallow hard. "And I probably would have lost my child." The words activate my gag reflex with vile tasting liquid that floods my tonsils.

Beck shakes his head; he tells me softly that everything will work out, and reminds me that I was the crafty one who came up with the plan to use Sabrina.

"I'm not crafty," I say, shaking my head. "I'm not scheming, or devious, or any of that. I don't even know if my cohort will pull this off or fall flat on her face. She sounds like she could be even more unstable that I am." I grimace, thinking back to Jackson's warning that she's nice, but kind of a dip. She confirmed she is both while on the phone with me.

"I don't know what I'll do if this doesn't go right, Beck, I can't even imagine the alternative."

"It will. You have to have some faith. One step at a time." He squeezes my shoulder, not intimately, but sort of like how a football coach would psyche up his wide receiver before a critical play. He heads back to Bailey, telling him to make sure the giraffe has a name. "No favorite animal can go unnamed," I hear him say.

I watch his back as he exits the kitchen, the movement of his hips, and the long strides of his legs that define a man who always knows exactly where he's going. Not married. No kids. I wonder if he has sacrificed everything else in his life to the pursuit of professional success. Does he have regrets of his own? Above all else, Beckett Brady strikes me as the kind of person who is guided by an overwhelming sense of right versus wrong. Much like Peter Brenner. He might take you down when you deserve it, yet he'll be the first one to stand behind you when you need propping up. He's also not one to buy an excuse when the truth would sound so much better if you were brave enough to let it.

Before that night in the bar, I used to walk with purpose myself. I used to be proud of who I was, how I had clawed my way out of a hovel, knowing that I could achieve so much more.

Funny how things can change a person from the inside out.

I walk over to the wall separating the kitchen from the living room and lean against the wooden molding I had helped my grandfather paint. I listen in on a heavy discussion over giraffe names. Beck tells Bailey that his giraffe will be stuck with its name for a very long time, so he'd better think about it for a while. Bailey begins throwing out suggestions that quickly launch him into another spasm of giggles.

"Stanley? No, Jim. No, wait. I got it! I will name him Momma-Beck, after you and Momma!"

I have to step away as a laugh almost blows my cover. I tiptoe over to the other side of the kitchen, fighting back a rush of fear so fierce I grip the sides of the sink with both hands to keep myself upright. My little boy has no idea how quickly everything could change. He could leave this place with a perfect stranger who has come to take him away from me. They will tell him it's for the best, that his mother is no better than her own parents, and society should have learned the first time around that some Carmichaels just aren't genetically coded to be responsible people. Then they will tell him something that will hurt me most of all. They will tell him that his mother has given up on him, she's never coming back, and she doesn't love him anymore. I can almost hear them saying, "Son, your mom is a bad person. She's going away for a long time. I'll bet she never loved you, anyway."

"No!"

It is louder than I intended, and it shoots right through the kitchen and into the living room, where happy conversation suddenly stops, and I hear two sets of legs moving toward me. Then two sets of arms reach for me at the same time.

"Momma, you okay? You scared me. Why are you crying again?"

"Bo, what's wrong? We're right here."

Two sweet faces peer in at me; I don't know which one to look at first.

We're right here.

"I'm so sorry," I begin. "I just, ah, I just bumped into this table here, and, ah, I hurt my hand." I bend down to Bailey's level and pull him tightly into me. "Sorry, Mr. B. I'm just fine. I didn't mean to worry you."

"Silly, Momma," he bursts free and runs over to the table. "Bad table! You shouldn't hurt my Momma." He takes one hand and gives the table a glancing blow. "See how you like it!"

"Yeah, you tell that table, Bailey. You tell it not to hurt Momma ever again." Beck is grinning, but he is looking at me like I'm a soft boiled egg with a cracked shell that's about to spill my guts all over the place.

"Hey, buddy. Can you go draw Momma-Beck a friend? Every giraffe needs a friend, right?"

"Yup! I'll go make a whole family. Maybe two babies so they can play together." Bailey scurries around the table and almost wipes out as his socks lose traction on the wood floor. He catches his balance and disappears around the corner to get back to work on expanding his circle of giraffes.

"I feel like I'm coming unhinged," I blurt out in short puffs. Beck shushes me.

"This is too much for anyone. Even for stubborn people like you." He reaches out to cradle my head. His bicep is like a pillow. "You have been so strong, Bo. For as long as I have known you, which is actually a long time, you have had to be so strong. Why did something like this have to happen to you?" It's just rhetorical, but it feels nice to hear anyway.

The full weight of my head lies along his arm. For two people who are virtual strangers, we've already spent too much time touching. As he strokes my head, I close my eyes and settle into the kind of darkness that feels more sensuous than comfortable. Sparks may be flying, but in this state of lowered defenses and high stress, it's just messed up to feel such erotic pings between us, especially with my son a room away.

I pull back. I can't give into this right now, it's dangerous. He's blurring the edges of my logic, and I'm allowing myself to need him. What if Beck becomes someone else I'll have to push away to protect.

"I don't know who I am around you …"

"Bo," he wraps my name in softness. "I'm here because you're in trouble and it's not your fault. You need my help, but I don't think I could leave now even if I wanted to," his voice becomes longing. "So spare me the mind games and the I-don't-need-you crap and just ... let ... go."

I squirm under his chin, stomach muscles clenched with labored breathing as I reach around his soft t-shirt to find even more hard muscle. His skin is dewy, inviting an almost visceral urge to dissolve into him. My body becomes a live wire ripped from its utility pole, jumpy and agitated, spooked by flashbacks of a young man who was tender with me when no one else was. Even though I was just a kid he happened to stumble upon during a call on some random night, I firmly believe that Detective Brady went to bed that night wondering where I was.

"We will get through this. Anderson will not win, and no one will take Bailey away. I promise you, we'll see the other side of this." There he goes again, with that word.

We.

They are two little letters that when put together have the power to change the world. When you are not alone anymore, fighting a giant that never tires and never backs down, your spirit is renewed by a hope so strong it's like an infusion straight into your veins.

As humans, we are not designed to be alone in this world. I should know. It was one of the first things I learned when I thought I'd be a doctor someday. Biology 101 brought the molecular explanation that each particle, strand of DNA, and proton inside us has a job. My professor told us that doctors should always blend biology with medicine, that one can never exclude the other.

One time, he brought in hundreds of magnets and gathered us around a table set up in the middle of the room. He took his overstuffed bag and emptied out a cascade of tiny silver balls that immediately began to move in every direction, desperate to latch onto another solid mass. He told us to lean in and watch.

"See here," he began, watching the small orbs like a proud parent. "They are entirely separate, yet drawn to each other by a force they can't deny. Our bodies are very much just like this, so are our souls."

At the end of the lesson, when we all needed to disperse to the next class, I hung back to watch the professor pile the balls back into his bag. One by one, with a gentle tug to break the connection, he threw them callously into the dark depths of his satchel. I made a vow to myself to remember the tiny balls when, one day, I would have the unfortunate task of telling a loved one that I couldn't save the sputtering life of a patient whose time had come. I would remember the bionic merger and apply that respect to the person lying lifeless in the bed. I knew that I would be the hand ripping them apart.

I look up, searching the endless blue of Beck's eyes, a million questions bouncing between us.

Why are we here together, against enormous odds and under the most bizarre of circumstances? Will we make it out of here? I think of Jackson, the only man I've ever loved who has released my culpability, forgiven me, but yet disappeared for good from my life.

I am not here with Jackson. I am here with Beck. Is he the connection I've been waiting to make this whole time? Or not?

Have I found the right ball at the bottom of the bag? Are we two biological particles giving in to an organic inertia, or …

… or is he simply a cop trying to crack my hardened exterior? That cold reality check makes me jerk back.

I shut it all down. I force myself to cut power to all these weird feelings swirling around us. I get it, he's good at this. He does this all the time, illuminating a person's doubts, fears, and most sacred secrets like a flashlight in a tunnel. He's an interrogator, for God's sake, mercilessly skillful at peeling back the layers of someone's identity.

I press my finger into my forehead to support the heavy lifting of such a puzzling deconstruction. I'm boxed in and scared shitless, indecently stripped to my deepest feelings. He could go in for the kill right now, take me down to the studs to figure out how my flaws and shortcomings have brought me to the edge of disaster. I wait for it like I always do, the crushing disappointment of realizing I have made yet another tie I will be forced to break because it's for the greater good.

Isn't it? If it is, he won't confirm.

"When did you know you wanted to be a cop?" I ask.

"The day I was born," he boldly answers right back. "Why?"

"Because I think you're really good at it. You have me spinning tighter than a licorice stick, and it's weird," I joke.

His lips pull back. It's so innocently suggestive I'm captivated. "Weird how? Wait, let me guess. You're used to being the smartest one in the room. Am I right?"

"You suck," I chuckle, but he's approaching again, and I'm immediately back on guard. What he says next is like a blast of frosty air on a sticky August night when even a sheet on the bed is too hot to touch.

"Stop fighting me. I know this is bad timing, but there's something going on with us, Bo. All right? I'll say it, it's out there now. I kinda like you, so stop pushing me away because you assume I'm going to criticize or judge you." He gets a tight lock on me again and thrusts me against him to hear him out.

"And you question whether you've done the right thing? Well, don't. Keeping Bailey was right, pure and simple, and you shouldn't have to explain that to anyone. Including me."

He gets it. He totally gets it. I smile. "You're worse than a girl," I chuckle. "You fight dirty, Detective Brady."

"Yeah, I'm not usually so in touch with my feminine side." He lays a soft touch on the tip of my nose. "You're a good mom," the growly whisper makes my pulse leap. "No matter how you got there and the alternative you considered, you're a good mom."

We have not fully discussed *how* I knew what fell out of Mackenzie Mason's handbag. I figured Beck thought I would recognize the prescription because I had studied medicine. Of course, he put two and two together and realized that I recognized the prescription because I had filled it for myself. What he just said is the complete and total truth of my life.

"Thank you."

I feel his hands retract, but as we separate, he slings a retort so unexpected after such a tender moment that I can't duck out of the way. It hits me square on, like a long needle into my muscle.

"Maybe someday you'll stop telling yourself that no one would want you, that's you're all used up, no good. Well, in case you're wondering, you're not as scary as you think you are. In fact, the right person won't be scared at all." He wags a finger at me, looking delicious and dangerous all at once.

"You are all bark, my dear …" he says, moving back toward the living room.

"… and absolutely no bite."

I stare at the swirls of dust on the floor. The front side of my body that had been pressed against Beck feels suddenly chilled, and woefully empty.

CHAPTER FORTY

The car smells like Italian subs, cigarette smoke, and old people. Troy uses his forearm muscles to keep the steering wheel from jerking the wobbly wheels right off the road. He had just hung up with Mac, making sure everything was in place for the presser. He checks his watch, figuring the senator's entourage should be back on 93-south, motoring toward Concord with plenty of time to ensure his speech on job creation hits just as TV stations are going live for their noon broadcasts.

The Governor of New Hampshire has been appropriately accommodating on this trip. By now, Troy felt like they were old friends. He and Anderson had been courting him for a long time. He'd played coy for a while, flirting with them like a cheap date, holding back his endorsement like a stingy kindergarten teacher with only one Hershey Kiss in her pocket. Troy had wondered what the fuck he was waiting for. Anderson was the best ticket in town, the only viable candidate in a sea of political half-asses who was on the right side of issues as sticky as carnival apples.

Troy agreed to allow one or two questions from strategically placed reporters at the presser today. He knew Anderson would handle it just fine; he had become so fluid on stage he was as graceful as a ballerina. As long as he wasn't distracted by perky tits or long flowing hair, Troy could almost guarantee Anderson would give a flawless performance today.

An image of Bo's face pops back into his head. It hadn't left since he'd first watched her staring back at him as she'd bounced down the pitted dirt road leading out of the apple orchard, and then again from under the street lamp.

Stupid girl.

One stupid girl and your entire operation could unravel. He had been hoping his old college friend could tie her up for a while, throw so much shit on her plate she'd gladly hand herself over to the first person who promised to make it stop. He thought she'd be buried in subterranean scandal for so long, Anderson would be at the tail end of his *second term* before she surfaced again, if she ever surfaced at all.

It had been simple enough. After finding the badly outdated cell phone Bo Carmichael left behind in the barn, he'd picked it apart. Finding enough information about her to work with, he put in a phone call to an old fraternity buddy chomping at the bit for the chance to find a higher calling in his life. Spencer Diaz had promised Troy he wouldn't let him down. Once they knew where Bo would be—thanks to a voicemail from her kid's doctor—Diaz said he would take care of the rest. A batch of junk in a plastic baggie was supposed to do the trick. In exchange, Troy promised him a nice spot on the presidential security roster.

So much for that.

She had slipped away before phase two of the operation could kick in. She was supposed to be fully engrossed in trying to keep her son right now, paying for a lawyer she couldn't afford, and keeping herself out of prison. Every minute she spent off his radar screen was a dangerous risk Troy could not allow to continue.

One phone call to one person who would listen to her crazy, delusional story was all it would take to bring them down.

Stupid girl!

Troy had a sudden thought of his mother. He must be tired if he allowed himself to think of her. What would she think of these depraved plans taking shape in his mind right now? Would she understand that he had no choice or would she clutch her crucifix and ask the good Lord for the strength it would take to denounce her own flesh and blood?

Troy knew what he had to do. Even if his mother was watching from her perch high over the clouds, he couldn't give in to regret or worry about repentance. His only savior now was the one who would guarantee him entry through the gilded gates of his earthly Candyland. Even though Anderson was imperfect on so many levels, he was exactly what Troy had made him. He was like an android with pliable tissue that Troy had nipped and tucked to hide the circuit board just below the surface.

He rolled down the window, noticing how it stuck like it was coming down on individual pegs.

Fucking shitbox!

Troy's mood was as black as the clouds racing in from the west. He checked his watch again, thinking that if all timed out as he planned, Anderson should be taking the stage in Concord at about the same time he was teaching the stupid girl a valuable lesson about what happens when you fuck with the wrong people.

CHAPTER FORTY-ONE

"Oh, *snap!*" Sabrina yelled, dropping the wireless mic she was trying to clip to the back of her pencil skirt and inspecting what was left of her right index fingernail.

Her photog looked up from the side of his camera. Greer Hanson was one of the most seasoned camera guys on staff, and couldn't figure out who he'd pissed off to get stuck with Sabrina. Whatever it was, he'd make sure it never happened again.

"Tell me you didn't break it," he said before she had the chance to thrust her mutilated manicure in his face.

"Well, of course I did."

"I don't mean your *nail*. I mean the mic. Tell me you didn't drop it."

"Jeesh, Greer. A little concern would be nice. This nail cost me a lot of money, you know."

"Well, *Sabrina,* a broken mic will cost me even more, *you know!*"

He grabbed the tiny metal box dangling next to Sabrina's hip, checked it for life, and then handed it back. "Let's try this again, shall we?"

Sabrina was already annoyed, and her flawless HD-ready, pancake makeup would soon show evidence of how skittish she felt on the inside. She could feel sweat starting to burst free from her hairline and make squiggly lines down over her temples. She didn't look to either side of her on the thin podium the reporters and photographers were assigned to. She couldn't pretend she was capable of making small talk with the network reporters who covered presidential politics as easily as she whipped out a buttery pie crust. They could take a ninety-minute press conference and convert it into thirty seconds of copy that covered every main point there was. It would take Sabrina all day to do that. She could tell from her periphery that the male reporters were leering at her, while the women were sizing her up and cursing the years and their almost constant overindulgence of coffee and fast food. A couple of them even lowered their eyes behind dark sunglass lenses to joke with each other about the days when they, too, believed that four-inch heels and being a reporter could peacefully coexist.

Sabrina paid them no attention. She even forgot about the jagged point of her typically unsullied fingernail. She was careful to make sure the mic's clip was firmly wrapped around the waistband of her skirt. She pulled the gray sweater over it to hide the cord and told Greer she was all set. He asked for a quick level, so she slowly counted to ten as he gave her the thumbs up around number six.

"All set," he said, meaning her audio was loud and clear.

Fabulous, Sabrina thought. Her personal destruction would not be interrupted by static.

Her reporter credentials hanging on a lanyard around her neck fluttered in the breeze. Sabrina reached for them, not to stop them from moving as much as she needed to give her hands something to do. Nervous energy flowed through her entire body. She thought again of her phone conversation with Jackson's friend. She had insisted that Senator Anderson was a very bad person who was trying to do very bad things. Beyond that, she said the less Sabrina knew about this, the better.

But Sabrina knew enough already. As the reporter from the biggest television station in the state, she would get first dibs at the senator when he opened it up for questions. Jackson's friend asked her if she could handle it. Could she handle the pressure of asking Senator Anderson a very specific, yet extremely embarrassing and career-threatening question?

'Can you do that,' she pressed Sabrina. *'Can you make absolutely certain you will be the reporter assigned to this press conference? Can you handle it once you're standing there with a camera rolling? I need you to be one hundred percent sure...'*

Sabrina had been honest. She explained that her boss would prefer to send the janitor to this event rather than her, but she would try. She never figured she'd actually get the nod. Jackson's friend had told her this could change her life, and before they hung up for the last time, she said she had complete faith in her.

Sabrina flinched as she drew her broken nail over her forehead, temporarily forgetting its talon status. She would have checked her makeup if she thought she could hold her compact steady, but her hands were shaking so badly she didn't want to risk it.

She had one job to do. She had one question to ask. She had burned the words she would say into her memory, spoken them only to herself so no one else had a clue that she was about to ignite the flames of what would become a funeral pyre.

Senator Declan Anderson's funeral pyre.

CHAPTER FORTY-TWO

I stand there on my grandfather's old floor, transfixed by feelings I didn't expect to have, elicited by a man I really don't know. Every emotion I have tried to suppress resurrected with the force of a stampeding water buffalo.

He's right about it all. I have systematically pushed away every person who has ever cared for me. Jackson, because I convinced myself I didn't deserve him. Peter Brenner, because I have to protect him from harm. I have made it a personal duty to ensure no one would ever hurt the people I love again.

But that someone may be me.

Dear God, I have done everything wrong! I am an idiot! Beck is right. My first inclination in life is to tackle everything head on with enough unyielding will to think I can handle it all on my own.

I sent Jackson away without giving him the chance to tell me he wanted to stay. I never gave *us* a chance to make the best of a crappy situation. I just assumed I was doing the right thing. Now I realize I may have done the exact opposite. If only I had been honest with Jackson. If only I had explained to him what had happened that night, maybe he would have stayed because it was *his choice* to stay. Maybe he would have forgiven me, folded me into his arms, and cried with me at the loss of our hopes and dreams. Maybe then, he would have welcomed this child into his life—loving him, loving me—because in his heart, we were his.

We will never be his. If I keep this up, we will never be anybody's.

I have to get out of here. I interrupt the giraffe drawing and tell Bailey to get his shoes on.

"I'm going to take Bailey up to the barn. Show him around a little. You can come if you want. Or, you can stay here …" I can't look at him. I can't look into his eyes.

"How about I give you some time with your son."

Just the way he phrases that pushes us apart.

I nod. "Okay, then. We'll be out back."

I can hear birds chirping, and wind blowing through crispy leaves, and my own footsteps falling on the patches of browning grass leading to the tall doors of my grandfather's barn. Otherwise, I am numb. My hand holds Bailey's, and even though I know it is there, I barely feel it. His chatter sounds like it is coming from the other side of a deep, dark tunnel. I feel broken.

"… right Momma?"

"Huh," I manage to mumble back, I don't know what he just asked me.

"This is where the horsies would live, right? And the piggies over there. And the kangaroos over there?" He is pointing to different sections of the barn, already filling it up with all the animals he sees in picture books at home.

"Yes on the horses and the pigs, but no for the kangaroos. They don't live on a farm, and it's too cold for them in New Hampshire. They live somewhere far away where the weather stays warm."

"Can we go see them someday? Can we go where it's always warm?"

"Sure, honey." I sound as deflated as a bounce house that's been stabbed with metal cleats. Bailey notices.

"What's a'matter now, Momma? Why are you sad again?"

I don't know how to answer that. I should explain some of what is going on right now. Maybe Bailey deserves to know the truth.

"Well, Bailey. I guess there's a lot happening right now and some of it is making me sad."

"Are you sad because you miss Peter? Or are you sad because you miss your grandpa?"

"All of the above. I guess all of that makes me a little sad. But you know what? Being here with you makes me very, very happy."

We are on the threshold of the barn door. I hoist Bailey up on one side of the step, while I take the other to balance us out. I wrap my hand around the black iron handle, take a deep breath in anticipation of the musty rush of air, and I push the door in. A flood of memories almost steals that breath away as I wait to hear my grandfather talking to his animals in low, hushed tones. Instead, there is silence. My grandfather is gone, his beloved animals are gone, but my son is right by my side. I have brought the newest Carmichael to claim his rightful place on the land he was born to stand on.

"Welcome home, Bailey." I force a whisper through a throat parched by emotion.

Echo Valley

Jennifer Vaughn

The light streams in through the door, making the long strands of cobwebs appear like strings of spun gold. I step in, though Bailey leaps ahead of me. He is wide-eyed, doing a slow circle to take in all the fascinating sights. I lean against the side of the door, running my palm over the worn paint on the wall where Feathers, my favorite horse, would lean her flank in an effort to get that irksome itch that her long wispy tail couldn't reach. I watch Bailey touching the iron bars that separate each stall. He steps into the one, laughing at the plume of dust that releases from the old sawdust on the floor.

"Who lived in here, Momma?"

"Feathers did. She was a beautiful chestnut mare."

"What that mean? She a chess-it nare?"

"No, buddy. A chestnut mare. It means she was mostly brown," I tell him, taking my hand to point to my nose. "But she had a white streak right down here, on the end of her nose."

"Oh, wow. Was she your friend?"

"Yes, Feathers was my favorite of all my grandfather's horses. I used to ride her through the woods back here."

My grandfather's knees wouldn't let him climb up into the saddle in his later years, so he would make me report back to him all the things I saw during my four-legged journeys through his sprawling backyard. As he sipped his coffee on the back porch, he would close his eyes and let his imagination carry him out of his rocking chair and on to the stiff, bony back of Feathers as we whipped through the meadow at full canter. I would tell him about the lupines that were so purple they almost matched the mountains slicing through the distant skyline. I would tell him about the northern hawk owl doing slow circles in the sky above us, watching us glide across the tall grass and the groundhog family that took up residence near the back fence. I would tell him the loons on the lake were calling for him, hollering out as we sped by. I can almost hear him.

"The loons will always welcome you home, Bo. No matter where you wind up in this big, ole world, the echo of the creatures here in the valley will always welcome you home again."

And now, under the most unexpected of circumstances, I am home.

Bailey hustles out of the stall and turns a corner to the main aisle where we used to milk the cows or exercise the horses when the snow got too high in the pasture to let them run free. His voice rebounds across the slanted wooden roof, alive with the awe of discovery.

"Momma, Momma, come check this out!" he yells over to me. I walk across the stone floor and up the small incline to where Bailey is running joyfully from one end to the other of the long pathway. "We got wires, and ropes, and buckets, and piles of brown grass."

"Hay. Those are hay bales. The animals used to eat that for dinner."

"Ewww, I don't want hay for dinner."

"Really? 'Cause I was thinking that's *exactly* what we'll have for dinner tonight." I start moving toward him, my arms outstretched and my fingers pulsing in and out in tickle motion.

He is running away from me, his short legs working double time to build distance between us so I can't catch him. Suddenly, he stops dead in his tracks and breaks out in the biggest ear-splitting grin I have ever seen.

"Peter!" he bellows so loudly my ears get a sharp pinch.

"Huh? Honey, no. We'll see Peter very soon, I promise—"

Bailey runs at me, then right past me, so fast he's almost a blur. "No, Momma. Peter's here!"

I whip my head around, half falling as I lose my balance. My eyes try to blink away what I can't believe I'm seeing.

Peter Brenner is on his knees, pulling Bailey into a giant hug.

Beck is standing right beside him.

CHAPTER FORTY-THREE

There are times when a photographic memory comes in handy, Troy thought. Like, right now, when he didn't need his notes to remember the path his cell's GPS had laid out to get him to the northern farm Bo Carmichael would take refuge at. Troy was betting it all that what Diaz had uncovered on a post-it note would lead him straight to her. He looked out at the empty highway and barren woods. What better place to lie low than this? There was nothing here. The isolation was perfect, ensuring that his nagging problem would be solved without a single witness for miles.

Who would have thought that a state populated by more wildlife than people would produce one nitwit woman who could unravel his meticulously prepared future? Troy had worried about a few of the skirts Anderson had taken up with, but never like this. This hairdresser was more like the plaid shirt guy at the factory—a total wild card who had seen a glimpse of who Anderson truly was.

Troy knew she had a kid. He had tried to be delicate about that. Clearly, his efforts had been rebuffed. That didn't feel good but nothing really did anymore. Troy promised himself that once he was standing just behind President Declan Anderson as he firmly laid his hand on the Bible to take the oath of office, he would think only of how his journey had ended and not the sacrifices made along the way.

The driver of the car on his left was staring at him.

Fuck you! Troy threw him a vicious glare but realized his new habit of thinking out loud probably looked very odd with no one else in the car. He slowed just a little to let the driver put some space between them. His undiagnosed ADD quickly looped him back to Bo and her kid. He felt his lips moving on mumbles again. A quick look in the rearview mirror showed no one around. He allowed his voice to rise, applying the skewed logic he lived by these days to inoculate himself against every human directive he had every learned.

It's not like anyone would miss them, he justified. This woman has lead a pathetic existence and Troy had no sympathy for people who fucked themselves by making poor choices. He had learned that Bo had been a smart girl who could have had a bright future. Instead, she turned tramp, barely a blip on the screen of life. Her kid would have probably ended up just like her. Yeah, two losers that no one needs or cares about. He allowed himself to believe that squashing this family wouldn't amount to much in the loss column.

Troy had become masterful at ignoring the one loose connection he still had to the part of himself that had once been a kind and decent human being. Every situation had a marketable opportunity. Either you seize it, or you allow it to seize you.

Given that Troy no longer allowed any gray area in his life, it was easy. Only his shrink would remind him of how dangerously simple it was to let that opportunity contaminate your principles.

The putrid air in the borrowed car was starting to give him a headache. Troy was thankful to see that he was only two exits away from the dirt road that would lead him to Bo. He knew her grandfather's farm was deserted. He knew there wasn't a neighbor around for miles. He also knew that not even the most supercharged battery on the most superior of cell phones would be able to hold a signal long enough for her to call for help. Bo Carmichael and her kid were all alone. No one would be coming to save her.

And, Troy hoped, no one would find her once he left.

Not for a very, very long time.

Ready to seize the opportunity, Troy drove on, mumbling to himself.

CHAPTER FORTY-FOUR

"Sabrina, stand by. You're thirty away," the producer's voice shot through Sabrina's head. She stood still on legs that feel like wood putty, thirty seconds from her live shot for the noon newscast. She will have roughly forty-five seconds to tell viewers where she is, and what Senator Declan Anderson plans to discuss during his press conference. She must also remind viewers to stay tuned, that once the candidate takes the stage, they will carry his remarks live. She wonders how she'll remember any of that because the only thing she can think is how she'd give her right arm and her cherished collection of Calphalon nonstick bakeware to not be here right now. She tries to find some saliva to moisten her mouth before her voice comes off sounding as flimsy and limp as the paper dolls she used to fashion wardrobes for in fifth grade.

Please, God, she says to herself. *I promise I will stop asking you to remove the cellulite I spotted on my ass last week. I'll even stop praying for a way to make butter a member of a food group. I'll even try to help out more. Like, for poor people, or women who think it's okay to mix plaid with stripes. I'll do anything, God. Just please let me not mess this up. Let me help Jackson's friend. Amen.*

"Sabrina, you're up. Go!"

Greer's finger points at her, a signal that she's up live on the air. She hits all the points she needs to, and even manages a tight smile as she nails her cue as precisely as a bowling ball slamming all the pins down. *She did it!*

"You're clear," the producer tells her. "We'll see you again for the presser. Nice job."

Sabrina pulls her earpiece out and sits down on the edge of the platform. She breathes in through her nose, exhales through her mouth. Whew! She got through the first part of her assignment, too bad the first part is also the easiest part.

After a few minutes, she hears the crowd start to shuffle back and forth with increasing anticipation. The reporters around her also jump to attention.

"He's here," they are saying, nudging their cameramen to make sure they are ready to roll.

Sabrina stands up, clamping her jaw shut because she can feel her teeth starting to chatter. She holds one hand out straight, trying to gauge how badly her nerves are firing. It is shaking so ferociously she quickly tucks it away behind her back.

Through the glaring noontime sun, Sabrina waits for the senator to step up the four steps it will take him to mount the stage. A beautiful dark-haired woman is the first to appear. She is holding a thick clipboard on the crook of her elbow, and talking into a cell phone at the same time. She looks behind her, nods, and the crowd goes wild as they catch a glance of the man who is handsome enough to make a grown woman cry, smart enough to fit in with the intellectual elite, yet folksy enough to remind the minimum wage earner that he still puts his pants on one leg at a time.

Just behind Declan Anderson is the governor. They make their way to the center of the stage, leaning over to clasp outstretched hands, waving to the poor slobs stuck in the back. The dark-haired girl doesn't follow. She remains near the stairs. The governor approaches the microphone and welcomes the crowd by making a few obligatory statements. Sabrina thrusts her earpiece back in, turning toward Greer and the lens of the camera, waiting for her producer to bring her back on for live coverage.

"Stand by. When the gov wraps, we'll go to you. Just set the scene and toss to Anderson. We'll take the whole thing live, and be ready to get the first question."

Sabrina nods. She's ready. This is it. As the governor throws an arm over his new best friend, the crowd roars. Greer's fingers next to his camera go from three, down to two, one, and then he points at her. She's live.

"And welcome back to the statehouse. I'm Sabrina Pressley with live coverage of Senator Declan Anderson's press conference. A huge crowd has assembled to hear his remarks on what we expect will cover the economy and, if elected, what his administration will do to create new jobs. The governor is just about to introduce Senator Anderson, let's listen in …"

Sabrina holds her face still as Greer pans the camera off beyond her shoulder, zooming in to the stage as the sound boosts to pick up Anderson's handheld microphone. She can see the dark-haired girl nodding at Anderson, smiling in a way that reminds Sabrina of the weird special report she had done the year before. The story was about a young girl who had been kidnapped by her babysitter and then forced to live with her in squalid conditions. Because the babysitter would occasionally throw some bologna at the girl, she began to associate her with food, and the good feeling of having a full stomach. Many months later, the child was found, but didn't want to go home. She had fallen into a distorted state of affection, thinking the babysitter was actually the one who had kept her safe and fed. Psychologists had explained to Sabrina that this bizarre paradoxical mix-up in the brain makes hostages feel adulation for their captors. Irrational, of course, given the gravity of what the hostages had endured, but present in their poor, abused minds nonetheless.

This beautiful yet forlorn woman watching Anderson from under a veil of dark hair had the same doughy expression on her face as that kidnapped child did as she faced her babysitter in court. Even though she was forced to reacclimatize herself back into a normal family, she likely longed for the days of moldy bologna and cheese.

"Could it be?" Sabrina thought aloud, getting a sharp response from the producer listening to her from the booth back at the station. Sabrina forgot her mic was still hot.

"Sorry ..." she whispered.

"Okay, but don't forget that you must get the first question, Sabrina. Alex *expects* us to have the first question."

Sabrina rolled her eyes, thinking how pathetic it was that Alex seemed to measure his manhood by his reporters' ability to snag the first question at any press conference carried live by multiple news outlets. Usually, she would give that only a half-assed effort. Today, however, she needed to be first for her own reasons.

She listened to the handsome man work the crowd, silently mouthing the words she had committed to memory because they were way too explosive to write down on paper. Jackson's friend had dictated exactly what she needed to say. Sabrina didn't ask about who was on the other side of this salacious scandal, and she almost didn't want to know. She said it was for Sabrina's own good that she didn't know. That way, when the shadow of doubt was planted, Sabrina could truthfully say that what she had been told was simply speculation from a credible source. Let Anderson have to do the bulk of the explaining. Looking at the dark-haired woman, Sabrina had an inkling that once the story broke, she'd figure it out on her own.

Anderson is pacing the stage, exuberantly reaching out to grasp knuckles raised before him. Sabrina has seen the act a zillion times before from these political types. They kiss cheeks, accept hugs from perfect strangers, pose for pictures, and mumble assurances that they understand exactly what it feels like to have four kids and no job, or a foreclosure notice arriving in the mailbox. Then they crawl into their air-conditioned SUVs with tinted windows while their personal driver hands them a tube of anti-bacterial hand sanitizer to wash off the grime the commoners left behind.

This one, though, seems worse than the rest. Disgusting in fact, Sabrina thought, as she pushed away the twinge of guilt over what she was about to do. Jackson's friend had told her not to give that a moment's worry, that when it all came out, she would be very proud of herself for doing the right thing. She told Sabrina that this press conference could be her legacy.

Sabrina rocked back on the narrow points of her skinny metal heels. She brushed back stray hairs that were tickling her eyes and took a deep breath until her lungs felt like they would burst. Since she had already spoken to God once today, she thought of her other life mentor. She figured that sending a mental message to Martha Stewart couldn't hurt, so as Declan Anderson approached the end of his impassioned address, Sabrina channeled Martha for strength and courage. After all, if a woman who was used to five-hundred-thread count sheets every night could survive on prison-issued bedding for five whole months, then Sabrina could certainly get through this.

She inched the pointed toe of her shoe closer to the edge of the reporter platform, leaning over to get the attention of Declan Anderson. She even pushed her chest out a little further to make herself more noticeable to the candidate who appeared to have a destructive liking of such things. She thought of Martha's message to her this morning. She willed herself to do something different and grand. As Anderson opened the floor to questions, she raised her arm so high she had a fleeting hope that for the sake of the reporter standing just below her, her deodorant is keeping up with her sweat glands.

She yells out as loudly as she can, "Senator Anderson, over here. Senator, Senator!"

Greer is rolling on the camera just behind her, her producer is waiting on the other side of her earpiece, and Alex is probably watching between fingers clasped over his eyes, waiting to see who Anderson will point to for the first reporter question.

Please, please, please. Let it be me, Sabrina thought. For God's sake, please let it be me!

Sabrina stretches further, pushing her sweater-clad perky chest out one ... more ... inch. *Please, you schmucky dog, look over here!*

"Ah, yes. You there, with the gray sweater. First question. Go ahead."

Declan Anderson flashes an easy smile at Sabrina, arrogantly waiting for the brain dead blonde reporter to choke out a softball question that he could knock right out of the park.

Sabrina recognizes that condescending smirk on his face. *Asshole*, she thinks, as she plants her feet firmly and rises to her full height, pulling back the boobs she had just used as fiercely as a warrior out on the battlefield.

She clenches her fist and prepares to fire him a fastball that will feel like his balls just got singed.

CHAPTER FORTY-FIVE

Bailey's face is bright red once it finally pulls out of the tight lock of Peter's arms. He is so excited he is doing bunny hops around Peter's waist.

I head straight for the arms that just let my son go, feeling both shock and elation to see him standing there next to Beck. He folds me into him and I breathe in all the smells that a girl usually associates with her dad.

"I can't believe you found us. I don't know where to begin, but I'm so sorry. I know you've probably been worried sick."

"I'm just so glad you're safe. I know more about all this than you think I know. But we need to talk. We need to make some plans, and I suppose you have some questions." He motions with his chin over to Beck, who is smiling sheepishly.

"Uh, yeah, just a few." I say, thinking how cleverly Beck had avoided having this discussion until he was good and ready. Peter swings Bailey back onto his hip.

"I see you've gotten to know my friend," he says, ruffling his hair. "He's a totally awesome police officer who I have known for a very long time."

"Yup, me and Beck are good friends now," Bailey confirms.

"Bo," Peter looks around for me.

"Right here," I tell him.

"I want you to know this man has been instrumental in helping me get to you. He never doubted you."

I nod, agreeing that without this detective on my side, I'd be as overdone as burnt toast. But how can this be? How can this detective and my self-appointed Fairy Godfather be standing here, in my grandfather's barn, acting like a long lost crime fighting duo who have just reconnected on my behalf?

Wonder Twin powers, activate!

Beck is standing with his hands on his hips, watching Peter and Bailey's reunion with a soft smile. He casts his eyes toward me, his expression telling me that he knows I'm trying to make sense of all of this.

"Peter was my very first boss. He taught me everything I know about being a good cop. He made me promise I wouldn't tell you about us until he got here. Once we were here, and you and Bailey were safe, I told him to give me some time with you to figure things out. He stayed away last night because he knew you'd be worried about him. But let me assure you, he is the finest officer I have ever known, not to mention indestructible, and I could only keep him away for so long. He insisted on being here."

I look into eyes that are as clear and blue as a cloudless sky. I get a vision of a young detective, eager to learn, so smart and determined. Peter must have seen that, too. It makes me swallow hard. Detective Brady learned from the best how to do his job with heart. But heart only gets you so far, and I'm not home free yet. Someone is still chasing me.

"If you found me, then I guess this place isn't entirely off the map, huh?" Peter nods at me.

"We need to keep that in mind, yes."

I gaze worriedly at Peter's craggy, yet loving face. Despite Beck's assurances, I feel such anguish for putting him in jeopardy; it's exactly what I wanted to avoid by not telling him about Anderson and his goon. I tug on Peter's elbow to make him put Bailey down so I can pull him away. He is on to me.

"Don't you start," he warns, his palm rising.

"Peter, no. Listen to me. This isn't safe for you. You're supposed to be swinging in your hammock right now, sipping an ice tea, and hauling your snowblower out of storage. You're retired! You shouldn't be here, risking everything you worked so hard--"

The hand is now full up.

"Bo Carmichael, let's get one thing straight, here. You and Bailey are in trouble. Far as I'm concerned, it's my trouble, too. Got it?"

I swallow what feels like a brick with rough edges. I give in and head straight for the inside of his arms again. I whisper something that is a mixture of *thank you* and *thank God for you*, and Peter gently pulls my dirty hair off my sweaty face. I have heard stories from daughters who claim a father's embrace holds mystical powers. It can melt away all the troubles of the world. It can thread back together all the pieces of a broken heart. It can even lure a smile out from behind a wall of hurt.

Feeling Peter Brenner wrap his thick arms around me makes me grateful that he is here, and for bringing all his mystical powers with him.

CHAPTER FORTY-SIX

Mackenzie Mason backs down one step on the narrow staircase next to the stage. She texts Troy that Anderson hit all his bullet points and was just about to take his first reporter question. She had instructed Anderson to look for the young blonde reporter who would be representing the state's largest television station. Troy had taught her that media relations in the early voting states were crucial. She had personally spoken to the station's news director several times, requesting live coverage for the presser, and lead story packages in the evening newscasts. In exchange, Anderson was to give the station's reporter the first question. A win-win all around.

How odd, she thought, as she waited for a return text from Troy that was already late in arriving. She knew he had some errands to run that he said were of a personal nature, but Troy always returned her texts. She wondered where he had gone. She leaned against the scaffolding of the stage, pulling one foot out of her pump and pressing it against the cool ground. Her legs were killing her. *Everything* was killing her. She hadn't felt like eating in weeks, her head throbbed like it was stuck in a vise, and her fashionably snug fitting suits felt tight and itchy against her swollen chest. She had been horrified this morning when the top button on her blazer seemed an ocean liner's length away from the hole it fit seamlessly into just last week.

She couldn't wait to get out of New Hampshire. So much had gone wrong here. Once she could get away from this campaign, get away from Declan, she could take a breath and figure out what to do with the rest of her life. She had some serious decisions to make and escaping this all-male judge and jury that had already tried to seal her fate was exactly what she needed. Mackenzie knew there would be hell to pay for not following through with instructions, but it was a risk she was willing to take.

She had been born the daughter of a staunchly Catholic couple. She had sat in a pew and recited the Psalms her entire life. She simply could not disconnect from the belief deep inside her that what she was being told to do went against the will of God. Her soul would be damned for all eternity. Her family would suffer great shame. For a thoroughly modern, high-achieving woman who had already broken more commandments than she could count; this one act was weighing heavily on her heart.

Troy had promised her a whirlwind of a journey. He said all she needed to do was work hard, be smart and dedicated, and shiny rewards would await her. She had done all of that and more. She had sacrificed what would have been a solid career on the Hill, blown off friends and family members, and become a walking zombie fueled by stale Ritz crackers and lukewarm coffee. She had given everything she had, and then she had dug deeper and found some leftovers to hand over, too. She promised herself she would try to stay true to who she was. She had failed miserably.

Mackenzie was no pretty-faced pushover. She had had long-term boyfriends and short-term lovers, and had discarded all of them as easily as she threw out the Sunday newspaper. She had been courted and adored by suitors who were rich, powerful, successful, young and old. None of them meant more to her than a few months of fun.

Until Declan Anderson came along and changed everything.

She knew he was a letch. She had booked plane tickets or hotel rooms for women she grew to loathe and despise. Women she started to feel a certain jealousy toward. Before she could stop herself, she was indulging in late night strategy sessions far past her usual bedtime and long after Troy and the other staffers had called it a day. She sipped room temperature Pinot, laughed at stupid jokes, and played the giddy tease until one night a gentle brush of elbows became a soft kiss on the cheek and whispered confessions of desire that was becoming too strong to ignore. Soon, Mackenzie was booking one less hotel room.

What was so wrong, really? She was bunking with the man she was falling in love with. He told her he was falling in love with her, too. He cried on her shoulder that his marriage was falling apart, his wife was a shrew, and he would get out. Just, not now. He needed to keep his family intact until the election was over. He asked Mackenzie to be patient, plying her with good sex, and sickly sweet promises.

"Can you do that for me, darlin'? Can you keep our love a little secret for just a while longer? I promise I'll make an honest woman out of you. I promise … I promise…"

Bullshit!

It had all been a lie. In fact, even her current predicament had been an accident caused by an overload of stress and exhaustion. Mackenzie had been away from home for so long she had forgotten to renew the prescription for her birth control pills. One day, she woke up feeling like her stomach was churning through raw sewage. As she raced out of the king-sized hotel bed still occupied by the sleeping senator, she barely turned the corner of the small bathroom in time to deposit her insides in the toilet. The sounds of her retching met with harsh, cold words hollered in from the other room, "For Christ's sake, Mac! Shut the fucking door. You're disgusting."

He had rolled over and gone back to sleep. Mackenzie had thrown up for an hour straight. And then, the next morning she was heaving all over again. And the morning after that, too. Eventually, it became clear that her problem was far worse than a bad batch of Chinese food or the Norwalk virus she'd picked up during a campaign stop at the nursing home.

She had allowed herself to be happy. She knew this might complicate things, but theirs would be a child born from love. She thought that once she told Declan about the baby he would hold her tight against him and tell her how thrilled he was. How they would have the best baby in the entire world, and together they could make it all work out.

Not so much. Mackenzie became the enemy. Her child became an unwanted aggravation, an image risk, an unforgivable mistake.

As the crowd roared for Senator Anderson, Mackenzie placed a flat palm against the lower half of her abdomen. She had started having conversations with her fetus, talking to it like a trusted friend who knew all her secrets. She promised it a good life, even if that meant she would raise it all on her own.

Mackenzie was leaving. She was prepared to say goodbye to Declan Anderson and Troy Olander and every other member of this wildly dysfunctional family. She thought about going home to the small Midwestern town her parents still lived in, volunteering at the free clinic once a week, and the food pantry two Mondays a month. She thought that might be the best place for her right now, given that she was about to become a rotund pregnant woman with no job, no baby-daddy, and a secret the size of Air Force One.

She twisted her foot back into her shoe to climb up the stairs and wait just beside the stage to escort Declan off after a sufficient number of reporter questions had been fielded. She checked her phone one final time for a text from Troy. Nothing. She found a spot next to the governor and first lady, and waited for the blonde reporter on the platform to holler out her question.

Once she heard what that question was, Mackenzie's sensitive stomach heaved and she promptly threw up before New Hampshire's most powerful couple could get out of the way. A dozen television cameras rolled as old coffee, half-chewed Tums, and partially digested stale Ritz crackers splattered like glue against carefully ironed dress pants and nude pantyhose.

Oh my God! What the hell was happening?

CHAPTER FORTY-SEVEN

We are sitting out in front of the barn on old Adirondack chairs my grandfather and I made many summers ago, trying to figure out where we can find a working television set to catch the noon newscast. Peter and Beck have been explaining to me everything they've been able to piece together about this thoroughly shameful effort to lock me away and misplace the key. I'm supplying further details of my own. I'm also starting to strongly dislike someone named Spencer Diaz.

Bailey is playing in the dirt, making a muddy chocolate cream pie with pinecones on top. He yells over to us whenever he finds a new ingredient to throw on top. So far, we have a few rocks, several broken twigs, and one dead horsefly.

I ask them if someone found my cell phone in the barn. I tried to call it that first day to see if anyone answered, but it was dead. At least that would explain how everyone seemed to know when the party would start.

"Don't know who has the phone, but Diaz was the one who knew about Bailey's appointment. He was also the officer who alerted DCYF to alleged drug activity in your apartment. He says the information was reported by concerned neighbors," Beck tells me.

"Yeah, hardly. I don't have any of those," I say wryly, thinking of the level of society that's represented in my apartment building.

"He's lying about that, but it was enough of an imminent danger report to get DCYF on your case. Bailey would have been seized and placed in state custody. Who knows what else they would have 'found' inside your apartment." Beck hooks his fingers into air quotes. It makes me shudder to think that another of those handy-dandy baggies would have miraculously appeared from underneath my couch, right there alongside Bailey's Bob The Builder front loader and old gum wrappers. If Beck hadn't warned me …

I turn to Peter. "He told me not to go home, Peter. He believed in me even while his buddies were selling me down the river. If he hadn't come to me beforehand I would have walked right into that."

"There aren't as many bad guys in this as you think," Beck explains. "Peter and I are pretty sure there are only a few. Those other officers were only following protocol. Your report did make you look like a real perp. A bad one at that."

I lean in over my knees and wrap my arms around the bony tops. We get back to our wickedly creative plot to air Anderson's dirty laundry, literally. Peter asked how I knew a television reporter willing to help, and I explain that she's the cousin of an old friend. I plead with my eyes for Peter not to push me further about *which* old friend, and he doesn't. I ask him what he managed to find out at the orchard, because I can't think of anything that would be left behind in the way of investigative tools.

"Well, after Mr. Bloomfield filled me in on what happened inside the barn," Peter begins, "Beck and I were able to put a few more things together. We still need to figure out who, under Anderson, has been running this sideshow. A person with as much to lose as a guy running for president won't be willing to get his hands dirty. Anderson is obviously aware that they need to deal with you, insisting on it even, but he's probably not in on the how. That way, when fists fly he is nowhere near the blood splatters." Peter finds a long sliver of wood on the side of his chair and pulls it out carefully until it is several inches long. "Bailey, look what I got. It's a piece of licorice you can put on your pie," he says, handing over the imaginary treat. Bailey pretends to take a bite and then plops it sideways over the mushy fly.

"Yummy! Peter, you get the first piece."

"I'd better," he says, but I notice his jaw tense up and his hands grip the sides of the chair. He looks poised to strike. Like a cobra. But strike, at what?

Suddenly, I hear a deep voice growling at us from behind. I get up from the chair so quickly it topples over behind me. Bailey screams. I follow the voice, turning around to find the tan man staring back at me from behind the barrel of a small, black gun.

"This just keeps getting better!" he expels at us with a ghastly pout. His eyes are wild, a sweaty sheen over his face that makes his dark skin look sick with fever. This is not the controlled, commanding political operative I first saw in the barn. Oh no, he's totally gone off the reservation. Way off. He's deranged!

The gun in his hand isn't nearly as scary as the sinking realization that this guy has clearly lost it.

"I can't catch a fucking break here, Bo! You had to call in the cavalry, huh? I should have taken you out in the parking lot while I had the chance."

Bailey scurries over to us, a flurry of arms and legs that frantically carry him away from the frightening man and directly into the middle of his mud pie. It oozes out in every direction.

"Momma, he scary!" he shrieks, barreling into me. "And he said the 'f' word," he squeaks out between terrified sniffles. I tuck him behind me thinking that right now the 'f' word is the least of my concerns.

CHAPTER FORTY-EIGHT

"*Excuse me, young lady?*" the senator warbles, as the crowd searches the risers to find the reporter who just threw a bucket full of icy cold water on their red-hot superstar.

"I was asking you, Senator Anderson, if you have any comment about reports that your staffer is pregnant, you're the father, and you're demanding she gets an abortion."

The crowd groans, the reporters on each side of her are dumbfounded, open-mouthed and silent, but the producer in Sabrina's ear is screaming, "What the fuck are you doing, Sabrina? Jesus Christ … cut audio, cut audio!" Sabrina plucks out her earpiece, letting the producer's screechy voice fade out.

Senator Declan Anderson looks green, but not nearly as green as the sleek-haired beauty Sabrina first noticed on the steps of the stage. The poor girl has just barfed all over the governor and his wife! She is bent over at the waist dry heaving. Sabrina sucks in her breath, thinking to herself, "*Holy hotcakes, she IS the one! This puke girl is the pregnant staffer!*"

Even though Jackson's friend isn't expecting any more from her than what she just delivered, Sabrina can't resist what tumbles out of her mouth next. And since no one has yet recovered from the shock of her first question, you could have heard a pin drop when Sabrina shouts out her equally searing follow-up.

"Senator, your staffer seems to have, uh, vomited. Is that because she has morning sickness, sir? Is she sick because she is pregnant? With your baby, sir?"

Back at the station, Alex is handed a paper bag. He hyperventilates into it until enough oxygen returns to his frenzied brain to settle his nervous system. He begins to think the most ditzy, ridiculously overblown caricature of a reporter he has ever hired, is about to have the last laugh.

He instructs his crew in the booth to stay on the shot. He makes a quick call to master control to extend live coverage through the stupid soap opera about to run. He hears the newsroom phones ringing off the hook. His general manager is coming toward him with both arms outstretched, a look of pure horror on his face.

"What the fuck did she just do to us?" he shrieks at Alex.

Alex chuckles, taking one more quick breath of the expended air inside the paper bag.

"I'll tell you exactly what she just did. Sabrina Pressley just made us the most important television station in the entire world."

The general manager snaps his head back like he just got smacked in the face. He starts to see what Alex sees: The video that will go viral, the station's call letters prominently featured every goddamned time someone clicks on the link, the requests for interviews, the advertising dollars that will follow. Every single time the public dismantling of Declan Anderson is viewed it will be *his station* that gets the credit for it.

"Huh," he mumbles, stroking the gray stubble on his chin and feeling like he just found a winning lottery ticket in the laundry.

"Maybe you're right."

"I'm right, all right," Alex says back. As he watches Sabrina Pressley in the monitor on the wall, he breaks out into a wide grin. He feels almost like a father sending his kid off to college on a full scholarship. He *made* this girl, for shit sake! He would earn his reputation back. He would be the most widely respected news director in the entire fucking industry.

He winks at the general manager who, just a couple seconds ago, would have happily drained out his body's entire volume of blood and tells him, "You can thank me later."

CHAPTER FORTY-NINE

Everything starts to move in fast forward. My grip on Bailey breaks as I feel him tugged from behind me. I turn to see where he went, but he has disappeared behind Peter. Beck takes my arm and roughly forces me behind him. I don't like that. I try to step back to the front of the pack, because I am the one the tan man really wants. Beck's arm is like a metal bar; it won't let me pass. Cop crisis training kicks in, they assume positions in front of Bailey and me while trying to lean on the perpetrator to stand down.

The tan man barks back, but in his frenzied mind, I'm the real mark here. His fixation to protect Anderson feeding a psychosis he associates with me, the barn and the unthinkable possibility that I'll spill the beans.

He can't lose! He sees Anderson—flawed as he may be—as his responsibility, his mission, his purpose.

"I wasn't going to …" I start to sputter, to diffuse, but fierce male voices shush me.

"Quiet Bo!" they snap, but just hearing my voice makes the tan man wince.

"You are stupid *and* selfish! Why did you bring them here? Too many fucking people! *Jesus Christ, you are ruining everything!*" The tan man wipes away sweat with his sleeve, his trigger finger getting a little shaky.

I can't let him do this. I have to stop him.

"I know, I know … let me …"

Two terse voices shut me down again. Peter and Beck will not allow it. They shut me up and push me further behind them, so I am able to once again grab Bailey. I squeeze his clammy hand in between my own and edge him further behind our human shield that has too few humans to make a difference. Even though they have spread their arms around either side of me, it doesn't change the fact that four people versus one unbalanced lunatic with a firearm is still a blow-out.

We can't win. I have brought together the only people in my life who have ever cared for me, and now they're about to die for it. The tan man's right; I am stupid and selfish.

I can feel Bailey's head pushing into the small of my back. He is breathing fast like he does when he has the flu and can't lift his head off the pillow.

My sweet boy. My unexpected gift. I can't lose him.
I won't lose him!

I turn all the way around so I am facing my son. I bend down into the dirt and let the fierce screech of the tan man telling me not to move fade out of my mind. I only see his little face. I wipe his tears and kiss his nose. His chin dips into my hand, and I pick him up. He feels weightless. I wrap my arms around him, breathing in his neck, burning his smell into my memory.

I rock back and forth like I used to when he was just a baby. Delicate, gentle sways, right and then left. I put my cheek next to his ear and start to sing. Our song. The only song that soothed him at night, the same one he now sings along with me when we're driving in the car, playing on the beach, or picking dandelions in the park. I will not let him know fear. His mommy is right here with him, just as I was in the very beginning.

Just Bailey and me.

I sing from my heart, with all the love I have in my entire being, to make my son feel safe for the few moments we have left.

"You are my sunshine … my only sunshine … you make me happy when skies are gray. You'll never know, dear … how much I love you … please don't take my sunshine away."

Shut up! Shut up!

The tan man roars. Peter and Beck fire back with police lingo, but Bailey and I are singing. Our eyes are locked, his chest rising against my own, our lifeblood shared in the lyrics of our special song. Once we finish the words, we start them over again.

My back is flush against both Peter and Beck, I can feel movement, I can hear more mumbling sounds, but I just keep singing. I rest my forehead on Bailey's, blurring my vision until I can see nothing but downy brown hair and moist eyelashes tickling my skin. He is so beautiful it steals my breath. Our moment of monumental peril was being diminished by the deepest love humans can ever know … the love for a child.

Thank you, God, for letting me feel this, if only for a short amount of time.

"You are my sunshine …" the tan man threatens to kill us all.

"My only sunshine …" because I have ruined everything.

"You make me happy …" he refuses to let a stupid hairdresser take him down.

"When skies are gray …" this was his one chance to take it all the way to the top.

"You'll never know dear …" it wasn't his fault that Anderson was a fucking pig.

"How much I love you …" he can't let it all fall apart; it's been his entire life.

"Please don't take … my sunshine … away…"

Voices rise, the ramrod straight backs against mine don't budge. I reinforce my grip on Bailey's back, holding him so tight I feel his ribs. I place another soft kiss on his blisteringly hot face. I inhale him in, close my eyes again to find the quiet, and I start to sing.

"You are my …"

Everything stops. My air escapes. My voice goes silent as the sound of a gunshot reverberates between my ears. I've never heard a gun fire so close, it's deafening. I can still feel Bailey filling my arms, but I don't know if I've been hit. I wait for a flood of pain. I feel nothing. The bodies holding me up break free. As my hearing returns, I think I catch something shouted that doesn't make any sense at all.

"Emily!"

Bailey wriggles away as I turn around to see what the hell just happened.

Emily Brenner is standing about eight feet from us; the handgun she just fired giving off a small trail of smoke from its tip. The tan man is hunched over, holding a shoulder that was just ripped apart by a perfectly placed bullet. Beck has one knee on his back, while he uses his free foot to kick the tan man's gun over to Peter.

I am stunned into silence by the timing of an unlikely rescue that only works in B movies. Peter puts the gun into his waistband, turns to make sure Bailey and I are safe, and then jogs over to his wife. He grips her by the elbows and leans down to look into her face.

"Sorry," I can hear her tell him.

"Sorry?" he scoffs. "For what?"

"For being late."

Peter laughs at her and then pulls her tightly against him. I watch from just behind them. I can hear Beck tell Peter to go find some rope in the barn to tie up the tan man until they can get a crew out. Bailey is leaning against my hip, sucking on one thumb, an old habit I thought we broke over a year ago. Who cares, let him use whatever vice he needs to right now.

Emily Brenner. The woman who has hated me, probably even blamed me for taking away her husband when he needed to be closest to her.

Has just saved my life.

I lower my head because it has become too heavy to hold up.

CHAPTER FIFTY

It's been a long time since my grandfather's kitchen held this many people. The table is full of coffee cups, fresh donuts, and one cup of chamomile tea. Emily Brenner is sipping from her Styrofoam cup with perfectly steady hands. She explained to Peter in a calm voice that he really shouldn't be all that surprised that she was able to find them in the nick of time.

"I'm a cop's wife. Don't you think by sheer osmosis I've picked up a few things along the way?"

She said she found Peter's notes scribbled on his desk blotter, and knew exactly where he kept his extra revolver. She was simply following the clues, and just like he does when he's working a case, she came prepared for anything.

"Unbelievable," Peter says. "How did you know where this place was, though?"

"Well," Emily begins, looking over at me. "I did some quick research, called a friend who works at the Registry of Deeds. Got an address, you know, it was easy."

"Easy?" Peter laughs. "Some of my finest detectives wouldn't have been able to make any sense of whatever I scribbled down in my office. I don't even remember myself. You, Emily, quite literally just saved all of our lives. And who the heck taught you to fire a gun like a sharpshooter?"

Emily takes another slow sip of her tea, and then allows herself a small smile.

"Body shot. Isn't that what you are supposed to do to bring someone down who is still valuable? Hit them in the body so they drop, but make sure they're still alive to spill their guts, right?"

"Damn straight," Beck gives her a wink. "You could be more valuable to law enforcement than your husband ever was. Besides, he's getting old and feeble anyway. Where you been hiding her, huh, Pete?"

"In plain sight. She's always been right there." Peter looks like he is seeing his wife for the first time in a long time. It is a tender moment that I feel slightly guilty to witness. I have so much to say to this woman, but I don't know where to begin. I stay quiet.

Once the tan man was safely roped up, he demanded a lawyer and access to the phone Beck turned up inside his car. His shoulder was pretty bloody, but Beck says the bullet went clean through so a good surgeon should be able to restore full function. While I was still coming out of my shock coma, Beck hustled down to the convenience store to make some calls, unwilling to trust the spotty cell service at the farm. The police and the ambulance should be here momentarily. The tan man will go first to the hospital, then once he's in recovery, Beck says he can be arraigned right there in his hospital bed.

Beck also told us that he caught a breaking news bulletin from the car radio, and watched some of the live local coverage of the Anderson press conference that was on the TV at the store.

"From what I could tell, Senator Declan Anderson is trying to sweep the beach. Sounds like he's got a whole lot of sand caught in some very uncomfortable places right now. Our girl came through after all."

I smiled at him. I didn't know if she could, but apparently Jackson's cousin played her role perfectly. Just the thought of this smarmy reprobate getting half of what he deserves is more gratifying than I thought it would be. It feels joyous, actually.

I walk into the living room to collect Beck's camping blanket, and the picture of the giraffe family Bailey is sending home with him. I fold up his blanket, taking a final drag of air from the soft plaid inside. I close my eyes and jump when I feel a hand on my shoulder.

"Come outside with me," Beck says softly.

"I'm just getting your stuff together. Your blanket and Bailey's picture," I say softly, handing him the pile.

"Walk me outside, let's give them a moment alone." He motions to Peter and Emily, still sitting at the table.

I nod, and follow him back through the kitchen and out the door. We go carefully down the porch steps and toward the Jeep. Bailey comes barreling out behind us.

"Beck, stop. Wait!" Bailey rushes into his arms, crumpling the giraffes while he squeezes him around the waist.

"Don't leave yet, please stay."

Beck tucks Bailey into his chest and returns an even tighter hug. I watch them with a small smile.

"I promise I'll be right back. You go wait for me, buddy. I'm not going anywhere. Not yet."

"Okay, Beck. I'll wait right here. Hurry up," Bailey's big grin holds no sadness, no shock, and no despair. Given what he's just witnessed it appears he is doing just fine.

Amazing.

Bailey scurries back up the stairs and into the kitchen. Once I know he's gone I turn back to Beck. His face is serene. His lips are closed tightly together, but pull into a half-smile as he looks down at me. I am almost lost in the blue tranquility of his gaze.

"Where do I even begin?" my voice is a throaty rasp.

"You don't have to begin anywhere. I already know everything you would say. Let's not do this to each other, okay?"

I am not in the proper frame of mind to make any sense right now, but I have to say something. Something worthwhile, defining, and important.

"Thank you doesn't begin to cover this. You … you … not only saved me, you saved my son …" the words come out as soft as the first drops of a summer rainstorm, but I hope he understands how deeply I mean them.

"*You* saved your son, Bo. *You did*. I just helped a little," he says, brushing a hair off my face. My skin ignites with his touch. I hear faint bird chirping all around us, cool air tickles the messy ponytail hanging down the back of my neck. I feel itchy beneath my clothes, restless and incomplete. I can't let this moment go. I reach deeper inside myself to flush out what I would normally tuck away. Even if that means acknowledging my own transgressions.

"I'm so sorry I said that to you before. It was out of line to suggest that you haven't known true love. Ignorant, really."

Beck shrugs. "It's true enough, I guess." His tone is somewhat weighed down by cynicism. Maybe Beck has his own personal transgressions.

"Why?"

"Because I've never had time for that stuff. My life is my job. It's all I've ever really wanted it to be."

I understand that. My life is Bailey. We have made the same journey so far, but I am getting a very strong feeling that we've both been stuck on the wrong track.

"I think some people would argue that's not enough." I mean for my statement to cover both of us.

"I've never thought that anything was missing. I didn't think I was the marrying type or the fatherly type. What happens if I don't make it home one night? Some poor family has to go on without me?" He shakes his head. "No, I wouldn't want that."

"But is it fair to deny yourself all the good that might bring? The nights when you do come home …" I shyly look away, breaking our gaze that feels like an electric pulse. The breeze kicks up. I hug my elbows to stay warm, not quite ready to head back in yet, but not sure I'm prepared to push this further.

Part of me wants to stay right here, where there is no noise or clutter, where endless space descends upward to meet peaks of rock and dirt that climb into the clouds. I have always held this place close to my heart but mostly because it reminded me of my grandfather and how it felt to be loved.

To be safe.

I am safe. Bailey is safe. My grandfather is not here, but Beck is. It's not that I would ever exchange one for the other, but the feelings floating around inside of me are eerily similar.

Beck shifts away from my loaded question. We talk a little more about Peter. I explain how Bailey's obsession with 9-1-1 innocuously led him straight to us.

"I had seen him around, of course, but didn't really know him until then. He's been like family to us, but I didn't want him involved in this mess. I would just die if anything ever happened to him. He and Emily, they've already suffered …" I fade out, preferring not to invoke the name of their dead son.

"He understands that, Bo. Not to say he wasn't pissed, because he's been just as worried about you. Trust me on that."

"He feels bad for me. He knows what total reprobates my parents are …"

"No, he doesn't feel bad for you. He loves you. There's a difference. Even a heartless lug like me knows that."

"Hey, I already apologized for that—" I start to turn back, expecting him to be smiling at me in jest. Instead, his face is serious. His eyes sweep over my nose, across my cheekbone, down to the fullness of my bottom lip.

His finger reaches out. It feels both rousing and numbing as it connects with the tender skin of my mouth. I don't think he sees the dirt smears on my cheeks, the lines where tears ran through the sweat on my face. I have never looked worse, but he doesn't seem to care.

"Maybe after today, everything could change," he says, his voice thick. "Maybe for both of us."

Sunlight hits me square in the face, along with a sanguine sensation that is beyond giddy or light. It's more far-reaching than that, a buzz inside my chest that doesn't hurt or alarm, but stirs and alerts. I feel fully charged.

"Maybe you're right," I don't recognize this sultry sound coming out of my mouth. Neither does Peter, who comes loping up between us holding Bailey's hand.

"Hope you're not getting sick, Bo, you sound awful."

"No, I'm fine," I gulp down embarrassment as the towering tension between me and Beck crumbles like dominoes. "We were just ... um ... just talking, and walking ..." Peter looks at me cockeyed.

"Sure you were," he says, but I can tell his senses are humming. Bailey jumps up on Beck, telling him that he wants to show him the stall where my favorite horse used to live.

"Okay, buddy, let's check it out. Then we need to think about heading home. It's time." He winks at me, gives Peter a small salute, and heads off toward the barn door with Bailey. Peter and I watch them for a while; neither of us feeling the need to address what we both know is going on.

CHAPTER FIFTY-ONE

"Are all of you free and willing to testify on behalf of this woman's ability as parent and provider?" the family court judge asks, raising his voice to make sure everyone who has gathered on my behalf in the courtroom can hear him.

They nod, some even adding a buoyant, "Yes, Your Honor."

I look behind me at the dozen or so people who have dusted off their most proper attire to come to court this morning to ensure DCYF that I am a fit and responsible parent.

It is just a formality at this point, but I couldn't help the nervous feeling I got walking into this courtroom. Just being here is unsettling. Peter gripped my hand as we walked up to the table at the front of the room, and told me again not to worry. He has been with me every step of the way. He and Beck pulled the petition to take Bailey away and made sure this was the first thing we took care of once we returned to Echo Valley. I look behind me at the first row. Peter winks at me. Sitting right beside him is Beck, who gives me a thumbs up. Just behind them, in the second row, are William, Ari, Jessie, and Gerry. They smile and give me a wave. Even Annie Bettencourt got up early today to make sure the judge knew that I was the best parent she's ever known, so much better, in fact, than her own grandson who seemed to father children like it was a hot trend, and then walk out on every one of them.

I turn back to listen to the judge, who is pulling apart a stack of paper and making notations on a few pages.

"Okay, Ms. Carmichael. Suffice it to say my only responsibility here today is to address the state's petition. I will vacate that, and make a note of the ample supply of character witnesses who are here in support of you."

He closes the packet of papers and leans over it with his elbows, removing the reading glasses from the end of his nose to address me directly.

"Again, it is not up to me what happens next, but let me say this," he begins. "I have the unfortunate task of removing children from their families every day. I do this to protect them from the very people they are, by nature, supposed to trust. I am disgusted and alarmed that the system failed you, Ms. Carmichael. You have my word that I will do everything in my power to make sure it never happens again."

"Thank you, Your Honor," I say quietly, as I hear an, "Amen to that" sputtered out from behind me.

"And, Bo?" he says again, as I register surprise that he would refer to me by my first name.

"Yes, Your Honor?"

"If anyone ever dares threaten to take your son from you again, you call me. Okay?"

I grin at the judge.

"Okay," I tell him.

"You're free to go. Good luck to you." He pushes my file aside and reaches for the next one sitting at the top of a pile that's as tall as my leg. Just another day in family court, I suppose, even though the thought of what this judge deals with on a regular basis makes me shudder.

"Onto the next," Peter says, taking me by the arm to the hallway of the courthouse where we are met by an old friend of his who has stepped up to handle the dismantling of the charges against me. Peter made sure he was on standby as soon as we got home.

Technically, because I skipped town to hide out at the farm, I have defaulted on my responsibility not to flee. The court immediately issued an arrest warrant, the DMV suspended my license, and I compounded my problems on paper. Peter and Beck sat me down to walk me through what would need to happen to clear it up. Even though everyone thinks Peter is a habitual offender on the golf course, he really only plays a couple of times a month. He does, however, always play with the same group, including a dear friend who is on the back nine of a life spent billing rich, white-collar criminals for his services to keep them out of prison. When Peter told him what had happened to me, he stepped in and took my case, gratis.

"Mornin' Bo, Pete," he says, holding a leather briefcase that is surprisingly scuffed for a man of his wealth and status. He notices me looking down at it. "Oh, don't you pay this old thing any attention. It's my good luck charm, been with me ever since law school. Given that I regularly enjoy senior citizen discounts and AARP conventions, that means it's damn old, just like me," he laughs.

"Actually, I like it, Mr. Sanborn. Good luck charms are nothing to scoff at. I also want you to know that am honored you would consider my family worthy of your time," I say, smiling at him. He has spoken to me at length over the phone, but this is the first time we have met.

"Ah, you stop it. What happened to you was a travesty. What kind of lawyer, or friend for that matter, would I be if I didn't step in to set things right?"

"You have my eternal thanks, Mr. Sanborn. If I have to supply you with free haircuts for the rest of my life, I will find a way to pay you back."

"Nonsense. This old dog keeps me loaded up on cold beers and grilled burgers at the clubhouse, that's all I need." He slaps Peter on the back as we move toward the exit. Next up is the district courthouse, where my motion to vacate the default awaits a judge's attention.

I ask them to go ahead, as I wait for the rest of my fan club to catch up. Ari, Jessie, William and Gerry wrap themselves around me, giving me hugs of support and words of encouragement. William has been marinating in outrage after hearing of what really made me sick on the side of the road that day. He says all that hotness on such an asshole is a total waste.

"You know, girl, I do believe that *Ander-skank* needs a good hard spanking, and not the kind that hurts so good, you know?"

"Ha, I think there are plenty of spanks to go around!"

I look at the faces of this motley crew that canceled all their morning clients to show up for me here. I never knew how much they cared.

"I can't thank you enough for being here for Bailey and me. It means the world, and I'm so sorry you were worried about us," I look into their eyes, and I stop at Gerry's. "You could have fired me, and yet you believed in me," I start.

"Oh, don't you worry, I fired you about fifty times behind your back," he says, trying to sound like a strict teacher. "But I knew something was really wrong. You would never not show up for me, Bo. I know that. You will always have a home in my salon."

He pulls me into a quick hug and tells his ducklings to follow him out to the car.

"We're heading back to work. You call me when this is all over. Then take the week off," he waves. I try to protest, but he's already walking away.

William yells back at me giving his rear end a little shake. "Thanks, Bo, worrying about you made me sick enough to drop three pounds. Lookin' pretty good under this hood, yeah?"

"Oh, yeah!" I laugh back.

"You have an interesting assortment of friends," Beck is next to me, smiling at the salon posse pulling away. "Ready to go?" he asks me, taking me by the arm. His fingers feel comforting and warm, a good feeling I'm getting somewhat used to.

"Let them ride over together," he says, motioning to Peter and my new lawyer, "I'll drive you over myself."

I say the only thing that comes to mind.

"Okay."

We make small talk in Beck's car. He updates me about the multi-state effort underway to find Spencer Diaz. My mouth turns in on the thought of the officer of the law who may be the most evil of this entire unsavory bunch. We now know how Diaz set it all up. He and the tan man, who actually has a name, go way back. Troy Olander needed a favor. Diaz was all too happy to oblige. He made a late night call to Judge Nelson to secure the warrant for my arrest, claiming he had a confidential informant telling him of my significant drug activity. Then, he called the bail commissioner personally, to ask for personal recognizance bail, but not to hurry, they'd wanted to work me for a while.

Beck's friend at DCYF also confirmed for us that Diaz had kick-started the whole process to take Bailey away by claiming a concerned neighbor had contacted him about Bailey's safety. That especially, made me despise him even more.

We could not confirm Diaz had taken the drugs, but there was already so much stacking up against him with his old buddy, Troy, ready to sell him down the river. Beck was also trying to put together the connection between Diaz and Judge Stanley Nelson. He told me about an early morning traffic stop he remembered Diaz going out on not too long ago. He had laughed about pulling over some guy for DWI, but when he rolled down the window, the dude looked like a lady.

At least from the waist down.

"Freak," Diaz had sputtered. "Fucking freak had on a hot pink thong and size twelve women's heels," he had shouted to the roomful of cops. Beck had wondered if the man wearing the thong was someone who would do anything to keep his clothing preferences on the down-low. He had checked the records from that night. Sure enough, even though Diaz had blabbed to anyone who would listen, there was no mention of the traffic stop and certainly no record of an arrest. He had let the guy go. Diaz had done a favor, and had asked for a favor in return. Beck had no way of proving it, but he had a strong feeling that Judge Stanley Nelson had a hankering for pretty undies. The warrant itself was legit, but the false swearing Diaz had given to get it was highly illegal, not to mention an all-around shitty thing for a police officer to do.

Troy Olander was under 24-hour suicide watch in the psychiatric unit at Concord Hospital. He wasn't even completely awake from the anesthesia before he spilled his guts. Beck had personally gone to his hospital room with a recorder in hand. The sordid details poured out of the political animal even though he knew he was about to cage himself. The gun was his, a necessary safeguard when you're traveling with a future president, he explained, but he had never fired it. He stopped guarding Anderson's reputation and unloaded like he was sitting before a priest in confession.

He told Beck that Bailey's doctor left a message about his appointment on my phone, and that's how they knew where I would be. He admitted that he thought that would be enough to take care of it. He said that Diaz made one final phone call to him before he took off, warning that I was on the run, but he was pretty sure where I was going. Beck berated himself for leaving behind an office full of clues that included the post-it he had scrawled *Carmichael farm* onto in bold pen.

"Diaz found our notes," Beck said, looking over at me sheepishly. "Lesson learned on this end, time to clean up my filthy office."

Beck said Troy would weave in and out of the story, offering resistance and then singing like a canary. He was obviously unstable and unsafe. When Beck explained it was unlikely Declan Anderson would ever face charges in connection to any of it, simply because Troy had never disclosed exactly what he was planning to do, the thoroughly defeated man had curled up into a ball, started to sob, and asked to see his shrink.

I shake my head at the senselessness, the absurd breadth of lunacy expressed by more than just one lone crazy person. They're a whole pack of crazy!

"You know, Beck," I begin. "The most insane aspect of this entire thing is that I never wanted to tell anyone. I wasn't going for some presidential bombshell. The only vengeance I wanted to enact against Anderson was not to vote for him. I just wanted to get home to Bailey and forget everything that had just happened."

"Their world is different, it's pretty hardcore. He's not the first, and probably won't be the last, high level political hack to lose his shit. He just pushed the envelope a tad too far." Beck touches the tip of my nose; a sweet habit he's developing. He knows my stomach is churning. "Do you want some coffee? I can swing through the drive-thru if you'd like," he asks.

"No, thank you. I don't know if I could keep it down." Beck nods and begins to massage the back of my neck with deep strokes against my skin. It feels like nirvana. I slide my eyes over to catch a glimpse of his profile. I can't get over how methodical he is, so patient, kind, and calm. I realize unraveling the sticky layers of conspiracies and staring down the barrel of a gun are events he's recovered from before, but I'm still a jumble of nerves.

"I'm not used to being a wanted woman, or trying to outrun an evil empire, or having a firearm cocked and loaded in my direction. I may fall short in many areas, but I try not to linger on the edge of life or death." Beck flashes a smile that tugs again at that invisible string attached to my stomach. Even though we haven't revisited that touchy conversation at the farm yet in detail, the feelings are still feverous.

What is it about this man?

"I understand. You've been through quite an ordeal. Unfortunately, Anderson's thug isn't the first of his kind to try and take me out. I guess I consider it a job hazard given the company I keep, but yes, it has been a devastating few days for you. Once this is over, and all the hype dies down, you should take a vacation …"

Yeah right! A vacation—on my salary—is simply ridiculous.

"No, Beck. I think that ship sailed a long time ago, and I don't mean the cruise ship, I mean the go-away-on-a-nice-vacation-with-your-significant-other vessel of good fortune."

He looks at me with the hint of a blush on his rugged face. "Yeah, I'm kind of stuck on shore myself. But I think we've established that already."

I look out the window. My man-radar may be low on batteries, but I suspect Detective Beckett Brady is flirting with me again, and I think I may be flirting right back.

I pinch the inside of my palm to snap myself out of it. I ask to borrow Beck's phone to check in on Bailey.

"Please. You worried about him? Don't be. You couldn't find a better babysitter in the entire Granite State. Emily will have him on his second batch of her world famous chocolate chip cookies by now. I'm sure he's totally fine, but you can call if you want," he says, plucking his cell phone from a black case attached to his belt. He's right, I'm being paranoid. Bailey is probably in better hands than he is when he's with me.

* * * *

Emily and I had taken a long stroll through the fields while we were waiting for the police to arrive at the farm. Peter had joined Beck and Bailey in the barn to give us some space. I tried to summarize everything that was firing around my brain, but I ended up sounding like I had the hiccups. Emily stopped walking and took my hand, which surprised me so much I jumped back out of her grasp.

"I don't blame you for being nervous around me," she said. "I haven't given you any reason not to be." She plopped down in the grass and took in a huge breath, closing her eyes in what looked to me like an attempt to rid herself of the negativity that had consumed her.

"How much do you love your son?" she asked me. I faltered, aware of how close I came to losing him.

"More than anything," I answered delicately, knowing whatever I said would hurt her.

"Well, that's how much I loved my boy. Our boy. Mine and Peter's. Tucker was my entire life. I was so devastated that it made me angry to see Peter getting better. Does that make any sense to you?"

I nodded. "Yes, I can see that."

"Instead of being grateful that Peter was trying to move on I was resentful. And, I think, a bit jealous." Emily pulled a blade of glass from the stretch of green next to her foot. "Jealous of you. And your little boy. I let my grief get the better of me, and for that I'm sorry." Emily's eyes were moist and for a fleeting moment, I felt every bit of her pain.

"I think that you came into Peter's life for a reason. And now, into my life. If it's okay with you, I'd like to spend some time getting to know you. And getting to know that little munchkin of yours that my husband seems to think is the bee's knees."

She let a single tear fall uninterrupted from her cheek. Once it cleared her face, she broke into a wide cleansing smile.

All she had to do was open her arms, and I fell right into them.

* * * *

"You're right," I say to Beck. "Bailey will probably want to move in. The Brenner house is powered by love and goodness and a steady flow of chocolate chip cookies."

Beck chuckles as he pulls into the courthouse parking lot, driving around back to the special spaces none of us regular people know about.

"We'll park back here, no paparazzi that way," he half-jokes. I have quickly become the media's flavor of the week. Me, and Jackson's cousin, that is. We have only spoken by phone, but I made certain she knows how deeply grateful I will always be. She is now making the rounds on the morning TV talk show circuit and entertaining six-figure job offers from network executives. She has refused to reveal the source of the tip—me—and hasn't commented on the announcement from Declan Anderson that he is withdrawing his candidacy for president due to personal reasons, or word that his wife has filed for divorce. Declan Anderson may not spend a single day in jail, but I do believe he will live out the rest of his pathetic life paying for his mistakes.

That alone, is good enough for me.

Beck pulls his car into an open garage bay deep inside the belly of the courthouse. He hops out and hits a switch that closes the door immediately behind us. Opening my door, he reaches in to help me climb out of the passenger seat. I put my hand inside of his as we walk to the secret door that pops us out near the storage room where old case files live. My fingers slip around Beck's as we walk through the quiet hallway toward the courtroom where my freebie lawyer will try to clear my name and give me back my life.

CHAPTER FIFTY-TWO

Peter and my lawyer are waiting for us to enter the courtroom. They convinced the judge to close the proceedings, which means no reporters or cameras will be allowed inside. Even though this is a juicy story that even I admit is impossible to resist, I have to protect Bailey. I have politely declined repeated requests for interviews and am anxiously awaiting the next big news story to come along and take the pressure off.

Peter gives me a quick hug before I sit down at the table on my side of the courtroom. "I'm right here behind you. Both of us are right here." He motions to Beck who smiles at me.

"It's okay, Bo. Everything will be just fine."

I know it will. I trust him. For some strange reason, I feel like I'll be able to trust him for the rest of my life. His blue eyes twinkle in the sun that streams in through the window. Peter nudges him, but the detective's eyes stay locked on mine. My lawyer says something to me, but I can't look away either. We stare at each other until the deep boom of the judge's gavel indicates that we're about to begin. I turn away from Beck with a shy smile. The tug in my stomach releases.

Here we go.

My lawyer sounds like a character in a John Grisham novel. His words are ripe with indignation and full of lawyer-y jargon I can't begin to understand. I keep my hands folded tightly together on the old wooden desk as he rails against the unholy charges filed against me, the emotional anguish I have endured, and the state's obligation to free an innocent woman before I launch the largest lawsuit in New Hampshire history. He uses that moment to point directly at the state prosecutor who has taken the hit to show up for this one. His boss told him to agree to drop the charges and get the hell out of the courthouse with a strict "no comment" for reporters. The state was already nursing a big black eye on this case, no need to talk about how much it hurt.

The judge listens politely. He allows the fiery lawyer his moment, but in the interest of moving more than just my case through his courtroom today, he eventually interrupts the overzealous showman.

"Duly noted, Mr. Sanborn," he begins. "On the motion to vacate the default on bail, I rule in Ms. Carmichael's favor. Furthermore, even though she is entitled to a hearing on the motion to vacate the charge of possession with intent to distribute, and for having an illegal substance in a police department, I would say there is overwhelming evidence sitting before me to make that wholly unnecessary."

Mr. Sanborn leans in and whispers in my ear, "This is perfect. You don't have to say a word here. Charges will be dropped. Of course, you can testify if you wish."

"No. I do not wish to testify. My statement was good enough for me."

"Okay, then."

"Your Honor, thank you for the expeditious manner in which you are processing our requests. And thank you to the state—for realizing its case was crap," he says mockingly and totally for effect.

The gavel comes back down as the judge declares my case officially closed.

The prosecutor is the first one to pack up and leave the courtroom. He stops at my table to offer his hand, wishing me the best of luck and apologizing for my inconvenience. I thank him, even though I think his choice of the word *inconvenience* is the understatement of the century.

Mr. Sanborn throws a stack of papers back into his brittle leather briefcase, patting it on the side as he clinks the gold locks together at the top.

"See?" he says, "she hasn't failed me yet." He gives me a hug and a kiss on the cheek. "Good luck, Bo. This was my pleasure entirely. This place feels like a vacation home to me," he says, looking around the courtroom where he carved out an entire career's worth of shining moments of victory.

"Thank you, Mr. Sanborn. Remember, now, you need a trim, or a golf caddy, or even someone to run out and get you takeout down the street, you call me," I hug him around his robust chest. "I will owe you forever."

Peter comes up behind me; Beck is on the other side. The doors to the courtroom are still closed, keeping the public at bay. Peter and Mr. Sanborn are going over details, exchanging paperwork that I need to keep. I feel my legs sway with a release of the exhaustion and worry that has drained my body's stock of resources.

I am free. I am free to go on with the life I used to be embarrassed about. Now, I can't wait to get back to the simplicity of it all. How grateful I am to have a job, people who care about me, and a little boy who is as resilient as an elastic band. Bailey has bounced back from all of this with the magical grace that childhood grants us before we know better than to risk getting by on hope alone.

As Peter and Mr. Sanborn walk together up the aisle of the courtroom, Beck hangs back. I know that he is waiting for me. I walk to him.

"This is all because of you," I say, trying to keep my voice steady and strong. "No one would have believed me that day. But you did. I can never repay you for that, but I promise to be a good mom and a non-drug-distributing member of our society for the rest of my life."

He laughs, and the sound of it makes my heart soar. The tug inside my stomach returns as I feel myself inching closer … closer … until finally, our lips touch for the first time.

For a girl who has put far too much on the back of hope already, I give in to the power of the elastic band and allow myself to believe again in anticipation of all good things.

"Come on," he says once we pull out of our embrace. "Let's go get your son."

THREE WEEKS LATER

"Momma, Momma, come on! We'll be late for Peter and Emily!"

Bailey has two fists clenched around the plastic bags of forks and spoons that I will be contributing to the cookout at the Brenner's house this afternoon. Emily had insisted that I have been through too much lately to worry about cooking a thing.

"I got it covered," she told me firmly. "You don't need to bring anything but yourselves."

I stayed up past midnight last night, frosting and sprinkling rainbow jimmies on top of a triple layer chocolate cake. I refuse to show up empty handed, and this decadent dessert has always been my specialty. Jackson used to tell me that if the best way to a man's heart was through his stomach, I could worm my way into his with my heap of deliciousness and still have room to spare.

For the first time in my life, it wasn't Jackson I was thinking of as I lovingly measured out the cocoa, flour, and baking soda for this one.

The sharp pain of losing him again has receded almost completely. I don't ache with guilt anymore. In fact, I can honestly say that I have finally moved on. Forward progress feels good. It feels right.

"Grab your sweatshirt, Mr. B. It might get chilly tonight."

"Okay, Momma. But hurry up, Peter and Emily are waiting for us! And Beck, too."

He smirks at me as he runs by to find a sweatshirt in his bedroom. I can hear him yelling out behind him—
"Momma and Beck-itt, sittin' in a tree, k-i-s-s-i-n-g … first comes love … then comes marriage … then comes Momma with a baby carriage …"

"*Bailey! Stop that!*" I insist, but my laugh bubbles up, egging him on.

"Sor--ree," he smirks at me, all cute and giggly. He swings back around the corner and grabs his forks and spoons again. "Can we go now?"

I fit one more layer of aluminum foil around the carefully placed toothpicks at the top of my cake to prevent the frosting from sticking to the top. I want this cake to be perfect.

"All right, buddy. Let's go," I say, carefully balancing the cake along my forearm as I reach for my keys. I pull the door behind me until I hear my flimsy lock connect. Next week, I am looking for a new apartment, one that is closer to Bailey's new full-time babysitters.

We sing along to Barney on the drive over to the Brenner's house. It is a trip that I make every other day to drop Bailey off with Emily while I go to work. Peter covers the remainder of the days by driving to us to pick him up. They tell me gas is way too expensive for me to make all those trips. Sometimes, they keep him for dinner so I can go out on a date.

Yes, a date!

Bailey screeches out from his partially open rear window as we approach the driveway and pull in. I beep twice and wave. Peter turns from the neighbor he's chatting with and rushes over to help us unload.

"Mr. B. I have a hot dog with your name on it, pal," he says, swinging Bailey up into his arms and planting a giant kiss on his cheek.

"Where's Emily?" Bailey asks, wriggling free.

"What? Emily? What the heck am I, chopped liver? Well, *excuuuse* me! She's over there, buddy. On the deck. Go say hi, she's been waiting for you to get here." Peter taps Bailey's bottom as he races off to find his favorite new babysitter who never falls asleep on him, and makes absolutely certain he never feels the need to dial 9-1-1 ever again. Not on her watch, anyway.

"Like two peas in a pod I tell you, Bo. You should see them in the kitchen. Bailey's almost a better cookie-maker than Emily is by now."

"No way, she'll always be the best. But he'll take a close second."

Peter pulls me in for a quick hug. "How you doin' kiddo?" he asks.

"Great. I'm doing really, really well. Work is busy, Gerry seems almost kind these days, and all my clients have forgiven me for having to reschedule them unexpectedly. I am almost back to complete and total normal."

"Reporters still bugging you?"

"Just one or two who seem to think that constant pestering will somehow turn a firm 'no' into a resounding 'yes'."

"You want me to make some more phone calls for you?"

"Nope, I can handle it. Thanks, anyway. Remember, you are now off the clock, Chief."

The relentless media was soundly rebuffed by my hometown. Echo Valley closed ranks, refusing to discuss me, or Bailey, or anything related to what happened. Finally, after years of speculating about how badly I must have messed up to wind up back home, it didn't matter anymore. I was one of them, and by God that meant something in New Hampshire. Peter even threatened a few of the most aggressive reporters with high crimes if they didn't back off.

He is fidgeting, something is on his mind, and he will say it whether I want to hear it or not. "I've lined up four showings for next Tuesday. But if I can make a suggestion, that condo complex going in right down the road would be perfect."

I reach in to grab my mountain of chocolate, and slap Peter's finger away from the side of the frosting. "Don't you dare, no grazing on my masterpiece."

He licks the tip of his finger to remove the trace of frosting residue, saying, "The condo, Bo. What do you think of the condo?"

"You are as persistent as a mosquito," I joke to him. Peter starts to protest, telling me that now is the perfect time to get in there with an offer and that I shouldn't worry about a down payment because The Bank of Brenner is wide open for business.

"No way. There is no way you and Emily are going—" The palm goes up.

"Just think about it. It was Emily's idea in the first place. You know me—I'm just a cheap, old, unemployed former cop."

"No, you're not," I begin. "Chief Brenner, you are the best thing that ever happened to me."

"Hey, hold up there!" Strong arms come around me from behind. "I thought I was the best thing that ever happened to you. Come on now, Bo, you can't play both sides here."

Just his voice alone makes me grin. I turn around and give Beck a kiss on the cheek.

"You are eavesdropping, Detective."

"Well, how could I not? Your car is so damn loud I could hear you coming from a mile away. Time to get that muffler taken care of. I'll take it in next week."

"It's okay, Beck, I can do it," Peter objects. "You're working, and I'm, well ... I'm not. Gives me something to do," he states. Another familiar voice chimes in.

"Good. You need to get out of the house! You're driving me crazy puttering around here." Emily comes up next to Beck and me. "Hi, honey. Let me see this chocolate wonder Bailey just told me about. You didn't need to do all this, you should be resting," she says, giving me a quick hug and looking inside the back seat.

"How much resting am I supposed to do? You all treat me like I'm recovering from open heart surgery, for gosh sake."

"Just like you said, Em, she's being stubborn about the condo," Peter begins, like I'm a petulant child who's resisting good advice. Emily pats my arm. "Oh, don't you worry about that now, sweetheart. We'll talk later. Once this guy has a thought in that big old head of his, it sticks around like peanut butter on bread. We'll work it all out."

The smell of a freshly lit gas grill rises on a breeze, tickling my nostrils and making my stomach growl. Emily tells Peter it's time to put the burgers on and help her carry out the bowls of potato salad. She starts to walk away then turns back to me. "Bo, before I forget, would it be okay if I took Bailey to the library this week for story hour? Some of my friends are bringing their grandchildren, and I'd like for him to come. I think he'd really enjoy being around other kids."

I nod. My eyes fill behind my sunglasses as I watch Emily and Peter walk back toward the front door of their well-kept home. My son comes tearing around the corner, trailed by the neighbor's five-year-old who is fast becoming Bailey's first BFF. I hear something about a Frisbee in the garage that they are desperate to get their hands on. Bailey makes a quick pit stop to say hello to Beck.

"Hi, Beck!" Bailey jumps full steam into Beck's outstretched arms.

"Hey, big guy." Beck's forearm muscles jump with the weight of my gigantic four-year-old. "How's my favorite nose guard doing?"

"Um, we are still ... discussing that, Beck. Four is a little young to be a football player."

"Not on my team it isn't. Don't worry, buddy, we'll talk her into it."

"Okay, bye-bye! I'm going to hunt turtles with Trevor." Bailey foregoes the Frisbee and then jumps out of Beck's arms to drag his friend down the slope of the backyard to a marshy puddle.

"Come on, Bo. He'll love it. That boy is built for football."

I am on the losing side of this argument. Beck is the head coach of the Echo Valley Tiny Mites football program, a storied franchise that begets kids barely waist high who can cut through a defensive line like a hot knife through butter. He says even though the season is already underway, there's plenty of room to fit Bailey on the roster. Peter told Beck to get it out of his system early, because once baseball season rolls around, Bailey is *all his*.

Really, though, I can't go wrong either way.

"Wow, what a beast of a cake!" he says. "Let me help you." Beck reaches over me to support the other half of the pan. "Pretty, smart, and she can bake, too. You are a keeper, Ms. Carmichael."

"And you are full of it, Mr. Brady."

We smile at each other and my stomach tugs again, but I'm getting used to that now. It's a nice feeling, a surprising jolt that I never thought I'd get for anyone other than Jackson. Beck's strong hands take the pan, but when he lifts it out, his head bumps the open car door and his chin dips into the top of my chocolate volcano. It looks like it just erupted on his mouth. I can't resist. I take my finger and wipe the frosting off his upper lip.

"Here, I shouldn't be the only one to get an early taste of this." He leans in, turning his head sideways to fit just under my nose. Our lips touch, and I get a solid transfer of chocolate.

"Hey, hey now. You two break it up already. Should have known not to leave you alone out here with a perfectly good cake." Peter slaps Beck on the back and takes the cake from his arms. "I got it from here. Come on, burgers and dogs are just about ready."

Peter yells down to Bailey and his friend to come on and eat, while Beck and I lean against the door of my car.

"I can't believe how much has changed," I say quietly as I watch Bailey run toward the fully set picnic table in the backyard that looks like it was staged by a crew from Good Housekeeping magazine. "I never thought I would fit into something like this."

"You mean, like, fit into a family?"

"Yeah, I guess that's what I mean. You know, given my own parents, and the other half of poor Bailey's equation, I figured all of this wasn't in the cards for us."

"Hmmm," Beck says, shaking his head. He knows more about me now than anyone ever has. He even knows every ugly detail about that night in college that changed everything. I was honest with Beck in a way that I never could be with Jackson or anyone else. He did not scold me for being careless, or chastise me for not coming clean about my secret. Instead, he held me tight and rocked me gently back and forth, as I let out years of sadness and frustration in giant, wracking sobs. When I was done, he wiped my tears away and kissed me softly. He didn't seem surprised or disappointed by what I had just poured out. I think he had more of a deep sadness for everything I had endured.

I'm not sure where this will go, but when I'm with him I feel alive. When I'm not, I think about him endlessly. It's different than with Jackson. I was just a kid. Now, I'm a woman. And Beck is all man.

I know that against all the odds I had stacked up for myself, I can love again. I'm already half-way there. My damaged heart is healing.

I hear boisterous laughter coming from the picnic table. Bailey is telling Peter and Emily about all the things he hopes Santa will bring him for Christmas this year. I hear Emily tell Bailey that she is making him his very own stocking to hang on her fireplace. I feel Beck's fingers wrap around mine as we walk toward the happy voices, the slightly charred hamburger rolls and perfectly chilled potato salad.

We swing our clasped hands together as Beck's voice carries up and away into the crisp fall air.

"Save me a cheeseburger," he yells, kissing my hand before releasing it to grab me a paper plate. As he passes it over he adds, "And save Bo here about five more."

They all chuckle over what has been a quick return of my infamously healthy appetite.

I slide in next to Beck. Bailey is across the table from me. Peter is at one end; Emily is at the other.

"Momma?"

"Yes, Bailey?"

"I was telling Trevor that I don't have a daddy like he does." The plastic forks go quiet against the paper plates. All eyes find us.

"That's right, Bailey. Your daddy isn't like Trevor's daddy."

Bailey takes a huge bite out of the end of his hot dog. In between chews, he continues. "Well, Trevor says that's okay."

"Yes, it is okay, honey."

"I know. I told Trevor that families come in all shapes and sizes."

I smile, recognizing the explanation from the book I read to Bailey sometimes to explain why moms and dads divorce, or if a parent dies, or when some jerk doesn't feel the need to acknowledge his offspring.

"Yes, they do, Bailey. Each family is special and different."

"Like ours," he says, with pieces of hot dog bun falling into his lap.

I look from Bailey over to Peter. My eyes move down the table to Emily. Finally, they find Beck.

"Yes, Bailey. Just like ours."

THE END

Acknowledgements

There is no greater experience for writing about the nitty-gritty, inner-workings of a presidential campaign than seeing one first hand. To every political operative I've encountered, thank you for sharing little snippets of your personalities, intensity, and all-out desire to win. You truly give your hearts and souls to your candidates, and it is a spectacular process to watch from the sidelines. My crime guy, New Hampshire State Police Major Crime Unit Detective Sergeant John Sonia, deserves a constant stream of thanks for everything you help me create. I very honestly could not do this without you. New Hampshire State Police Captain Greg Ferry, you always answer my texts and make me laugh. Thank you so very much for sharing your expertise and personality. Los Angeles Police Detective II Kristin Merrill, thank you for the checks and balances. Attorney Mark Stevens, my thanks for helping break down the law until I understand how to effectively put it into words. To Greg Kretschmar, your red barn *is* Echo Valley. I am a forever fan of your humor, talent, and wit, but also the goodness with which you live your life. Thank you for capturing the beauty of New Hampshire, and letting me borrow it.

To the hardest working publishing team in the business, I owe you so much. Waldorf Publishing runs on pure adrenaline, and heart. Barbara Terry, Danielle Van, and Beth Stifflemire, I appreciate your passion, humor and hard-charging ambition working on my behalf. To Mark Isaac, thank you for taking our cover image ideas and carrying them across the finish line. To editors Carol McCrow, and Elisabeth Pennella, I so deeply appreciate your attention to my details. Carol, your sweet notes make my day.

To my mom, Betty Vaughn, my cherished early reader, I love you so. My dad, who doesn't read much but thinks I'm a super writer anyway, you remain the best man I've ever known. So much of Peter Brenner is you. To Brad, Brody, and Darby, I can write about love and family because I have been blessed with you. My greatest joys lie within all that you are, and I'm so proud that you're mine.

Author Bio

Jennifer Vaughn is a longtime member of the award-winning news team at WMUR-TV, in Manchester, New Hampshire, and the author of *Last Flight Out*, *Throw Away Girls*, and *Legacy Girls*. As the evening anchor, Jennifer has lead coverage that has earned Edward R. Murrow, Associated Press, and New Hampshire Association of Broadcasters Awards.

She is also the recipient of multiple Emmy nominations, the Red Cross Sword of Hope Award, and had her debut novel, *Last Flight Out*, featured in the Swag Bag at the Daytime Emmy Awards in Beverly Hills, CA, in 2013. Jennifer has had prominent roles in internationally-televised presidential debates alongside CNN, ABC News, and FOX News, has anchored election night coverage for both national and state contests and provided political analysis for national radio and television news outlets.

She's interviewed every sitting president and presidential candidate since 1999, supporting WMUR's extensive first-in-the-nation presidential primary coverage. Jennifer has covered everything from Super Bowls, world championship parades, ABC's *Extreme*

Home Makeover, deadly natural disasters, and medical breakthroughs, though her favorite stories are the personal ones that showcase triumph over tragedy, and give hope to the human spirit.

An avid contributor to charities that direct funds and support to cancer patients, Jennifer donated all proceeds from the sale of *Last Flight Out* to local organizations. Learn more at www.jvwrites.com.